D0394240

A Wizard in Chaos

BOOKS BY CHRISTOPHER STASHEFF

The Warlock

The Warlock in Spite of Himself
King Kobold Revived
The Warlock Unlocked
Escape Velocity
The Warlock Enraged
The Warlock Wandering
The Warlock Is Missing
The Warlock Heretical
The Warlock's Companion
The Warlock Insane
The Warlock Rock
Warlock and Son

The Rogue Wizard

A Wizard in Mind
A Wizard in Bedlam
A Wizard in War
A Wizard in Peace
A Wizard in Chaos

The Warlock's Heirs

A Wizard in Absentia
M'Lady Witch
Quicksilver's Knight

Starship Troupers

A Company of Stars
We Open on Venus
A Slight Detour

The Rhyming Wizard

Her Majesty's Wizard
The Oathbound Wizard
The Witch Doctor
The Secular Wizard
My Son the Wizard

The StarStone

The Shaman
The Sage

Christopher Stasheff

A Wizard in Chaos

A Tom Doherty Associates Book
New York

This is a work of fiction. All the characters and events portrayed in this novel are either fictitious or are used fictitiously.

A WIZARD IN CHAOS

This book is printed on acid-free paper.

A Tor Book
Published by Tom Doherty Associates, Inc.
175 Fifth Avenue
New York, NY 10010

Tor Books on the World Wide Web:
http://www.tor.com

Library of Congress Cataloging-in-Publication Data

Stasheff, Christopher.
A wizard in chaos / Christopher Stasheff.—1st ed.
p. cm.
"A Tom Doherty Associates book."
ISBN 0-312-86032-3 (hardcover)
I. Title.
PS3569.T3363W586 1997
813′.54—dc21 97-23603
CIP

First Edition: December 1997

Printed in the United States of America

0 9 8 7 6 5 4 3 2 1

A Wizard in Chaos

1

The roar of battle filled Cort's ears, deafening him. He couldn't even hear the bellow as the enemy soldier swung his broadsword. He only saw the man's mouth gaping.

Cort caught the blow on his shield. It jarred his arm all the way to the shoulder, but he couldn't hear the blade ring. He pivoted and stabbed crosswise at the foeman's sword arm. The man rolled back, catching Cort's blade on his own, but was too slow trying to return the stroke. Cort let his blade's rebound help him in swinging up, over, and down at the man's shoulder. The soldier's mouth widened in an unheard scream as he fell away.

Even in the thick of battle, Cort felt elation that he hadn't had to kill the man. He stood in the forefront of his men on guard, waiting for another enemy boot soldier to fill the place of the one who had fallen—but surprisingly, no one came. Instead, three of the enemy turned and ran from the unceasing blows of Cort's own soldiers. He stood a moment, staring in disbelief. Then a grin of triumph split his face, and a yell of victory from all his platoon split the air. The raw energy of it seemed to strike the enemy in the back and push them on; they ran, then ran faster as Cort's men redoubled their yelling.

Young Aulin leaped forward to chase, howling like a madman.

"Stop him!" Cort cried, and Sergeant Otto leaped after Aulin, two soldiers following him. They caught the boy and sent him spinning back into line. *Thanks be,* Cort thought. It was the third rule of battle every new recruit had to learn: Never chase a routed enemy. Too many of them had been known to turn and fight when you had come too far from the safety of your own lines.

Watching the enemy run, Cort could only think that it was no surprise. They'd been raw farm boys, probably pressed into service by their boss on a week's notice, when he'd found out the Boss of Zutaine had hired the Blue Company to march against him. They hadn't stood a chance against seasoned professionals. It was a wonder they had lasted half an hour!

"We're not just going to let them run, are we, lieutenant?" his master sergeant growled.

"Of course not, Sergeant Otto," Cort replied, "but we wait for the captain's signal."

A bugle rang out, its clear high note piercing the shouting. The Blue Company responded with a massed cheer and started forward.

"Advance!" Cort told the master sergeant, and the man turned to bawl the order to the platoon. They marched forward, picking their way over and through the bodies of the fallen. Cort knew the sight would trouble him horribly when the battle lust had faded, but for now, his heart sang high with the knowledge that boot after boot had attacked him and fallen, but he still walked!

They came to the top of the rise, and Cort saw the bullies in the distance, spurring their way past their own soldiers, knocking them aside in their haste to escape. Their bouncers followed hard on their heels, also mounted—but far ahead, the Blue

Company's reserves came charging down from the pine forest where the captain had hidden them. They had carefully worked their way around the hills and behind the enemy's lines. Now they proved their worth, surrounding the bullies, catching the reins of their rearing warhorses and pulling their heads down, then hauling their masters off their backs. More troopers cut off the bouncers and unhorsed them, too. They let the boots go, running past the Blue Company on either side—common soldiers brought no ransom. Now and then, a boot slowed as if realizing he should defend his masters, but half a dozen Blue Company pikemen turned, bellowing, to change his mind, and the boot ran on in the midst of his fellows.

"No ransoms for us this time," the master sergeant grumbled.

"You weren't thinking of hiding a bouncer away to ransom on your own, were you?" Cort asked with a grin.

"No, of course not, lieutenant!" Sergeant Otto said quickly. "You know me better than that!"

Actually, Cort knew the man well enough to be sure that was exactly what Otto would have done if he'd had the chance, and never mind that a lowly noncom couldn't hold a man of higher rank prisoner. The bouncers' armor alone would have been worth a year's pay for the master sergeant, though the noncom probably would have kept the horseman's sword. "Share and share alike," he reminded Sergeant Otto. "Whoever captures the bullies and bouncers the Blue Company ransoms, we all share equally." They almost never caught a boss, of course.

"I know that!" Sergeant Otto said, then realized Cort had been saying it for the benefit of the three new men who had survived the battle. "After all, the reserves may have caught them, but we're the ones who fought the battle and drove the bullies and their bouncers into the reserves' arms!"

He took a cue well, Cort thought. "We'll have our turn at being reserves, sergeant. Let's just hope that we don't have to charge the enemy to turn the battle when our time comes."

"I'll hope indeed," Otto said with a grin. "There's a farm I'd like to buy, lieutenant, but it's back home in the Domain of Evenstern, not here on a battlefield!"

The recruits behind him forced an uneasy laugh.

They were still marching, but the enemy boots had fled into the pine forest themselves, and the Blue Company held the field.

"There he goes!" Otto pointed at the top of a bald hill, where a horseman, silhouetted against the sky, had turned his horse and ridden down out of sight in the midst of his bodyguards.

Cort nodded. "So the Boss of Wicksley loses the day—and we lose the boss."

Otto shrugged. "Didn't think we'd catch him, did you, lieutenant? Bosses always make sure they'll be safe, no matter who loses."

"He might be caught yet," Cort disagreed, "if he tries to rally what's left of his men."

"More likely he'll ride home to his castle and bar his gates against the Boss of Zutaine." Otto was as tactful as old noncoms have to be, when they're trying to educate brash young officers—not that Cort was new to the trade anymore, having survived a dozen battles. He was a veteran now, so Otto paid him respect as well as tact. "Of course, if Zutaine besieges him, we won't be in on it."

"No, the boss will just use his household troops," Cort agreed. "Can't have a mercenary captain taking Wicksley Castle away from him, can he?" He was very much aware of the new soldiers behind him listening wide-eyed, soaking up every bit of knowledge of soldiering that they could. "A captain does become a boss now and then, but the bosses don't want to let it happen any more often than they can help."

"Suits me." Otto made a face. "I hate siege duty. Give me a clean death in battle, say I, not a lingering one from disease or petty quarreling." He was still aware of the learning going on behind him.

The bugle blew again, and Cort quickly said, "Halt," before Sergeant Otto could turn and bawl it to the troopers.

It never occurred to Cort to wonder why foot soldiers were called "boots" if they fought for a boss, but "troopers" or "soldiers" in a mercenary army, or why their horsemen and junior officers were called "cavalry" and "lieutenants" instead of "bouncers." It was just the way it was, just the way it had always been, just as the men who commanded the mercenary armies were "captains," not "bullies," and the men who ruled a whole district with its dozen or so bullies were called "bosses."

It did occur to him to wonder which of the bodies on the ground were alive, and which dead. "Winnow the bodies, men! Cart the live ones to the surgeons, and bury the dead."

"Why bury them if they're not Blue Company troopers, lieutenant?" one of the new men asked, frowning.

"Because their bodies will rot and spread disease through all of us! Plant them and let them make next year's crops rich, men! And remember the songs your village sage taught you. Sing them while you lower their bodies down and cover them up. We don't want their ghosts walking, any more than their diseases, or the Fair Folk summoning them forth to be mindless slaves!"

The raw soldiers blanched, and turned to start hunting.

"It'll keep them from having the shakes for a little while, at least," Cort told his master sergeant.

"Yes, but the weakness will be worse when it hits, for having seen so many dead bodies in a single day," Otto predicted. "At least they should lose their stomachs pretty early on, so we'll have an excuse to send them off to rest."

Cort remembered his first battle and shuddered. "I suppose they have to go through it all, don't they?"

"If they want to stay in this trade, they do," Otto returned. "Of course, after today, all three of them may decide to resign and take their chances with their boss's draft."

"I wouldn't blame them for a second," Cort said grimly.

"Then again, today they've seen how the boots were driven on in front of the bouncers, to take the worst blows and the highest death count," Otto observed.

"And seen how you and I led our men and took our chances right along with them," Cort said. "I wouldn't blame them for quitting, sergeant, but their chances for living will be a lot better with us."

Otto nodded. "You've lived almost four years since you joined up, sir, and I've lived nearly ten. We've both seen comrades fall all around us, but nowhere nearly so many as if we'd stayed home and fought for our bullies. No, all in all, I'd rather be a sergeant than a brute."

Cort knew that "brute" was only the bosses' name for a non-com, but he appreciated the double meaning anyway.

"But you, sir, you've seen how the bouncers may be wounded and captured, but seldom killed." Otto looked up at his young master with a glint in his eye. "Your chances for long life are better with a bully instead of a captain, at least until you start your own company. Why stay?"

"Because I'd rather have a quick grave than a long prison term while I waited for my bully to save up the ransom money," Cort answered shortly.

That wasn't it, of course, and by Otto's approving nod, he knew the sergeant knew it. It was simply that Cort couldn't have brought himself to have driven plowboys before him to their deaths—and Otto knew that, too.

He turned away, wrenching his mind away from his embarrassing lack of hardness. "You take half the men and search our ground to the east, sergeant, while I take the rest to the west."

"Yes, sir! Ho! Squads one and two! With me! Squads three and four! Follow the lieutenant!"

Cort started off, back toward the knoll where the Blue Company's flag stood, eyes on the ground now. Even from this distance, he could see the occasional plain rough-woven tunic of a serf who hadn't been a soldier. His mouth tightened in a grimace; he tasted bile. There were always a few plowboys who didn't move fast enough and were ground to mincemeat between the two armies. There were always a few serf women whom the soldiers found right after the battle, when blood lust and plain lust were both high, and those women were ground up in a different way, before an officer or bouncer could stop it—if he wanted to stop it. It was tragic, but there was no help for it; it happened so often that it was just part of war.

Over the horizon from Cort, in a pasture screened on two sides by woods and on the third by a mountain, the great golden ship came spinning down to the ground, light as a ballerina, in the middle of a pasture. It was so noiseless that even the cows sleeping nearby didn't look up.

The ramp extended, sliding down from the ship to the ground. Gar led the mare down its slope, Dirk following with the stallion. They had caught and tamed the two horses in a wilderness a thousand miles away, but had only been gentling the beasts for two weeks. They were still half-wild, but Gar was a projective telepath, so the mare went quietly under his spell. The stallion jerked his head against the bridle, though, rolling his eyes.

"Spare a thought for my mount!" Dirk called.

Gar glanced back, and the stallion quieted.

They came down onto firm ground, and both horses seemed to relax, though their flanks still quivered. "Not bad for their first spaceship ride," Dirk said. "Did you have to keep them hypnotized the whole way?"

"Probably not," Gar said, "but it was only a fifteen-minute hop, so I kept them in trances just to be on the safe side." He raised his voice a little. "Back to orbit, Herkimer. Stay tuned."

"I will await your communications, Magnus," said the resonant voice of the ship's computer. It called its owner by his birthname, not the nickname he had won on his travels. "Good luck."

The ramp drew back in, and the huge disk rose silently, spinning away into the night, until it was only one more star among many.

"How far to the nearest castle?" Dirk said.

"About a dozen miles, but there was a battle going on there this afternoon, and the troops seemed to be celebrating as we were coming in for a landing," Gar answered. "We might do better to head for the nearest town."

"Let's hear it for city lights." Dirk mounted.

So did Gar. They rode off side by side toward the dim track that Herkimer's night-sight program had shown them.

"How about this," Dirk suggested. "We ride together until we're sure the way is reasonably safe, then split up to spy out the lay of the land and what's on it."

"My instincts are against it," Gar said, frowning. "There're too many evils that can happen to one of us alone."

"Yes, especially on a planet like this, founded by a group of very idealistic, quasi-religious anarchists. I guess they managed to stay peaceful, living under colony domes, long enough to Terraform the continent."

Gar nodded. "Then, when the land was ready for the seeds of Terran plants, they opted for the primitive life, going out to farm and live in small villages of prefab huts, with no government higher than a village meeting." He sighed. "How could they possibly have thought it could last?"

"They figured they could all just imitate the saintly lives of their sages," Dirk reminded him, "and that would keep them from hurting one another or offending one another—or so say the historical notes in the databank. Voila! No need for government!"

"Not exactly hard-headed realists, then."

Dirk nodded. "I'll bet they were determined not to depend on high-tech agriculture or sophisticated birth control techniques."

"But they did depend on human nature being considerably more virtuous than it is," Gar said darkly.

"So they fell back into a medieval standard of living."

"They were probably idealistic enough not to mind the hardships," Gar sighed. "I wonder what went wrong?"

"What went wrong?" Dirk asked. "Just look at those pictures we took from orbit! Castles on the hilltops with people in satins and furs walking the courtyards, packs of men in armor on horseback, and people in rags plowing the fields! What do you *think* went wrong?"

"Well, yes, that much is obvious," Gar admitted, "but I'd like to know the details. They do seem to have strayed into some form of government."

"Only locally," Dirk said grimly. "How many battles did we spot from orbit? A dozen?"

"Seventeen," Gar admitted. "None of them very big, though."

"Tell that to the men who died in them! And if we just happened in on a day when seventeen battles were in progress, what are the odds that it was an ordinary day?"

"Fairly good," Gar agreed, "though coincidences do happen . . ."

"But not very often. Look at it this way—their ancestors got what they wanted: no government. They just didn't expect it to result in open season for robbers."

"Oh, come now. Isn't that going it a bit strong, calling the local aristocracy robbers?"

"How do you suppose they got those castles? And how can they be aristocracy if there's no king or queen to grant them their titles?"

"Why, they appointed themselves, of course," Gar said mildly. "That's what *my* ancestors did."

"But forgot to appoint a king," Dirk reminded him, "so there's no one to keep them from chewing each other up every year or three, and the common people with them." He shook his head. "No matter how you slice it, there's too much trouble for the two of us to ferret out together—it'd take six months! If we're apart, we can cover twice as much territory and find twice as many problems—or twice as many solutions. Who knows? Maybe we just came down during a dynastic quarrel, and all we have to do is help the right side win."

"Assuming we can define 'right,' under these circumstances," Gar said drily.

"Whichever candidate will be best for the people."

"Easy to say, not so easy to see. Besides, you don't really believe the situation is that simple."

"No, I don't," Dirk sighed. "The peasants are in too much misery to have been oppressed by war for only a year or two. But it could be we're near the end of the local version of the Hundred Years' War."

"Even five could do it," Gar said grimly. "My friend, if I say it's too dangerous to split up, and I'm the one with the psi powers, then it's *really* dangerous."

"It was pretty dangerous where I grew up," Dirk pointed out, "especially since, if I'd been caught, I wouldn't have been only a runaway churl—I'd also have been guilty of treason. But I survived, and I hadn't even met you."

Gar rode in silence, his face stony.

Dirk recognized the reaction to a telling point. "Besides, I'm the one who *doesn't* have a virtual ESP arsenal, so if I'm suggesting we split up, I've got to be fairly sure I'll be safe."

"Not necessarily; I know your dedication," Gar countered. "Still, I'm your friend, not your master. If you want to go, I have no business trying to stop you."

Dirk looked up sharply, wondering if he detected hurt, especially since his big friend's face was still stony. "Don't worry, old son," he said gently. "We can stay in touch with these new toys Herkimer made us." He touched the thick iron brooch that held his cloak. Underneath the enamel, it was an integrated circuit with a miniscule audio pickup; the whole surface acted as a loudspeaker. "Of course, we don't want the peasants getting frightened by talking brooches, so if I need you, I'll chirp like a cricket."

"Yes, well, I hope I won't be in the middle of a battle when you call," Gar said with irony. "Let's plan on comparing notes every evening, shall we? That's a good time to go off by one's self for a few minutes."

"Or to shut the door," Dirk agreed. "Let's state the question we're trying to answer clearly and briefly, then—that always helps when you're trying to find clues to the solution."

"A good idea." Gar was coming out of his melancholy. "We need to resolve whether or not this constant warfare is good for the people as a whole."

"It can't possibly be," Dirk grunted, "but I suppose there's a chance that there's a government under it that would be good for the people, if we could ever get rid of whoever's causing the fighting."

"Or stop the governments themselves from fighting," Gar agreed. "After all, it's not the first planet we've seen that had constant warfare."

"No, but there's a certain vividness to this one that suggests a high degree of dedication," Dirk said with a shudder.

"Try to keep an open mind," Gar urged. "The fighting might be a ritualized political process, with an equally ritualized way of avoiding killing or maiming people, like the Terran Native Americans' custom of counting coup."

"I'll try to keep it in mind," Dirk sighed, "but I doubt it highly."

"I know what you mean. We've never seen a planet where there was so much fighting going on at one time."

"Could be their busy season," Dirk suggested without much hope. "What if we decide this constant warfare isn't just a freak outbreak, though, and can't possibly be good for the people?"

"Then we have to seriously consider the possibility that it must be stopped, and that the governments that cause it, or the lack of governments, need replacing."

"And if they do," said Dirk, "how do we go about replacing them?"

"One question at a time, my friend," Gar said, smiling. "We'll deal with that one if we come to it."

His concentration on the plight of the people had let him ignore the mare; she tossed her head and reared. Gar turned to her, pulling down on the bridle, sending a soothing thought. She came back to all fours, calming considerably.

"Gentling does go faster with your special gifts," Dirk admitted. "You don't suppose they could work on the local lords, do you?"

"Probably," Gar said, "but it would be totally unethical—unless they were so cruel that virtually any method of stopping them, and saving their peasants, would be morally acceptable."

"And if things got that bad, we might as well just lob in a small bomb." Dirk sighed. "Would have been nice if we could have done it the quick way."

"Imposed attitudes seldom last, anyway," Gar told him.

The Boss of Zutaine didn't want to pay off the Blue Company once the battle was done, of course, but he knew he might need them again, and what was worse, he knew he could look down from his battlements to see them camped all around the foot of the hill on which his castle stood, hungover and staggering with headaches, but nonetheless in a perfect position to besiege him. If they did, he knew the siege wouldn't last long. He wasn't fool enough to think that his twenty-three armored bruisers and their ragtag collections of plowboys would stand a chance against a thousand hardened professionals. So he paid—eight times eight times eight gold marks, and an extra eight into the bargain as a token of the boss's goodwill. Two lieutenants counted the pieces out on a chequerboard, stacking the coins four high on each square, then sweeping them into a sack and stacking the next set.

Cort watched, feeling only awe, not greed. There was a certain beauty to the metal as it flashed in the sunlight. He didn't believe the alchemists who claimed it was the purest metal in the universe—too much blood was spilled for it—but it was pretty. Five hundred twelve pieces of gold, each worth twenty silver coins! Eight pieces of silver for each trooper, ten for each lieutenant, one hundred forty for the captain, and two thousand plus eight extra for the Company treasury! But they had fought long and hard for that money, and the pay of those who had died wouldn't be shared out among the living—it would go to the families they had left behind, though it wouldn't last long and couldn't possibly make up for the loss.

So the boss and the captain parted with mutual expressions of gratitude and respect, both knowing that the Blue Company might be hired to fight against Zutaine within the year, and Captain Devers turned his troops to march away.

"Two thousand for the company!" grumbled a soldier who had just survived his first battle. "That's a funny way of saying 'for the captain!'"

"Don't let your tongue wag to make a fool of you," Cort told him. "That treasury makes sure we won't starve if there's no work."

"Aye," said the sergeant, "and it's out of that hoard that Captain Devers sends a silver coin every other month, to each of the families of his troopers who have died."

The young fool stared. "I've never heard of a mercenary captain doing that!"

"They don't," the sergeant growled. "Devers does. That's why I stay with his Blue Company."

The captain paid the lieutenants, and each of them paid their men. Then they marched off on leave, each platoon bent on visiting a different village—the whole company together would have destroyed any town—each roaring to begin celebrating, eager to infest the inns, make the brewers and harlots rich, pester the decent women, and pick fights with the civilian men.

Cort had other plans, though. He had dropped a hint in

each sergeant's ear, and each sergeant had mentioned the town of Bozzeratle as his men were discussing possible destinations—so it wasn't quite by accident that Cort's platoon was marching toward the town in which his fiancée lived.

2

Gar rode out of the forest onto the road, and the merchant shouted, "Bandits!" The spear he used for a staff snapped down, leveled at Gar's stomach. One of his drivers plucked an arrow from his quiver and nocked it in one smooth motion while the other drivers swung their bows around from their backs and strung them.

"Peace, peace!" Gar held up his hands. "I'm no bandit! My name is Gar Pike, and I'm a mercenary looking for honest work!"

"What did you say?" The merchant frowned. "Oh—'honest work.' I can scarcely understand you, your accent's so thick."

He wouldn't have understood Gar at all, a week before. The local dialect had drifted so far from Galactic Standard that Gar had taken quite a while puzzling out the vowel shifts, wandering through markets and sitting in taverns listening, then trying a halting imitation of their words. Now he could at least be understood.

The spear and bow held steady, and the rest of the drivers nocked arrows and drew.

"A soldier for hire?" The merchant frowned with suspicion. He was lean and tall, as these people went, looking hard enough to be a bandit himself, though his tunic and leggins were of broadcloth instead of homespun, with a sleeveless, knee-length robe over them. His colors were all brown and green, the better to blend into the forest around him. "How can we be sure you're honest, not some bandit sent to strike from inside while your mates attack? What proof can you give?"

"No proof at all," Gar said cheerfully, "except for this letter." He had tucked the rolled parchment into the collar of his tunic, where they could see it easily; now he drew it out slowly and tossed it to the merchant. The man caught it and unrolled it, frowning as he studied it.

Gar studied him in return. He'd been surprised to see anything resembling a merchant in such a war-torn country, but he couldn't think what else a commoner with a string of mules loaded with huge packs might be, especially since he was dressed a bit better than his helpers. A merchant had to look prosperous, after all, or no one would have confidence in the goods he sold. With the warlords constantly battling each other, trade should have been very risky indeed—a merchant could never know when a band of soldiers would descend on him to confiscate his goods. He guessed that this man, and the few others like him, must have become very good at finding out where the battles were, and planning routes that kept them far from the skirmishes.

"I can scarcely make out these words," the merchant complained.

"It comes from very far away," Gar explained. It did—about fifty light-years. "They don't speak the language the way you do here."

"Hardly the same language at all," the merchant grumbled.

One more strike against the possibility of any sort of law or order on this planet. A strong government would have tried to keep things from changing too much, and words would take on new forms very slowly if at all. The fact that Galactic Standard had evolved into a local dialect whose speakers could scarcely understand its parent language meant there wasn't anything to put the brakes on the headlong rush into confusion.

"Never heard of this Paolo Braccalese," the merchant grumbled.

"As I say, he's very far away," Gar told him.

"But he speaks well of you." The merchant rolled up the parchment with sudden decision and thrust it back at Gar. "And we can surely use someone of your size. All right, you're hired. I'm Ralke, and I'm your master now—but if you betray us, you'll be looking for some new guts."

So Gar joined the caravan—and that afternoon, the bandits attacked.

They burst from the roadside trees howling like banshees, pikes up to skewer the drivers. Mules bawled and balked, and Gar barely had time to draw his sword. The driver-archer shouted even as he drew and loosed; then the next arrow was on his bowstring, and the other drivers had strung their bows, but the bandits were in among them, stabbing and swinging. One driver screamed as he fell from his mule.

"At them, lads! They don't want your goods, they want your lives!" Ralke shouted as he parried a stabbing pike, then chopped off its head.

"Only goods!" one bandit shouted. "Throw down your weapons and we'll spare you! We only want the goods to sell!" Then he snarled and swung the headless spear shaft at the merchant's head.

Gar turned a pike with his shield and thrust into the bandit's shoulder, roaring. The man fell back, and Gar turned, spurring his horse, riding back along the line of mules, chopping pikeheads and slashing at soldiers, bellowing bloody murder. The bandits fell back from the terrible giant long enough for the drivers to launch a flight of arrows. Several of the bandits fell, howling and clutching at shafts. Their mates shouted in rage and charged the drivers again, screaming, "Die, scum!"

The drivers dropped their bows and yanked short swords

from the scabbards on their saddles. Another driver fell howling, a pike gash pumping blood, but Gar turned and chopped through the shaft, then struck the bandit on his steel cap. The blow rang, the man fell—and suddenly, the bandits were turning, running, leaping, disappearing back into the trees.

"Nock arrows!" Ralke shouted. "They might come again!"

"We'd better see to the wounded." Gar started to dismount.

But Ralke shouted, "No! Let the drivers do the bandaging! You stay on guard! Johann!"

"Aye?" said one of the driver-archers.

"Tie up those soldiers. Karl! Watch the fallen ones and make sure none of them swings on Johann!"

Karl nodded and moved over to the prisoners, hard-faced.

Gar hesitated, then swung back into the saddle again, glancing at the trees, then at the half-dozen bandits who lay groaning and writhing on the ground—except for two who lay very still. He was amazed how well-equipped they were, each wearing a hardened leather breastplate and a steel cap.

Then he realized that they were all dressed alike.

"Master Ralke!" he cried. "They aren't common bandits—they're soldiers!"

"Yes, out of work and on furlough," Ralke said grimly. "But soldiers will be ashamed of being beaten off by a train of traders, so they're all the more likely to come back than common bandits would be. I was wise to invest in your services, Gar Pike. If it hadn't been for you roaring like an ogre and slashing like a windmill, they would have slain us all!"

"Would they really?" Gar turned to him with a troubled frown.

"I've seen it happen," Ralke answered, and two of his drivers nodded.

"I only escaped by pretending to be dead," one said.

"I ran," the other told him, "I was lucky. I looked back and saw the rest of my caravan being slaughtered."

"Haven't been guarding merchants long, have you?" Ralke asked, frowning up at him.

"Not in this land, no," Gar said carefully. "The bandits in Talipon weren't quite so thorough."

"Well, common bandits aren't, either," Ralke said. "They just want the goods, and if we gave them up without a fight, they might even leave us without a blow."

"But what would we have to sell at the next town, then?" one of the drivers asked. "And with nothing to sell, what would we eat?"

"I didn't work and save for ten years until I could buy my first cargo, just to make some bandit richer," Ralke huffed.

The drivers all nodded, and Gar guessed they were hoping to do the same. "But soldiers are different?"

"Of course. They don't dare let us live, you see," Ralke told him. "If their captain found out about it, he'd flog them within an inch of their lives."

Gar stared. "You mean they weren't acting on their captain's orders?"

" 'Course not," Ralke huffed, and a driver explained, "We're too small for a captain to notice, but his soldiers might try to pick up some easy money."

"We just have to make sure it's not easy," another driver said grimly.

"There's truth in that," Ralke said. "We don't even have to be able to beat them, just wound them badly, be able to kill even one of them. They face death on the battlefield every few weeks—why take a chance on it with a merchant caravan?"

"So they only attacked us because they thought we were weaker than they were," Gar inferred.

"That they did, and I would have thought the mere sight of you would have turned them away," Ralke said.

Gar shook his head. "Professionals always know they can beat an amateur hands down. They just didn't know that I'd been in an army, too."

"They didn't know that we'd faced bandits five times before, either," one of the drivers said grimly.

"Unpleasant surprises all around," Gar agreed.

"For your own merit, give us some healing!" one of the bandit soldiers cried.

Ralke glanced again at his own wounded men. "They're almost done bandaging their fellows. They'll get to you in a minute. There's none of you so badly hurt that you can't wait a little."

Actually, one of them had been, but Gar had been doing a little telekinetic first aid, pinching off an artery until he could make its severed wall grow back together. "What will you do with them, Master Ralke?"

"Leave them tied up," Ralke said simply. "But we'll leave a note for their captain, too, explaining that they were trying to rob merchants."

"No!" a fallen soldier cried. "He'll flog us soggy, you know he will!"

"Be glad you'll live," Ralke said grimly.

"Will he really?" Gar asked. "Flog them, I mean."

"The captain? He will, and all their squadron with them—so as soon as we're gone, they'll come out of the trees to help their fellows and destroy the note." Ralke shrugged. "No matter. Sooner or later, one of them will grow angry with the others and tell the captain for revenge."

The fallen mercenary spat at him. It fell short.

"I hope you cast a spear better than that," Ralke countered. Then he explained to Gar, "Most of the mercenary companies have very strict rules about looting the people who might hire them next time—and you never know what town a merchant's from, so most of the captains are careful to leave us alone. Their soldiers, though, think that's foolish."

"Done, Master Ralke." Johann came up to him, wiping blood off his hands. "That will hold them till their mates get them to the company surgeon. I'd love to hear the story they're going to tell him as to how they came by those wounds!"

"It'll be a champion fable for sure," Ralke agreed. "Too bad none of them can write well enough to copy it for us to read later. Enough time spent on them, lads. Lash our own men to their saddles and be off!"

They moved on, even the three wounded drivers riding. None of the wounds was terribly severe, though one would have been without Gar's invisible help. Two men wore slings, but only needed one hand to ride and encourage the mules.

As soon as they were out of sight of the fallen mercenaries, Gar said, "You know that none of those soldiers will really tell the captain, of course."

"I know, but I have to let them think I believe they will, or they'll call in some of their comrades to track us down," Ralke said. "I recognized their colors, though. They're the Badger Company. Their captain is probably a good customer at the taverns at Therngee Town, just over those hills." He pointed at the range ahead. "When we stop there to trade, I'll leave him a note telling what his men have done and describing the one with the long scar on his cheek. That will probably be enough for him to recognize, and if he knows one, he'll know their whole squadron." He shook his head. "Few enough of us merchants survive, what with bandits and wild beasts and bosses who decide to take our goods without paying us. We don't need the hazards of the professional soldiers, too."

"I'm surprised to see so much greed here, Master Ralke," Gar said. "In my far-off land, no one uses money, or tries to take anyone else's goods."

"Oh, don't they, now! And how do they pay their taxes?"

"There aren't any." Gar tried to describe the original settlement on this planet. "There aren't any bosses to demand them. There aren't any cities, either, only villages, and the people get together in the evenings to discuss their problems, and work out any disputes."

Ralke barked laughter, short, sharp, and sarcastic. "That must be a golden land indeed! The old tales tell us that our ancestors lived like that, hundreds of years ago—but there are always greedy people being born, and people who are better at fighting than anyone else and see no reason why they should sweat digging and hoeing in the fields when they can just take what they want from people who're weaker."

"That's how the bullies began, eh?"

"Bullies indeed! But they found out quickly enough that some bullies were stronger than others, and could beat them all one by one if they didn't do as they were told—bigger thugs who put together armies of bullies, each of whom had his own band of bruisers, and that's how the bosses came to be."

Gar nodded; folklore confirmed his guess. "And the merchants?"

Again the bark of laughter. "Mercenaries came first, but taxes came before any. I told you that the bullies took what they wanted instead of working to raise crops, weave cloth, or build houses. Well, the bosses made the bullies gather the food and cloth for them, and the bullies, not to be outdone, appointed their best bruisers to collect the goods, and not just enough for the bosses, of course, but for themselves, too . . ."

"And the bruisers decided to take a little extra for themselves."

"Most surely. The upshot of it was that they took everything but the bare necessities the common people needed to keep them alive. They took their jewelry, too, the necklaces and bracelets of amber and shells that the people had made for themselves—and when they brought them back to the boss, he recognized some of the beads as being of gold."

"And all the old tales told how much gold was worth," Gar interpreted.

Ralke nodded. "Children's tales, and stories from old books. The boss told the people of that village that they could keep half of their next year's crops, if they gave him more gold beads instead. He gave each of his bruisers a few gold beads as part of their pay, and they gave them to their boots. The boots took them back to the village and traded them for food and drink—and trade and money were both born."

Reborn, rather. Gar was more sure than ever that philosophy could never triumph over human nature. "And gold gave rise to mercenaries?"

"Well, it gave the bosses a way to pay soldiers without keeping them as part of their household forever. For that, there are some who say that mercenaries invented money, or were the cause of that invention, at least—and they may be right."

"Don't the old tales tell?" Gar asked.

Ralke shrugged. "The tales say that Langobard, the first captain, was one of the few left alive when two bosses fought over his people's village and chewed it up in the fighting. Langobard gathered the few others who lived and took to the greenwood. I don't know if they were the first bandits, but they've certainly become the most famous! In the next few years, others whose villages had been burned came to join him, as well as those who disobeyed the bosses, turning on their tax collectors and killing them. His band became the largest and richest in the forest, preying off the tax collectors and, later, the parties of bruisers sent to kill them. At last the Boss of Tungri, who claimed the forest, came himself with all his army to slay the bandits, and Langobard knew his day was done, unless he could invent a scheme to delay the boss."

"I take it he was very inventive."

"Oh, most surely! He sent a band to raid the borders of the boss's neighbor, the Bully of Staucheim, and the bully called on his master, the Boss of Dolgobran, who called up all his bullies and their men and marched off against Tungri."

"But Tungri didn't know about it, being deep in the woods chasing Langobard."

"He found out quickly enough. The messenger reached him the next morning, as his army was breaking camp among the trees. Tungri cursed and turned his men to ride home—but as they came to a meadow, they found Langobard and his men drawn up awaiting them under a white flag. Langobard told the boss that he and his men were tired of living like wild animals and offered their services to him in exchange for new clothes and a year's food, so that they would no longer need to rob tax collectors. I'm sure the taste was sour in Tungri's mouth, but he needed to ride against Dolgobran without delay, and didn't dare lose men in a fight with Langobard."

"Plus, having Langobard's troops on his side couldn't hurt," Gar observed.

"Indeed not! He struck his deal with Langobard and marched against Dolgobran forthwith. They won the day, and Tungri paid Langobard out of Dolgobran's granaries. Thus were the mercenaries born."

"Did Tungri ever learn why Dolgobran marched against him?"

"Of course, but he never learned where the raiders had come from." Ralke chuckled. "The common folk did, but the bosses never heard the tale till Langobard, Dolgobran, and Tungri were long in their graves. By that time, there were so many bands of mercenaries, and the bosses needed their services so badly, that there was no taking revenge, and no point in it, either."

"A shrewd man, this Langobard," Gar observed.

Ralke nodded. "He lived out his life till old age took him in his bed, and which of us can ask for more?"

Well, there were a great many people on a great many worlds in the galaxy who could ask for more, such as happiness, full bellies, and a few little luxuries. Gar took it as a measure of this land's desperation, that the people's highest dream was simply to survive. "You must be asking for more than being allowed to live until you die, Master Ralke, or you wouldn't risk your life carrying goods from one town to another."

"The hope of making a better life for wife and children make a man do foolish things." But Ralke grinned. "Besides, I like the thrill of it, and the chance that I'll be paid better than a soldier in the end."

"I'm not sure many troopers think of their work as thrilling," Gar said drily. "Still, you could have become some sort of craftsman—let's say a silversmith. Even the bosses must have to pay a man well if there aren't very many who can do the work."

"Ah, but for that, you have to have a talent for crafting things well." Ralke held up wide hands with short, thick fingers. "I have no gift in working with silver, or with wood or clay for that matter—but I do seem to have a knack for striking a good bargain."

"And for fighting?" Gar asked.

"That too, yes. My father was a mercenary, though he never stayed in one place long enough to marry. I, at least, can come home to a wife at the end of each trading journey."

If you live, Gar thought, but didn't say so. Ralke was silent for a minute, too, and Gar had a notion the words ran through the other man's mind, as well. He didn't try to read his thoughts, though—there wasn't reason enough.

Cort's men began to grumble as they passed town after town in their march to liberty. Sergeant Otto finally said, "All the other platoons have already stopped, lieutenant, and it's almost sunset. Why are we still going?"

"For the same reason we kept marching last month, and the month before," Cort told him. "Why did only the Sky and Indigo platoons stop at the first village?"

"Why," said the master sergeant, "because there weren't enough inns and whores there for more than . . ." His voice ran out as his face turned thoughtful. "Well, it's true that Bozzeratle Town is fresher—the landlord at the inn gladder to see us, and the whores, too. They aren't as jaded, either."

"The farther away the village, the more welcome we are," Cort told him. "Still, there are limits to that welcome. Remind the men to watch their manners."

"Be sure that I will," Sergeant Otto said grimly, then called back to his staff sergeants, "Bozzeratle Town! Tell 'em not to go throwing their weight around! We want to be welcome next month, too!"

The men answered with a shout of joy. An hour later, they marched into Bozzeratle and burst into the inn.

Cort stayed long enough to drink a flagon, and to make sure his sergeants were staying vigilant and not drinking too much. The soldiers *were* drinking too much, of course—that was half the reason why they'd come. But they were jovial and, if not actually polite, at least not offering harm to anyone, particularly the serving wenches, though they joked with them and praised their charms. Drunk or sober, they all knew the captain's rule: If the wench offered herself, all well and good to accept, but if she didn't, no soldier of the Blue Company could even ask. That didn't mean that none of them would, of course, but it did mean that the sergeant would be there to stop him before he frightened anyone. The better companies were very strict as to how their soldiers treated civilians—you never knew which town, or even village, might scrape up the money to hire you next month.

Satisfied that all was as much under control as it could be, Cort went out the door, walking quickly in the gathering darkness, back to the town's central street, then left into a lane that was just as broad, and boasted tall houses with wide lawns. Lamps on top of poles burned here and there, giving the street a dim light, far more than the rest of the village had. Every house had a lamp burning by the door, too. This was where the more prosperous citizens lived, the ones who had become vital to the bosses' security or comfort in one way or another—retired officers, a merchant or two, and the local doctor.

Cort hurried up the flagstone walk of the third house on the right and thumped the knocker. After a few moments, a face appeared at the door, stared in surprise, then opened it. "Lieutenant Cort!" said the aging man with the candelabra in his hand. "What a surprise!"

He didn't look pleased—nervous, in fact—but Cort didn't

notice that in his hurry. "The captain never tells us ahead of time when we'll have liberty," he said, by way of apology. "Good to see you again, Barley. Are your master and mistress in—and Miss Violet?"

"The master and mistress, of course! This way, if you will, lieutenant. They're in the sitting room." Barley turned away, and Cort followed him eagerly. He had been dreaming of Violet every night, and whenever there was a free moment during the day. It had been a month since he had seen her. Her raven ringlets, her warm brown eyes, her full red lips curved in a coquettish smile—his heart skipped a beat at the mere thought of her, and soon he would see her!

3

Madam, master—Lieutenant Cort has come to call." Cort pushed past the butler, pulse thumping, smile wide with anticipation. Bruiser Ellsworth and his wife were rising to greet him, he alert, watchful, ready for anything—but she looked troubled, even, perhaps, afraid.

Alarm vibrated through Cort. "Is Violet well?"

"Oh, yes, quite well, young man," Mistress Ellsworth said, "but she isn't at home."

"Well, that's a relief. I was afraid—I mean—"

"A young man is always afraid for the young woman who has caught his eye," Bruiser Ellsworth said, "and rightly so, in a world like ours. Violet is well, but she isn't with us just now. Will you sit, lieutenant?"

"Yes, thank you, sir." Cort took the chair the older man indicated.

"Port, I think, Barley," Ellsworth said. The butler nodded, turning away to leave the room.

An awkward silence fell, but Cort didn't mind it, really; he reveled in the warmth and home-feeling of the house and of Violet's parents. All were solid and stable, reassuring in the way the two older people clasped hands still, even at their age. Mistress Ellsworth's figure was matronly, but scarcely portly, and she was still handsome, with hints of the beauty she had been in her youth. She wore a long, dark-blue gown with a broad white collar, her gold-and-silver hair in a coil that seemed more like a coronet. As for her husband, the title "bruiser" seemed very ill-fitting—he was still muscular and sharp-eyed, of course, but his hair had streaks of silver now, his beard and mustache were almost completely gray, and he seemed so prosperous and contented that it was hard to imagine him as a man of war.

As to the room, it was pleasant, somehow combining luxury and thrift, letting the visitor know that the owners had more than enough money, but were careful how they spent it. A fire burned in a small fireplace, only waist high, but tiled and with a mantelpiece elaborately carved. The walls were painted butter-yellow, reflecting the fire's glow with warmth, and the walnut flooring was polished to a similar glow. A brightly patterned carpet covered most of it. Furniture consisted of only a chest against one wall and a settee on one side of the fireplace facing the two chairs on the other, all of dark, carved wood, all padded, all solid and comfortable. It was more than spartan, less than extravagant, and very much a home.

The bruiser stirred and broke the silence. "So you've won your battle, then?"

"Aye, and only two small wounds to show for it," Cort confirmed. "How did you know, sir?"

"Well, the lack of serious wounds spoke somewhat, but the energy and eagerness in you spoke more. A mercenary is downcast when he's lost a battle, lieutenant, and not only because he's lost the second half of his pay."

"I don't think the boss was any too happy about having to pay that," Cort said with a grin.

"They never are," the bruiser assured him. "Fifteen years as a mercenary, though, and only twice did I see a boss or a bully try to renege on that second payment when we'd won his war for him." His smile was hard. "We took it from them both, of course."

Cort remembered the clash of arms and a boss crying "Enough, enough!" "They don't try it often."

Ellsworth nodded. "Bruisers and boots only fight once a year or so, and a quarter of our force is always straight from the plow. Mercenaries fight every month. There are few bosses indeed who can stand against even one free company."

Cort frowned. "Then why . . ." He caught himself in time, realizing his rudeness. "Excuse me, sir."

"Why did I take service with a boss and become a bruiser instead of trying to build my own free company?" Ellsworth smiled. "Well asked, young man, and the more so because you'll have to make the choice yourself, some day. Well, a bruiser's life is more certain—when you only fight once a year, there's twelve more chances you'll come home to your wife and children alive. And the pay is just as good as a lieutenant's. True, a captain has greater income, but greater expenses, too, and a greater risk of losing all. Even if my boss were beaten and he had to yield some of his land, I'd still be his man, and still have the income of the farms he bids me supervise for him."

"And if yours were the lands he yielded to the victor, the new boss would probably still have you watch over his new farmers for him." Cort nodded.

"Oh, he might have a mercenary officer who wanted to become his bruiser," Ellsworth said, with a grin that as much as said that was how he'd come by his own land and title. "Even then, though, I'd still be my boss's man, and though my family would have to yield this house to the new bruiser, we'd still have housing within the boss's castle."

"It is a more certain life," Cort agreed. "In fact, it's enough to make me wonder why any man would become a captain."

"Wealth," Ellsworth said simply. "If a captain manages to hold a winning company together for even ten years, he can retire as rich as any boss. But the price is heavy, young man. I've seen very few who married before they retired, and fifty is late to begin a family."

Cort thought about that—then suddenly thought about nothing, because there, through the great window facing the front of the house, he saw his Violet coming down the walk, laughing, bright-eyed, vivacious, beautiful, thoroughly desirable . . .

And on the arm of a young civilian, gazing up into his face, and there was no mistaking the light in her eyes—it was love.

Cort hadn't been aware he'd come to his feet, but Ellsworth was saying, "Sit down, now, lieutenant, sit down. It's not as though you'd been betrothed, after all, and a maiden does have the right to change her mind as her heart tells her—a right, and even a duty."

"You could have told me."

"We were warming to it," Dame Ellsworth said, voice trembling.

It was true, Cort realized—the bruiser had led the conversation to marrying, and not marrying. Ten minutes more, and he probably would have broken the news to Cort as gently as he could.

"Thank you for trying to be kind," he said in a brittle voice that he scarcely recognized as his own. "I'd better go."

"Surely not!" Dame Ellsworth protested, and there was definitely fear in her voice now. Cort would have told her not to worry, he wouldn't beat up his rival right there on her doorstep, but his anger choked him to silence. He strode to the door, yanked it open, and went out and down the path, walking quickly, but managing a stiff "Good evening" to Violet and her swain as he passed by. She stared at him in shock that turned quickly to fear, and the young man looked up with a scowl that turned to wariness as he recognized a mercenary officer. He was soft as a slug, Cort thought with disgust, but he had to admit the man was handsome, and jealousy gnawed at his vitals. He walked even faster, through the gateposts and out into the street, Violet's wail of distress fading behind him.

His stride ate up the ground, even though he was stiff with hurt and rage. Blind misery choked him, choked his mind; it was ten minutes before his thoughts cleared enough to realize where his feet were taking him: not to the inn, but down a side street to the row of cheap taverns, where his rowdiest men would be carousing, taverns that served brandy, not ale, taverns where they didn't mind a bit of brawling, and the wenches were outright whores.

Cort wasn't sure which he needed most: the whore, the brandy, or the brawl. Then he decided there was no need to choose, and strode on down a street that rapidly narrowed to an alley and left the broad ways, and the lights, behind.

By sunset, the merchant caravan had come out of the woods and was plodding across a wide, flat land with low grass and, here and there, cattle grazing. *Too little water for good farming,* Gar thought. A hill bulged up in the middle of the flatness, seeming very much out of place, its sides sweeping up in a slope gentle enough for cattle to graze on, its top a perfect dome. Gar had a notion a gas bubble had been trapped in molten rock there, in the early days of the planet when everything was in flux.

Master Ralke looked about him anxiously. "I don't like this, don't like it at all. We're too much of a danger to those mercenaries—they don't dare have us bear word to their captain."

"Wouldn't they be more afraid to attack you again?" Gar asked. "After all, if their captain would flog them for stealing, what will he do to them for murder?"

Ralke cast him a peculiar look. "What womb did you just crawl out of? If we hadn't fought them off, they'd have killed us all!"

Gar stared. "Killed us? Just for a few mule-loads of goods?"

"They're mercenaries," Ralke said. "Killing means nothing to them. They do it for money every time they go into battle. Why not do it for loot?"

Gar felt a chill down his back. "Then we'd better find ourselves a campsite we can defend easily, where they won't have much chance of sneaking up on us."

"Where, on a flat and featureless plain?" Ralke demanded.

"The plain is our friend," Gar told him. "There's nowhere to hide, no cover to help them sneak up on us. But atop that hill would be even better." He pointed.

"On top of a Hollow Hill? Are you mad?" Ralke cried. "But I forget—you're a foreigner. Don't you have them at home?"

"Not like that one, no." Gar said, bemused. "How do you know it's hollow?"

"Because it's a dome! Those are the hills the Fair Folk choose for their palaces!"

"Fair Folk? What are they?"

"Bad luck just to talk about! Not even a boss dares bring their displeasure down upon him! Armies never fight in the shadow of their hills, for fear the Fair Folk will be angry and come out to slay them all with their magic!"

It did sound something like the Wee Folk of Gar's home planet—but it also sounded useful. "Then let's camp on its slopes, if the mercenaries are afraid to attack us there."

"Oh, wise indeed," Ralke said, with withering scorn. "We'll be safe from the bandits, sure enough—but the Fair Folk will come out and kidnap us all! I think perhaps I had better choose our campsite, soldier!"

"If you will," Gar sighed. "I'd suggest right out in the middle of the plain, though, and as close to the hill as is safe. After all, if we're afraid of the Fair Folk, maybe the soldiers will be even more so." Superstition, he reflected, had its uses.

Cort was almost to the tavern alley when he heard the call for help—the scream, rather; a young woman's scream, high, piercing, and terrified. His anger instantly transmuted into savage joy—action was the tonic his wounded heart needed. Cort ran toward the cry, kicking garbage out of the way as he went. He skidded around a corner and saw three of his own soldiers laughing and dancing about a young civilian and his lady. She clung to his arm, effectively barring him from drawing his sword, but he flourished his torch valiantly, thrusting it at any soldier who came too close. The troopers laughed and jeered at him.

"Come, pretty boy! Draw your tin sword, so we can chop it off!"

"Chop off the hand with it," a second soldier said, and guffawed.

"No need to get hurt," the third soldier advised. "Just walk on home and leave her to us. We'll be her escort." He leaped in, hand reaching for the girl.

"Get away from her!" the young man shouted, thrusting with the torch. The soldier laughed, stepped aside, and plucked the torch from his fingers. His mates howled with glee and stepped in, fists pumping. The young man fought valiantly with his single arm for about fifteen seconds before a haymaker caught him on the side of the head. He slumped to the ground.

"Tenn-*hut*!" Cort barked, and the three troopers came to attention out of sheer reflex. One had the good sense to hold the torch up anyway.

"You mangy scum!" Cort prowled about them, though all his instincts screamed to join them in their sport, not stop them. After all, it was a civilian man who had stolen his sweetheart, and a civilian woman who had hurt him. But he was an officer, and had his duties to his captain. "What in blazes do you think you're doing? What's the captain's one rule about civilians?"

"Leave 'em alone, sir," one of the soldiers said through stiff lips.

"Too right, leave them alone!"

"Unless they swings first, lieutenant," one of the other men objected.

"First, and often, and show no sign of stopping! Don't even try to tell me this lad was attacking you, trooper! Or were you afraid his lady might beat you to a pulp?"

The trooper reddened, but held his brace.

"You lousy excuses for human beings!" Cort raged. He couldn't yell at Violet, after all, but he could damn well yell at his own men—especially since they deserved it. "You scrapings from the trash barrel! You slime off the bottom of a boat! Fifty women willing to go with you for a coin, and you have to pick on a maiden!"

"There was a long line, lieutenant," one of the men offered.

"What, were you afraid you'd be too drunk by the time your turn came? Well, it's going to be a hell of a lot longer wait now, trooper—a month or more!"

One of them, a newbie, opened his mouth to protest, but Cort bellowed, "And if you don't look sharp, you'll spend that month in the guardhouse! Now apologize to this lady! *And* her escort! Of course, I don't expect you know how to be polite, so I'll show you!" He turned to the young woman, who was kneeling with her escort's head in her lap, sobbing.

The tears left Cort at a loss, so he did the only thing he could. Doffing his cap, he said, "My deepest apologies, young lady. My troopers are a bunch of ruffians who ought to be kept in a cage. I humbly ask your pardon for their misbehavior."

The young man blinked, gave his head a shake, then stared up at Cort in alarm.

"They won't trouble you again, sir," Cort assured him. "My most humble apologies. I can only say that they were drunk and didn't really know what they were doing."

"But we do!"

Cort spun about and saw six hard faces lit by another torch. Three of them carried quarterstaves, three carried naked swords. They wore no uniforms, and with a sinking heart, Cort realized what they were—an amateur citizens' patrol, cobbled together as soon as they'd heard the soldiers had come to town.

"Our fellow townsman down with his lady cowering by him, four soldiers standing over them—oh, we know what they were doing, all right! Beat their heads in, men!"

The citizens shouted and started forward. The woman screamed.

"Guard!" Cort shouted, and his three troopers spun about, pulling out the only weapons they had: their daggers. Cort's sword and dagger hissed out of their sheaths, and the citizens hesitated; even outnumbered and underarmed, the professional soldiers were frightening.

Then the citizen leader snarled and started forward.

"Protect yourselves!" Cort shouted.

Daggers whipped up; the professionals caught the slashing swords on their knives, then slammed punches to the stomachs. Two of the citizens folded, but the staff-men waded in over them, and the third swordsman swung at Cort.

"Truce!" he shouted, even as he caught the man's blade on his own. "I've called them off! Truce!"

The swordsman grinned, and Cort realized the man thought he had the soldiers on the run. "Footpad!" the civilian shouted, and swung again.

Cort parried with his own blade, suddenly afraid of these amateurs, even more afraid of the captain's rage if he found they'd slain even one civilian, but most afraid of all that he might have to tell his hard-boiled fighting men to let themselves go. "Put down your swords, and we'll sheathe our daggers!" he cried. "We don't want to hurt you!"

"Don't want *us* to hurt *you,* you mean!" the swordsman called back, and thrust at him. Cort whirled aside, struck the blade down with his own, then kicked the man in the belly. He folded, but the girl's escort had recovered, and leaped for Cort with his own sword out, shouting, "Bastard!"

Cort just barely caught the blade on his dagger, then lifted his sword to parry, ready to thrust if he had to, the command to unleash his human hounds on the tip of his tongue.

But a quarterstaff struck downward, knocking both blades aside, and a strongly accented voice rang in Cort's ears, crying, "Put up your weapons! Soldiers and townsfolk both! Put up your weapons, or I'll break them all, and you into the bargain!"

Whoever he was, he was already behind Cort. The officer spun and saw that quarterstaff whirling, then lashing out to crack against one of the civilian's staves and leaping back into its whirl. Another civilian reached up his staff with a shout; the stranger struck it out of his hands. The third townsman dropped his staff, holding his hands high.

"Stand!" Cort roared, and the three soldiers froze.

The civilian swordsman thrust at the stranger, who leaped aside, his staff whirling. It cracked down on the blade near the hilt, and the sword flew clattering along the street. Its owner yelped with pain and nursed his hand.

One of the soldiers started for the sword. He barely leaned toward it before Cort snapped, "Hold!" and the man froze, tilting to the side.

Cort turned to the young woman's escort. "Sheathe your sword, and I will, too. If we don't, that madman will break both our blades."

"Oh, you'd better believe it!" the stranger assured them.

Watching them warily, the escort sheathed his weapon slowly. Cort matched him movement for movement, then turned to the stranger, making sure he could still see the escort out of the corner of his eye.

One look at the stranger, even by guttering torchlight, and Cort knew why he'd been able to fight them all to a standstill. The staff was sheathed with a foot of iron on its tips, which made it both harder and heavier—and when something like that spun so fast as to be a blur, as the stranger had done, it was equal to a sword indeed. "I've never seen your style of fighting before," he said.

The man smiled, showing a lot of teeth. "Want to see it again?"

Cort shuddered, more at his look than at the thought of the danger. "Thank you, no. Who are you, anyway?"

"Dirk Dulaine, at your service." The stranger turned to the

civilians. "I'm from out of town, in case you hadn't noticed."

"From far away, by your accent." The leader glowered, still nursing his hand.

"Far away indeed," Dirk agreed, "so I don't particularly care about you or these soldiers—but I don't like seeing a young woman in danger, either. If you'll all put up your weapons and let her go home with her escort now, I won't need to swing again."

"We could make mincemeat of him," one of the soldiers blustered.

"Be still, you fool!" his mate snapped, and the man fell silent, glancing at the other soldiers in surprise and fright.

"Let the young couple walk out of sight, and we'll go," the citizen growled.

"Officer, bid your men step aside," the stranger advised.

"Back, two steps!" Cort barked, and his men retreated. Cort bowed. "Gentleman, lady—again, my apologies."

"Taken, with thanks." The escort finally remembered his manners, then led his lady out of the torchlight, still gasping in little, sobbing breaths. They passed down the alley, and the two groups stood stiffly, watching each other warily.

"Out of sight, I said," the stranger reminded them.

The couple reached the end of the lane and turned into the alley that led to the main street.

Dirk stepped back, lowering his staff. "Okay. You guys can kill each other now, for all I care."

The civilian leader darted to pick up his sword.

4

The swordsman reached for the hilt and shouted with pain.

"Here, let me see." Dirk went over to him and felt the civilian's hand with his left. The man yelped, and Dirk growled, "I *was* being gentle, damn it! Don't worry, it'll heal. I just sprained your wrist for you, that's all. You!" he called to one of the soldiers. "Stick his sword in his scabbard for him!"

The trooper glanced at Cort, who nodded, realizing what a stroke of diplomacy it was. The trooper didn't—he eyed both the civilian and Dirk's staff with great wariness as he picked up the sword. The other civilians tensed as he did, but when he slid the blade into its scabbard and stepped back, they relaxed a little.

"That's very nice," the stranger said with sarcasm. "Back to your own lines, thank you."

Again, the soldier glanced at Cort; again, Cort nodded, and the soldier stepped back beside his comrades.

"Now!" Dirk slammed one end of his staff against the cobbles and leaned on it. Soldiers and civilians both tensed, leaning in, ready to jump, realizing that it would take the stranger time to lift that staff again, and if they were quick enough . . .

Dirk favored the soldiers with a wolfish grin, then flashed it at the civilians. Both sides leaned back with a grumble of disappointment—the stranger was ready for just such an attack, even inviting it.

"That's better." Dirk leaned on his staff so completely that it was a virtual insult. "Okay—somebody want to tell me what this was all about?"

The soldiers glanced at one another uncertainly, and Cort gave them the tiniest shake of his head—if any of them were to speak, it would be him.

The civilian's leader said, "We heard a woman scream, so we came running. We saw one of our own men on the ground with his lady beside him, cowering before four soldiers. Oh, we knew what was happening, all right!"

"Meaning you assumed the worst," Dirk corrected. He turned to the soldiers. "Were they right?"

"My men were drunk and a bit overeager," Cort admitted, "but by the time these . . . gentlemen . . . came, I had heard the scream myself, come at the run, and already shouted my men back. I had the situation in hand."

The civilians muttered at that, and their leader frowned, suddenly doubting his own righteousness.

"You were so eager to protect your own that you almost started a bloodbath when the crisis was over," Dirk told them. He raised a palm to forestall the civilians' protests. "Oh, you were right to worry, sure enough, but when you saw an officer, you should at least have asked before you started swinging. I'll gladly admit that when soldiers are out on liberty, civilians should travel in packs, but you were a little too late this time, and a little too eager." He turned back to Cort. "Though truth to tell, I'd say your men were spoiling for a fight, too."

"They'll be spoiled enough, you may be sure," Cort said, with a glare at his men. They paled a little, and stiffened to attention again.

"Not as much as they might have been," Dirk reminded him.

"The young couple are safe, after all, though the young man will have a few bruises."

The civilians all started talking at once.

"Of course, the soldiers have a few lumps, too," Dirk told them, with a glare that shut them up, "and since both sides seem to have pounded each other equally . . ." (his voice shifted to a parody of politeness) ". . . might I ask that all of you *back off*?"

The civilians jumped, and even Cort felt the impulse to hop at the whiplash of the words.

The civilians' leader frowned. "Who're you to go telling us what to do?"

"The man with the staff," Dirk said with a grin, "who knows how to use it better than any of you."

Cort and the civilian leader eyed each other with suspicion, but Cort said, "No harm done, after all, or at least, nothing that will last."

"And other civilians might be in danger, while you stand here chattering," Dirk pointed out.

The civilians frowned at that, and their leader said, "Well . . . as long as all is under control here . . ."

"It is," Cort said. "I assure you of that."

"So do I," Dirk told them.

"We'll be about our rounds, then," the civilian leader said. "Keep your men leashed, now!"

"I will." Cort reined in his temper.

The civilians turned away, muttering to each other, and went out of the alley.

Cort relaxed with a sigh. "I could almost wish we'd taught those arrogant townsmen a lesson—but I have to thank you for making peace, stranger."

The soldiers grumbled with disappointment.

"Yes, I know, I wanted a brawl, too," Cort sympathized. Then his voice hardened. "What the *hell* did you think you were doing, jumping a civilian and his girl? Were you so overcharged that you couldn't wait your turn with the professionals? Or did you think you might nod off before you got to the head of the line? What're you using for brains—porridge? Why, you fly-infested, drink-sodden, stumbling, stuffed bearskins! Put your heads together, and maybe you can realize how much trouble this town could make for you if you had so much as *touched* that woman! If the captain hears about this, he'll flog you so raw that you'll be wanting new backs even more than new brains!"

"He—he won't, will he, sir?" one of the troopers asked in a shaky voice. "Hear about it, I mean."

Cort took a deep breath for another blast, then sank under a tidal wave of sympathy. He knew how the men felt tonight, knew exactly how they felt. "No, I won't tell him—and you'd better hope for all you're worth that the civilians don't! But if I catch one of you lousy apes so much as looking cross-eyed at a townsman even one more time, I'll turn you into dogmeat!"

The soldiers snapped to attention again.

"Get back to the inn, now," Cort ordered, "and lock yourselves in your room! Dis-*miss*!"

The soldiers relaxed and turned away grumbling—but they moved quickly. When they were out of the alley, Cort turned to Dirk. "You took a bad chance there, stranger."

"Not really," Dirk told him. "The civilians were putting on a brave show, but they'd already had enough of fighting with professionals. You and your men might have been enjoying the brawl, but I knew you wanted to end it quickly, so all I had to do was give you both an excuse."

In spite of himself, Cort grinned. "A face-saver, eh?"

"Call it a chance to retire with dignity," Dirk temporized.

"But why take the chance?" Cort asked. "It was none of your affair, and you might have been beaten senseless."

"Not much risk of that." Dirk flashed him the toothy grin again. "Besides, I've been out of work a while, and I was getting rusty. I needed a little dust-up."

"So did I," Cort said grimly. "I was disappointed not to have it, but I'm glad the captain won't have a major brawl to find out about." Then he gave Dirk a keen glance. "Mercenary, eh? And your band lost so badly it was scattered?"

"Something of the sort," Dirk agreed. "That, and being a free lance by nature. I don't like to stay too long with any one band."

"Don't like to stay peaceful too long, either, by the look of you," Cort said. Then a sudden, huge, soul-weariness engulfed him. "The hell with it all! Come on back to the inn, stranger, so I can thank you properly with a flagon of brandy."

The stranger raised an eyebrow. "More to it than a run-in with a bunch of overgrown delinquents, eh? Sure, I'll be glad to drink your brandy. Maybe you can give me a point or two about the locals. Seems to be a lot I don't know about who, what, where, and why."

"Yes, by your accent, you would be from far away, wouldn't you?" Cort asked. "Still, brandy's the same in any language, friend—or at least, the taste is."

"True enough. Drink first, talk later." Dirk fell in beside the lieutenant as they started walking. "Of course, if we're going to the inn you sent your men back to, you can just happen to be keeping an eye on them."

"I can keep an eye on those who are there," Cort said grimly, "and count the rest as they come in."

"Well, if you need to go out for the occasional patrol, I'll come along." Dirk grinned again. "Might be fun."

Cort eyed him with misgiving. "I only know two kinds of soldiers who think fighting's fun: the ones who have never been in a battle, and the ones who have seen so much war they've gone crazy with it."

"You forgot the third kind," Dirk told him.

He said it with such a nonchalant air that Cort couldn't help smiling. "Third kind? What's that?"

"Soldiers on leave," Dirk said. "Sometimes they don't even need to get drunk first."

* * *

Gar surveyed the line in front of them with a frown. "I'm used to merchants and farmers lining up to wait for the gate to open, Master Ralke, but these men don't look like either."

The town wall was only about twelve feet high, but the dark gray stone of which it was made gave it a very forbidding appearance. The dozen or so wagons lined up in front of the great leaves of the gate were driven by hard-eyed men wearing the same livery as the guards who lined the roadway to either side, armed with pikes and halberds.

"You must come from a fat country indeed!" Ralke said. "There isn't a merchant in the lot, nor a farmer, only soldiers." He glanced at Gar. "Did you hide your sword and dagger, as I . . . Yes, I see you did."

"I understand why, now—they don't like the competition." Gar shook his head sadly. "But why are soldiers driving the wagons?"

"Boots, lad, not soldiers. We call them boots when their boss is a bully. They're driving because they're tax collectors, and that's why they've so many guards. As to lining up to wait for the panels to open, they could come in any time. There just happen to be more of them here in midmorning, because they all set out from last night's camping at more or less the same time."

"I take it very few of the villages pay in coin, then?"

"You take it rightly; few villagers have coin with which to pay. They never have extra crops to sell, since the boss takes them all. He's the one who does the selling and has all the gold."

"What does he buy with it?"

"Mercenaries for his next war, mostly, but he'll have a few coins left over to buy some spices and fine cloths for himself and his family, and that's where we come in."

It didn't take terribly long to reach the gates. The wagons being driven by boots rolled on in with scarcely a nod to the guards. But when Master Ralke stepped up with the first of his mules, the gate guards clashed their pikes together to bar his way. "Vairudingugoink?" one of them demanded.

"This is what takes the time," Ralke told Gar. "I don't speak the dialect of this city."

Gar wondered if he himself could, if they would just speak enough of it.

Ralke pointed to himself, then cupped his hand and pantomimed dropping coins into it, then waved back at his caravan, saying, "Merchant."

"Awmeshen!" The guard nodded, then held out a cupped palm and scratched it. "Bayeedcawminnaloutre!"

"Entry fee," Ralke explained to Gar, and slipped two large silver coins from a slit-pocket behind his belt. He placed them in the guard's hand; the man nodded with satisfaction, and the two halberds parted. The guard pointed at a stone building atop a low hill in the center of the town and said, "Zeedeebaasfirs!"

Ralke nodded, pointing from himself to the castle in one smooth movement, then called to his drivers and led them through the gate. Gar rode beside him on his horse. The guards eyed him suspiciously, and Gar felt as though they could see through his cloak to the sword hanging across his back, but they said nothing as the caravan rode on in. Gar loosed a pent-up breath. "What's the name of this town, Master Ralke?"

"Loutre." Ralke gave him a shrewd glance. "Heard of it, have you?"

"Only from that gate guard."

Ralke's eyes widened. "You speak their language?"

"No, but I know several others, and I can guess from the way the words seem alike."

"Oh, you can, can you?" Ralke growled. "What did that guard say?"

"I was just beginning to be able to understand him at the end there, but I couldn't figure out what 'Loutre' meant. Without that, I suspect the last two things he said were 'Pay to come into Loutre' and 'See the boss first.' "

"Good guesses," Ralke approved, "but you could have worked that out from his gestures. Still, keep trying to puzzle out the words—it would be handy to have someone on my side who could understand the language."

"I'll work on it," Gar promised. He didn't bother telling Master Ralke that he had really been matching the words to the guard's thoughts. Why burden the poor merchant with more than he needed to know?

Down the broad boulevard they went, broad enough for ten soldiers to march side by side, then up the winding road to the castle. The guard at the drawbridge challenged them again, but didn't demand any money, only insisted on looking under the wrappings of the mules' loads as they came in. They went under the portcullis, through the entry-tunnel, and into the courtyard. There, Master Ralke directed them over against a wall, where the drivers unloaded the mules and opened the bundles. Gar pitched in and helped, but was careful to keep his sword hidden. When the goods were all laid out, the drivers led the mules away to feed and curry while Ralke strolled along the line of luxurious cloths and rare foods, seeming nonchalant but actually vigilant.

Gar kept him company. "What do we do now?"

"Wait," Ralke told him, "for the boss's convenience."

"Oh. He has to inspect the goods before you're allowed to take them down to the marketplace?"

"He has to inspect them, all right." Ralke grinned, showing his teeth. "Inspect them and take what he likes. If he takes more than a few items, he'll probably pay for them."

" 'Probably?' You mean you could lose your whole cargo right here?"

"Could, yes. Inside his own domain, and especially inside his own town and castle, a boss can do anything he damn well pleases."

"His whim is the only law, eh?"

Ralke frowned up at him. "Law? What's law? Another one of your foreign words?"

"Why . . . yes," Gar stammered, completely taken aback that

the merchant didn't even have the concept. "But you don't think he will take everything?"

"Why, no. He knows that if he leaves me nothing, I won't be able to come back with more—and he values these little luxuries I bring from the great world outside. Him, or his wife."

"Market forces." Gar nodded.

Again, Ralke gave him a peculiar look. "What market ever had force?"

Gar just stared at him for a moment. Then he said, "Perhaps more than you know, Master Ralke, but this isn't the place to speak of it. Remind me to discuss the subject when we're back on the road."

"Certainly no time now." Ralke gave him a nudge instead of pointing. "Here comes the boss."

Gar turned and saw a tall, stocky man approaching with a woman almost as tall as himself, fingers lightly touching his arm. She was gray-haired, but didn't have many lines in her face, and walked with the grace of a woman in her thirties. Gar remembered that, on a medieval world like this, she might well *be* in her thirties. Her gown was blue velvet, her hair caught in a net whose threads were golden, and her husband wore brocade, with a scarlet cloak of fine red wool. He was gray-haired, too, his face lined and weathered from a life of campaigning. He walked with a slight limp, and his broadsword swung at his hip.

Behind them came a slender man in gray broadcloth, his black hair short in a bowl cut, his angular face impassive, but a gleam in his eye.

The boss stopped opposite Ralke and said something in an affable tone. The short, slight man said, with a heavy accent, "The boss greets you, merchant, and asks what you have to show him today,"

"Good! A translator!" Ralke muttered to Gar. "That will make dealings a good bit easier."

It probably would, Gar thought—except that he was sure the

boss had said, "Well, merchant! I trust you had an easy journey!" and nothing yet about Ralke's stock in trade.

The merchant bowed to the boss, saying, "I am honored by the boss's interest. For this trip, I have fine linen, purple dye, silk, satin, and many spices and dried fruits."

The translator turned and repeated the words to the boss and his wife, listened to their replies, and turned back to Ralke. "The boss will look over your goods."

"I am pleased he finds them worthy of regard," Ralke said smoothly, and the translator delivered the message to the boss and his wife.

But Gar, listening not to a foreign language, but to a different dialect of his native tongue, and listening not just with his ears but also with his mind, knew the boss had said, "Ah, good! We have been wanting more purple dye for new liveries for our boot-men!" His wife had replied, "The cooks have almost used up all the cloves and orange rind, husband. Has he those?" The translator had told them that Ralke had answered, "Alas! It has been a bad year for southern crops, Your Honors. Such things are rare, and high in cost."

Ralke frowned. "Why do the boss and his lady look disgruntled?"

"Because the boss has fought a war this year," the translator said, "and has little money for luxuries."

Now Gar knew what the gleam in the translator's eye was—not interest, but mischief.

Ralke frowned. "That's not welcome news! I had hoped for good profits this season."

The boss said something, and the translator turned to listen. Gar leaned over and muttered quickly, "You may make a good profit after all. The translator isn't telling you what the boss really said."

Ralke turned to stare at him. "You've worked out the language already? You can understand him?"

Gar just had time to nod before the boss turned to say something to Ralke, frowning. The translator interpreted, "The boss will take all your purple dye. He offers you a silver mark for each pound."

"A silver mark!" Ralke cried. "It cost me more than that! The southern folk make it from sea snails, and it takes thousands of them for a pound of dye! It's very expensive!"

"It has been a bad year for the boss," the translator replied.

"It will be a worse year for you, if he finds out you're lying about what he said," Gar informed the man. "He told Master Ralke that he wouldn't pay more than three silver marks for each pound."

The translator stared at him, thunderstruck, and Ralke stifled a grin.

5

"You did not tell me your man spoke my language," the translator said slowly, "but he is mistaken. Why would I lie?"

Gar started to answer, *Because you enjoy making trouble,* but Ralke forestalled him. "You would lie because the boss will leave it to you to draw the money from the treasury and bring it to me. You'll give me what I think the boss agreed upon and keep the rest for yourself."

The look the translator gave him was pure hatred.

The boss said something, and the translator turned to answer.

"The boss wants to know what you're talking about," Gar murmured, "and the translator is telling him he can't repeat it, because what you're saying is so insulting."

"None of that!" Ralke said sharply. He turned and bowed to the boss and his wife again. "Tell them I have only the highest respect for them, and was only discussing how many marks there are to a silver pound."

The translator flashed him a glare that should have shriveled him, but turned back to interpret.

"He told the boss what you really said this time," Gar said.

"Fortune favored me when you joined our caravan, Gar Pike!" Ralke forced a smile for the translator. "It seems you and I shall do business of our own, interpreter. I'm Ralke; who are you?"

"My name is only for my friends," the interpreter snapped, but the boss cleared his throat with impatience, and the translator gave him a guilty glance as he added, "and for my business associates. I am Torgi." He turned to the boss and gave a brief explanation.

"He's just telling them that you're trying to be friendly by exchanging names with him," Gar muttered. "He's giving them your name, too."

"As though they didn't have it already," Ralke returned.

Torgi turned back to them. "What do you suggest?"

"That you interpret my prices accurately," Ralke told him, "but I'll raise them by one part in five. Then after the sale, you and I will split that one part, half each."

"One part in ten is better than nothing," Torgi grumbled.

"Much better than your boss learning how you were garbling his words," Gar reminded.

Torgi's glare would have seen him convicted for poisoning on a civilized world, but he could only say, "I agree to your terms. Now, how much do you want for the dye?"

"I had hoped for three silver marks and a copper mark," Ralke sighed, "but the boss's offer will give me some profit, at least."

Torgi turned and translated faithfully. The boss smiled and glanced at his wife, who beamed up at him and nodded. He turned back to speak in a lofty but kindly tone.

"He will give you the copper mark for each pound," Torgi translated, "but trusts you will be as moderate as you may in your other prices."

"The boss is very gracious," Ralke said, with a smile and a little bow at the couple.

The bargaining proceeded smoothly from that point, and when they were done, Ralke was looking quite satisfied, because the boss and his wife had bought half his stock and had paid him a fair price. The boss said something with a smile, and Torgi told

Ralke, "His Honor has enjoyed dealing with you, and trusts you will visit his castle on your next journey."

"I will be honored by his hospitality," Ralke said, with yet another bow.

Torgi translated; the boss smiled benignly, satisfied, but told Torgi one more thing as he turned away. Torgi said a few words and bowed.

"He told Torgi to get the money and pay us," Gar muttered.

"I will fetch the money," Torgi told them. "Then you will be on your way quickly, yes?"

"We'll pack while you're gone," Ralke assured him.

"You will go, too." Torgi gave Gar a look that promised revenge. "We shall meet again, be sure."

"I'll look forward to it," Gar said, in a tone of great politeness.

"Brandy," Cort told the serving wench. "The whole bottle."

She smiled knowingly and turned away.

"Rough day, huh?" Dirk said, with a sympathetic look.

"Oh, the *day* was fine," Cort told him. "It's the night that's been an ordeal."

"Girl trouble, eh?"

Cort looked up, amazed.

"It couldn't have been that little dust-up back in the alley," Dirk explained. "Compared to battle, that was a piece of cake. So if you're on leave, it had to be a woman."

"You're shrewd, stranger," Cort said slowly, "and you know the ways of soldiers. How long have you been a mercenary?"

"All totaled? Maybe a year." Dirk smiled at Cort's skeptical look and explained, "I'm a free lance. I sign up for bodyguard jobs as often as army, and the captains usually hire me for just one battle."

"Can't be signing on as an officer, then," Cort said, frowning. "A captain wouldn't want a stranger in his cadre."

"Right on the mark. I'm a sergeant."

"Only if you sign up with a mercenary company," Cort said

with a smile. "Sign up with a boss around here and you're a brute."

"That your term for a noncom?"

"Their term," Cort corrected. "Mercenaries use the old words—old enough that we don't know where they came from. But we have to know the others. After all, any of us might want to join a boss someday." He saddened suddenly, thinking of Squire Ellsworth—and, therefore, of Violet.

"So a sergeant is a brute," Dirk said briskly. "Might be apt, at that. What's a lieutenant?"

"A bruiser," Cort explained, "and with the bosses, he rides a horse and wears heavy armor. Mercenaries have whole companies of cavalry, lightly armed, and they can dance circles around the bruisers while they cut them to shreds."

"I take it a bully is a captain?"

"Yes, and the boss is a general. Sometimes the boss will appoint one bully to command the others, but that's the only case where there's a rank in between."

"Other countries, other ways." Dirk sighed. "At least it's no worse than trying to understand navy ranks and insignia."

The bottle landed on the table, then two mugs. It was a measure of Cort's state of mind that he didn't even glance at the wench, only pushed some coppers over as he told Dirk, "I've heard of navies—fighting sailors, aren't they?"

"Yes, and I only served with them once. Never again! I don't like having the ground move under me when I'm trying to thrust and parry. As soon as the ship docked, I signed off, and that's how I came to your country."

"The seacoast is far away," Cort commented. "You must have been quite a time, coming this far inland."

Dirk shrugged. "One job led to another, each farther away from salt water, which was just fine with me. I was captured in the last battle, and being a stranger just hired for the duration, the captain didn't think I was worth ransoming. So I went to work for the boss who had caught me."

Cort grinned slowly. "Why not? If the captain wasn't loyal enough to ransom you, then you had no loyalty to worry you. But didn't the boss realize you wouldn't be any more faithful to him?"

"I don't think bosses really worry about loyalty," Dirk said slowly, "just about belting you if they think you've betrayed them. Still, the issue didn't come up. I fought in one more of your little wars, somehow survived, and that was it. Didn't even stay long enough to figure out that boss, bully, bruiser, brute, and boot were like rank names."

"He paid you off?"

"Yeah, with my freedom. That's how I ransomed myself."

"Ah! Yes, that would make sense." Cort nodded, enjoying the talk—it kept his mind off Violet. "Especially since, once you were free, he would have had to pay you."

"Exactly. He didn't have another war brewing at the moment, so he dismissed me rather than give me silver. I signed on as a merchant's guard, took a short stint as a tax collector and hated it, and started riding the roads looking for work."

"You've been at liberty ever since, then?"

"Yes. Nice way of saying 'out of work,' isn't it? But I'm a long way from home, and much though I'd like to go back, I don't know if I'm willing to sign on as a sailor again."

"Make enough money to buy passage on a merchant ship, then," Cort suggested.

"I'm working on it."

"You'll never make it one job at a time," Cort said, with certainty. "Sign on full-time with a mercenary company, stay with them a year or so and save your money behind your belt instead of spending it on easy women and watered brandy, and you'll have enough."

"I suppose I'll have to," Dirk sighed. "I don't like being tied down to one place that long, though."

"No other way," Cort pointed out, "and you're more likely to be killed hiring out battle by battle, than by joining with a company of men who depend on you as you depend on them. A free lance gets put in the front line every time."

"Don't I know it," Dirk said wryly.

"I could use another sergeant," Cort said slowly. "My master sergeant has been talking retirement for some time, and the captain's been telling me he has too many recruits—he needs to set up another platoon. Why not try some steady work for a change?"

"Why, thanks." Dirk straightened, looking surprised. "I really don't know enough about you to accept, though." He grinned suddenly. "But to tell you the truth, I'm inclined to accept."

"I hope you do." Cort smiled. "Learn more about me, then. Ask."

"Well, for starters, what's the name of your company, and who's your captain?"

"Yes, that might be handy to know, mightn't it?" Cort said with a laugh. "Well, we're Captain Devers's Blue Company, my lad, and proud of it. We've taken our share of losses, it's true, but we've had far more victories."

"That's a track record I can live with. What about you yourself, though, lieutenant? How did you get into this line of work? Not exactly the most secure future in the world."

"A grave is very secure." Cort sobered suddenly. He didn't like the feeling, so he took another drink. "As to the chances of staying out of that grave, well, they're better as a peasant hoeing crops, but it's a lousy life, with never enough to eat and a house that might blow down around your ears."

"I didn't think you had the look of a peasant," Dirk observed.

"Of course not," Cort said impatiently, "but I grew up playing with their children, then learning to rule them. I'm the third son of a bully. Do you have the Third Son rule where you come from?"

"First son to stay with the estate, second for the army, third for the navy?"

"You must have grown up near the sea. Close, but here the first son becomes his father's chief bruiser, then a bully when his father dies. The second joins the mercenaries, which gives the bully an 'in' if he needs a troop. The third goes out into the hills to find a sage, so he can sit at a teacher's feet and learn how to save the souls of his whole family."

"At least you believe in souls," Dirk said. "I take it you didn't want to become a sage?"

Cort shook his head, mouth a grim line. "I still have hopes of marrying. Oh, I know the stories about the village girls visiting the male sages to learn the arts of love, just as the village boys go to the female sages, but I wanted a wife, home, children . . ." His gaze drifted away, Violet's sweet face coming into his mind's eye again, bringing with it a melancholy so sudden and powerful that he feared that he might weep.

"That the only reason you didn't go into philosophy?" Dirk asked. "Not the best reason for becoming a soldier, I'd say."

Suddenly, and rather oddly, Cort was very much aware that he was on trial here. He shrugged off the mood and turned back to Dirk, wondering why on earth he should care what the man thought—but he did. "My spirit was too active and restless, so I took service as a mercenary. Being a bully's son, I started as a sergeant and moved up to licutenant two months later."

"And the life suits you?"

Cort shrugged. "Every life ends in death, but at least a soldier has a chance to fight. The risks are greater, but the pay is better, too. The work suits me—life becomes very vivid, very intense, in battle. Yes, the sight of a sword slicing at me sets fear burning through me, but it sets me afire with the lust for life, too, and there's no feeling like victory, when the battle's done and many lie dead but you're still alive. It even makes the panic and horror of defeat worthwhile, just knowing that there will be another victory some day—and the camaraderie of men who have lived through a battle together, and know they can depend on one another no matter how much they hate one another's guts, is closer than anything else I've experienced. That's why my men obey me—not because I'm a bully's son, and not because I can beat any of them into the ground, but because I've done my best to keep them alive, and the battle's come and gone, but we're all still here."

He drew breath, amazed that he had talked for so long, but Dirk only nodded, looking very serious. "Yes. I think I'd like serving with an officer who feels that way about his men."

"Stout man!" Cort grinned as he clasped Dirk's hand. Then he fished a silver mark from his belt-purse and set it in Dirk's palm. "There's the coin of enlistment. Welcome to the Blue Company, Sergeant Dulaine."

"Thank you, lieutenant," Dirk said, grinning. "What's my first duty?"

"On liberty? To get drunk and make the whores rich. For an officer, though, it's a bit different. On leave, I spend most of my time watching out for my men, breaking up fights before they start and calming outraged burghers. I even patrol the streets." Cort set his hands on the edge of the table and shoved himself to his feet—but the table shoved back, and he half fell into his chair again, looking about him in stunned amazement.

"No patroling tonight, I think." Dirk stood slowly and helped Cort to his feet. "Drank more than you knew, and faster, didn't you? Well, keeping the troops in line is sergeant's work, really; lieutenants just keep the sergeants honest. Introduce me to your men, lieutenant, and let me take the watch."

"But I always . . ."

"Not tonight." Dirk didn't mention that Cort was obviously in the mood to get drunk, dead drunk. "Let me earn that mark you just gave me."

"All right." Cort decided that it did sound like a good idea—and wondered why it was so hard to think, so hard to keep shoving Violet out of his mind. He took a badge from behind his belt, one with three chevrons on it, and waved it in the general direction of Dirk's chest. "Here's your rank, until we can get you livery."

Dirk intercepted the badge before sticking could turn into

stabbing and pinned it on his tunic. "Handsome piece of jewelry, that. Okay, lieutenant, take me to meet the boys."

They rode out through the gates of Loutre with Master Ralke in high spirits. "A very profitable stop, Gar Pike, and a pleasant one, thanks to your knowledge of the language. Really, I'll have to give you a bonus when this is done!"

"I won't refuse it," Gar said with a grin.

"Worth it ten times over! We sold the whole cargo, and bought another worth half again what we paid for it! Off to Zangaret Town, now, where they value the kind of gauds these Loutre folk make!"

"Good dealing almost makes the hazards worth it, eh? But if you have to deal with translators like that all the time, it's a wonder you ever make a profit at all!"

Ralke's smile turned to a frown on the instant. "A wonder indeed, and most men who go trading come home in beggary, if they come home at all! No, friend, I did well indeed when I hired you."

"Thank you," Gar said, trying to sound flattered. "So there aren't very many merchants, then?"

"So few that we all know each other, even those we've never met. Oscar of Drellan deals far to the west, selling the silks made along that coast; he wishes to buy the sort of plates and cups these Loutrens make, and Holger of Alberg buys them from me to trade with Oscar for his silks, then brings the silks to sell to me. Lotar of Silace carries cloves and pomegranates up from the south with many more spices as well; he trades them to Albert of Rehem, who barters them to me for the ivory I buy from Krenel of Grelholm with the stout woolen cloth woven in Wurm. Krenel brings the walrus tusks and narwhal horns down from Marl of Rohr, whom I've never seen but who trades his ivories for the cloth I buy from the Wurmers. I could go on for half an hour, but not much more; we are all known to one another, and have each built up a band of drivers who are as strong a set of fighters as any mercenary squadron. We are the ones who've survived."

Gar shuddered. "A risky trade indeed!"

"But a profitable one. If I live to retire, I'll have as much wealth as any boss, though I'll be careful to hide it well and be sure few people know about it. My house is already a virtual fortress, and I'll make it even more so as I grow older. There are peasants aplenty who are glad to move their families into my compound, train with weapons, and do an honest day's labor in the warehouses. They'll have new tunics of stout cloth every year for their pains, real cottages that keep the drafts out instead of the tumbledown huts most live in, and three pounds of bread and one of vegetables every day for each family, with meat once a week and fish twice. That's fat living indeed, for most poor folk."

"So even in your retirement, you'll be working hard managing all those people and warehousing goods for other merchants," Gar deduced.

"Yes, but I won't have to go out on the road again. Five more years of good trading, and I'll manage it! What say you to five years of steady employment, friend Gar?"

Gar noticed how quickly he'd been promoted from stranger to friend. "It's an attractive offer, Master Ralke, and I'll think very seriously about it. Before I can settle into one job that way, though, I've some personal affairs I must set straight."

"Ah!" Ralke nodded. "A woman, an inheritance, or a revenge—no, don't tell me. I don't want to know! But when your score is settled, friend, remember where you'll find a safe berth, with Ralke of the town of Firith, and glad I'll be of your company!" He frowned suddenly. "You won't bring another war down on us, will you?"

"Just the opposite, if I can manage it," Gar told him. "I hope to prevent a war, not fight one."

Ralke raised a palm, turning his face away. "I won't ask how. But I'm glad to hear it." He turned back to Gar. "The bosses let a few of us trade, for without us, they'd never have the luxuries they want so badly. After all, what's the point in being a boss if you can't live better than a peasant?"

Gar could have said that for some men, power was enough in itself, but he had the good sense to hold his tongue.

"In war, though, all such unspoken agreements go by the board," Ralke continued. "When bosses send their bullies before them to fight one another, any luckless merchant who gets caught between is ground into the dirt and his goods destroyed. We survive by learning ahead of time who's fighting whom and where, then going far away from their battleground. But there's always the fear that someone will start a war too fast for us to learn of it, and we'll have to leave our goods and flee for our lives." He nodded. "Done that more than once myself, I have. No, war's bad for business. It boosts our losses and reduces our markets." He grinned suddenly. "If I were a smith or an armorer, I own I'd welcome war, for all the business it would bring me." He frowned again. "But I'm not a smith, I'm a merchant, and I'll support any man who works for peace!"

"I'll remember that," Gar assured him. Then he stiffened, as though hearing something.

"What is it?" Ralke demanded.

"Boots, a score of them to our dozen by the sound, heavily armed and running down a hidden trail ahead and to our right!"

"You've keen ears, friend," Ralke said, "but I don't doubt you." He turned away to bawl battle orders to his drivers.

6

The boots burst out of the underbrush, bellowing like bulls spotting a trespasser. They must have been watching the caravan, because they didn't seem at all surprised to see the mules drawn up in a circle and the drivers spaced around them evenly, bucklers on their arms and arrows on their bowstrings. The first flight took out eight boots. The other twelve roared even louder and kept on coming.

They were too close for a second flight of arrows. The drivers dropped their bows and pulled out short swords, axes, or iron-banded quarterstaves.

"Treachery!" Ralke shouted. "They wear the livery of the Boss of Loutre! We're betrayed!"

"Don't be too quick to blame the boss," Gar snapped, then thrust at a boot. The man twisted aside, but so did Gar's sword, slicing through the cloth just below his breastplate and leaving a line of blood. The man howled in shock and swung with his battleaxe.

Gar sidestepped, bringing up his buckler to turn the axe's edge, but three boots had converged on him, and he had to duck to avoid the spearpoint aimed at his head. The edge seared fire across the back of his neck. He bellowed with the pain and dropped down to a crouch. The boots, thinking he had fallen, all jammed in with a cry of victory. Gar stabbed upward, catching one man in the shoulder, then yanked the sword out as he shot to his feet, catching a second attacker on the side of the head with his shield.

But the third drove in from the front, howling in anger. His spearpoint jammed on Gar's chain mail, but a stab of pain told him the tip had scored a rib. He thrust at the man's face. The boot leaped back with a scream, an inch away from the sword's tip—and fell, his feet tangled with his fallen mate's legs. Gar kicked him on the helmet and stepped over the dazed man to meet two more boots running toward him.

One spear stabbed low, the other stabbed high. Gar caught the one on his sword blade and the other on his buckler. The high-stabber reversed his spear like a quarterstaff and drove the butt into Gar's belly. Gar fell to his knees, gagging but managing to lift his buckler to fend off another stab. The other man gave a shout of victory as he thrust, a shout that turned to a gurgle as an arrow pierced his throat. His eyes bulged; he fell.

Three drivers came running up to dispatch the other spearman, one of the first attackers who was struggling to his feet. But Gar was scuttling forward on his knees, managing to wheeze, "Save who you can!" and breaking off the tip of the arrow, then yanking the shaft out of the fallen man's neck. Blood spurted—the honed edge of the arrowhead had severed the carotid artery—but Gar pressed his thumb and forefinger over entrance and exit wounds, choking out, "He's lucky—it only struck muscle!" as he reached with his mind frantically to knit cell to cell, holding back the rush of blood while the artery wall healed and grew firm again.

The drivers stared at him, amazed by such mercy, then turned away to bandage the few enemies who still had a chance—and, of course, their own.

Satisfied that the man would live, Gar snatched the fellow's belt off, flipped its owner over, and bound his hands. Then he looked up to see Ralke staring down at him. "I have to have at least one of them alive," Gar said by way of explanation. "More if I can."

"Well, you've succeeded in that, and in saving us all," Ralke told him. "Three of them came for you, and that left two of my drivers free to help their mates. They knocked over two boots, and the four of them helped four more, and . . . Well, you drew so much of their attack that my men finished them off easily. Only one of our drivers is down with a spearhead in his thigh. The others are bleeding, but they can walk."

"Let me see the man with the spear wound." Gar scrambled to his feet. "While I'm bandaging him, tie up the others and find me their sergeant, if he's still alive."

"The brute?" Ralke grinned. "Oh, he's alive, all right. He came for me, but he wasn't a trained swordsman. He'll live, worse luck."

"Then I need to talk with him. But first, the driver."

It took Gar ten minutes to make sure the driver was all right. By luck, the spearhead had missed both arteries and veins, and Gar was able to start the flesh healing as he poured on brandy and bandaged the wound. Then he turned to the sergeant.

He knelt beside the man, whose teeth were gritted against the pain of the wound in his shoulder. Gar lifted his head and shoulders, none too gently, and listened with his mind as he demanded, "Why did your boss send you to steal our goods?"

"Because he wanted them," the man grunted, but the face that flashed through his mind wasn't the boss's.

Gar shook him, and the sergeant cried out in pain. "You're so used to lying that it's become a habit with you," Gar told him. "Think! You have nothing to gain by telling a falsehood, and I'll know if you do! It was Torgi the Translator who sent you after us! Is he that spiteful a man?"

At last fear showed on the sergeant's face. "How did you know that?"

"It was there in your face for those who know how to read the eyes," Gar told him, "and I can guess his reason, but I want to hear it from you. Tell! Was it only spite, or did he want the money?"

Superstition shadowed the man's eyes.

Gar decided to nudge him. "Your name is Hannok, and you haven't told me that. That, too, is clear to see for those who know how to read faces."

The sergeant who didn't shrink from a sword or a mace now paled with fear of unknown powers. "He wanted the other part-in-twenty."

"Was that his only reason, though? How much did he pay you?"

"Twelve silver marks," the sergeant admitted.

"That was the other half of the amount Torgi's lie hid." Ralke, too, was eyeing Gar with something like fear.

"So it wasn't greed alone," Gar inferred. "He has a little power, and doesn't want anyone infringing on it."

"He could also be afraid that we'd reveal his treachery to his boss," Ralke said heavily.

"A good guess. My advice, Master Ralke, is for us to quit this domain and do it quickly, for we have an enemy here who won't rest until he sees us dead. That was what you were supposed to do, wasn't it, Hannok?"

"It was," the sergeant admitted.

"Even leaving may not do," Ralke said, frowning. "Tell me, Brute Hannok, is Torgi's post only that of translator? Surely there isn't enough work for him in that function alone."

"He's the boss's steward," Hannok growled.

"And every boss has a steward," Ralke said heavily. "If they take up Torgi's cause, we'll be lost."

"They don't dare," Gar told him, "for his cause is that of betraying his lord. Any steward caught aiding him will be dismissed from his post at the least, hanged at the worst. They'd do better condemning Torgi, and I don't doubt they will, if his perfidy becomes known."

"Which is all the more reason why he has to kill us." Ralke nodded. "Yes, I see. But we can't go back and tell the Boss of Loutre, for Torgi will have assassins waiting, and it won't do any good to swear secrecy, for Torgi won't believe us."

Gar frowned. "How do you know that?"

"Because anyone that close to a boss is too deeply enmeshed in intrigue to be able to believe anybody's oath."

Gar saw a chance to apply a little more pressure. "But if none of the boots come back, Torgi might assume we've all killed each other."

"Six of us got away!" Hannok blurted. "They were hidden on the hillside, and I didn't give them the signal to join in!"

Ralke didn't need to be a telepath to see through that one. "Nonsense! When your first six fell, you would have called in the rest."

"I'll pay you!" Hannok declared. "The whole twelve marks will be yours if you let us live! Come, you're a merchant—why're you doing this, if not for money?"

"We'd like to keep our lives, too," Gar reminded him. "Money isn't much use to dead men."

"On the other hand," Ralke said, "if you gave us the money *and* your oath to say we're dead, we could let you all go."

"Done!"

"Master Ralke!" Gar cried. "You're not thinking of . . ."

"But I am," Ralke said. "As Brute Hannok has said, I do this for money, and I'm used to taking risks. If he swears we're dead, the chance of Torgi learning otherwise is small enough to be worth taking."

"Well, you pay me to fight your enemies," Gar said, scowling, "and I've given you the best advice I can. If you choose to ignore it, I can't stop you."

"You've a bargain, Brute Hannok." Ralke reached down.

Hannok clasped his hand and used it to pull himself to his feet. "You won't be sorry for this, merchant." He reached inside his tunic. Gar swung up a hand, ready to strike, but Hannok only pulled out a purse. He set it in Ralke's hand. "Count it—but if you don't mind, I'll set my men to making litters while you do."

It took the boots much longer to cut poles and stretch cloaks over them than it took Ralke to count the silver. The boots loaded their wounded mates, and the one dead one, onto the litters and turned away up the hillside.

"I'll remember you for your mercy, sir," Hannok promised him.

"Don't," Ralke requested. "Forget me, brute. Completely. Please."

The brute grinned and raised a hand in salute. Then he turned away and led his men back along the road.

"Mount!" Ralke cried, and the drivers who could still ride swung up onto their mules. Litters between them carried the two wounded.

As they rode off, Gar asked, "You don't really think Hannok will tell Torgi we're dead, do you?"

"Of course not," Ralke said. "We killed one of his men and wounded most of the others, including him. He'll want revenge, and will be back leading a larger force. But he won't find us."

Gar frowned. "How will you stop him?"

"Because I know the country almost as well as any of his boots," Ralke said, "and better, in terms of finding bolt-holes. There's a cave not far off where we can hide our goods and a few of the drivers to guard them."

"Why not all of us?"

"Because it's not that big, and because we could never keep that many mules quiet long enough for the boots to march by."

"Then where will we hide?" Gar asked.

"There's a peasant village not far from here," Ralke told him. "We can hide among them easily enough."

"But they'll be risking their lives!"

"Not really," Ralke told him, "and the poor folk will do anything for a few coppers. I should know—I was born one of them, and so were all my men. But there's the other reason, too."

"Which is?"

"A chance to strike back at the boots and the boss in some small way." Ralke flashed him a grin. "Oh, they'll help us, right enough."

Gar could scarcely tell where the fields left off and the village began. The only clue was a large circle of bare, beaten earth with the smoldering remains of a communal fire in its center. Around it stood a ring of low, moldering haystacks—or at least, that was what Gar took them for at first. But when Ralke said, "Here's our hiding place," Gar looked more closely and saw holes in each haystack, pointing toward the central fire. These were actually shelters where people lived!

Ralke held up a hand to halt the caravan—only twenty bare-backed donkeys now, with ten riders and two wounded men on litters. Then he called out, "Headman Bilar! It's Ralke who calls!"

A head popped out of one of the huts, almost as unkempt as the thatch above it. Then a body followed it, and Gar had to throttle back a gasp of dismay. The man was old, ancient, bald on top with a fringe of long hair stringy with dirt and snarled from never knowing a comb. It straggled into his beard and down his back, not that Gar could tell where beard left off and hair began, for both were light gray. All he wore was a sort of sack made of coarse brown cloth, faded to tan but darkened by dirt. His arms and legs were scrawny and scarred here and there from work accidents, and his feet were bare, the soles toughened almost to horn—but he was alive, Gar realized. He wondered how many of his generation could have said the same.

The oldster came up to Ralke and said, "Greet ye, merchant!"

"And I greet you." Ralke held up a palm. "How go the crops, gaffer?"

"They'm still stand, sair, thank 'ee. No war this year yet."

"And the rain has been good." Ralke nodded. "Where's Bilar?"

"He'm in t' fields, sair. Will 'ee have us call 'im in?"

"I think so," Ralke said slowly.

The gaffer turned and gestured. Several other heads had poked out of doorways, now that the old man had shown them it was safe. One of them nodded and shot away running—a boy of six or seven, Gar decided, wearing only a loincloth.

The women began to come out, with children clinging to their skirts. They wore their hair shoulder length or longer, tousled and snarled, mostly of varying shades of brown with here and there a blonde or redhead. A few were slender and had no wrinkles in their faces or arms—presumably young. Most of them had thickened with maturity and childbearing, though, and even those whose hair hadn't begun to gray already had nets of wrinkles on their faces. The gray-heads, many of whom were balding, also had wrinkled skin on arms and hands—and presumably legs, though there was little of them to be seen. They wore the same sacklike garment as the old man, except for the ones who had babes in arms, beginning to nurse again now that the alarm was past. These women wore the sacklike garment cut in two, so that they could lift the waist of the "blouse" to expose a nipple for the baby.

Gar felt not the slightest stirring of desire. What repelled him most wasn't the lack of grooming nor the dowdiness of their clothes, but the air of resignation and defeat they all wore. The whole village seemed immersed in sadness.

Several old men hobbled out on canes to sit by the doorways in the sunshine. Only the one Ralke had called "gaffer" was fit enough to walk unaided.

Gar noticed that there were far fewer old men than old women.

"Sit 'ee down, sair," the gaffer said to Ralke. The merchant complied, and Gar sat with him. "If 'ee has aught to sell, though," the gaffer said, "I'm afeard we have nowt to buy with."

"It's always so, gaffer. We'll give you what little news we have for free."

"Thank 'ee, sair, thank 'ee!" The gaffer beckoned, and all

the people came crowding around. Even the old men hauled themselves to their feet and tottered over to hear Ralke begin the news.

Gar quickly became lost. It seemed to be only a list of which boss was fighting which, and what bully had raided what other boss's bully's border. It was relieved by the occasional account of a bully who had been hanged for betraying his lord, and the odd boss who had been killed on the battlefield, losing his domain completely to his enemy. Ralke added in reports of good crops, and reports of droughts which were fortunately distant.

The villagers hung on his every word, for even though all the stories were only variations on a common theme, they were news of the world beyond the boundaries of their bully's fields.

Finally there was a shout, and they looked up to see a middle-aged man wearing only a loincloth come trotting in behind the boy. The crowd pulled back, and the headman stepped up to Ralke, who stood to greet him. Breathing hard, the headman nodded and said, "Greet you, merchant."

"Greet you, headman." Ralke grinned. "It has been a long year, but not a bad one, from what your villagers tell me."

"Not bad at all," Bilar said, more with relief than with satisfaction. "The crops were good, and the bully left us enough flax to make new clothes. He even sent us meat once a month, and only took three girls for his bed."

"A good year indeed," Ralke said, with a very forced smile.

"That doesn't mean we have anything to buy with, though."

"But we do," Ralke said.

Murmurs of wonder went through the camp.

"We ask a night's food and lodging of you," Ralke explained. "I'll pay two copper coins for each man."

Bilar frowned. "How's this, merchant? Every other year you come, you and your men camp in the village common!"

"Yes, but every other year, we haven't had boots chasing us."

A whirlwind of hubbub and speculation caught up all the villagers, filled with fear and protest.

Bilar's frown deepened. "The boss would hang us all for traitors!"

"The boss doesn't know about it," Ralke told him. "His steward has sent the soldiers out to hunt us down. We beat them off once, but they'll come again."

"The steward would be a bad enemy, too." But Bilar seemed relieved. He glanced up at Gar and said, "We could say you forced us."

"You could," Ralke agreed.

"How would we hide you? Where would another dozen men have come from?"

"My men will strip down to loincloths and go out into the fields. They'll lash sticks together to form sleds, and harness the mules to draw them for haywains—you are haying, aren't you?"

Bilar nodded, a gleam in his eye. "Then come nightfall, we bury 'em under the hay, yes?" He jabbed a thumb at Gar. "Take a heap o' hay to cover him!"

"It would," Ralke agreed. "He and I would both stay in your houses. I'll wear a tunic—you must have one or two waiting to be mended. Gar will lie against the wall, and you can cover him with straw and rags, to pretend he's a bed."

"Might work," Bilar said, "and if they find him, we can always say we feared to anger him." He looked up and down Gar's great length and said, "Even boots'd believe that."

"I'd believe it, too," Gar said. "Sometimes I even scare myself."

Bilar threw back his head and laughed. Then he said, "I'll ask." He turned back to beckon his people around him. Excited, they came, crowding into a huddle, and a torrent of talk poured forth. The other grown men came running in from the field and joined the huddle. Furious argument erupted.

Ralke leaned back, arms folded. "They'll come to it eventually," he said.

"This isn't the first time you've left a few coppers among them, is it?" Gar asked.

Ralke looked up, startled, then nodded slowly, his face a mask. "As I told you—I was born and grew up in a village like this."

"How'd you get out?"

"There's only one way for a man—as a boot or a soldier. I was lucky enough for a mercenary company to come along."

Gar nodded. "And for a woman?"

"A boss's bed," Ralke said, "then a bully's. After that, she can stay and go among his boots, if she wishes, and make a job of it. If she's lucky, she might get a chance to follow a mercenary company to a town."

Gar began to realize that the mercenary companies were the bright hope of the young here—a bright hope that usually ended with death in combat, or with being worn out in prostitution. "Master Ralke, I was wondering . . . the gaffer who greeted us, how old is he?"

"Forty," Ralke said, watching Gar's face closely. "Bilar is thirty."

Gar's face stayed imperturbable, no matter what he was feeling. "I was afraid of that."

The huddle broke up, and Headman Bilar came back to them. "We'll do it. Where's your copper, merchant?"

Gar found he could almost hope Ralke was broke.

Cort led Dirk to the front of the room and turned to face the tables that had somehow become emptied of civilians and filled with soldiers. He took a deep breath, then bellowed, "Atten-*shun!*"

The clatter of overturned benches was drowned out by the double stamping of fifty pairs of boots.

Into the sudden silence Cort said, "Men, let me introduce you to Sergeant Dirk Dulaine." He paused, bracing his feet against the room's odd tendency to sway, then went on, finding he had to be very careful to speak clearly. "He's joining the Blue Company. When we get back to headquarters, I expect the captain will want to give him a platoon of his own. Any one of you might be in it."

The soldiers stood like statues, eyes straight to the front, but Cort could fairly hear their brains clicking as the point worked its way home. No soldier wanted to have a sergeant with a grudge against him; therefore, it behooved them all to be very hospitable to the new arrival.

"At ease!" Cort barked, and the room resounded with another stamp as the men set their feet eighteen inches apart and slapped their hands together behind their backs. Cort turned to Dirk. "Care to have a word with the men, Sergeant Dulaine?"

"Yeah." Dirk grinned like a shark and stepped forward into the tension generated by forty-three hostile gazes, most of the men wondering what the hell he was doing walking in as a sergeant when all of them had been working their way up from private for a year or more.

The other three knew the answer. They'd been in the alley facing the citizen's committee.

"I'll be taking the watch tonight, so your poor overworked lieutenant can get some shut-eye while the master sergeant's out trying to keep your mates from stepping into the mud too deep." Dirk grinned around at them. "Anyone got a problem with that?"

"Yeah," a voice called. "I got a problem with that."

Dirk turned to look—then looked up, and up and up, until he finally found the grinning face on top of all the muscle.

7

B*ig* wasn't the word for this soldier—he was huge, at least six foot five and more than two hundred thirty pounds of solid muscle.

"Shut it, Korgash!" Cort rapped out. "This man has the right to command you because I say he has!"

"True," Dirk agreed, "but if I have to go running to you to back up every order I give, lieutenant, I might as well not be here." After all, Korgash wasn't really all that impressive to a man who had Gar Pike for a friend. "I think I'd better prove to Private Korgash that I can enforce my own orders."

"Corporal!" Korgash pointed to the two chevrons on his sleeve.

"You were until now," Dirk told him.

"You think you can take off one of my stripes?" Korgash grinned down at Dirk. "Come and get it!"

Dirk strode across the room and reached up for Korgash's stripe. The big man's grin widened as he snatched Dirk's tunic at his throat and lifted him off the floor.

Dirk kicked him in the belly.

Korgash dropped him with a strangled shout of fury, doubling over. Dirk landed lightly and stepped in to throw a haymaker.

The other soldiers shouted in outrage.

Even doubled over in pain, Korgash managed to raise a fist to block, and Dirk stepped in to drive his left into the corporal's face. Korgash caught his hand, though, and squeezed. Dirk yelped, pulling his left back.

The other soldiers cheered and started pushing the tables back to leave a nice, wide ring for the match.

Korgash managed to draw a breath and was just starting to grin again when Dirk slammed his right into Korgash's face. This time, he followed through.

The big man bellowed and stood upright, letting go of Dirk's left, and Dirk shot another right into Korgash's belly, where his foot had hit. Korgash blocked with a shout of anger, then slammed a punch at Dirk's head.

Cort couldn't follow what happened next, because it was too fast, but somehow, Korgash was flying through the air. He landed with a jar that shook the room, with Dirk still holding on to his wrist—so Korgash bellowed anger and yanked Dirk down on top of him, slamming a punch at the sergeant's head. Dirk rolled, though, and somehow the punch caught his left shoulder instead of hitting his chin. His face whitened with pain, but he clamped his jaw shut even as he rolled and came up to his feet.

Korgash scrambled up, too, mouth open in a roar that Cort couldn't hear because the other soldiers were shouting so loudly, but the corporal hadn't quite straightened before Dirk's fist caught him on the chin. Korgash's head snapped up, and Dirk slammed into him full-body. What exactly he did, Cort couldn't see, but the corporal fell over backwards and landed hard. He was slow to move, and his mates went crazy, shouting for him to get up.

Dirk stepped back, breathing hard and massaging his left shoulder.

Korgash finally pushed himself up to sit, shaking his head to clear it. He saw Dirk and shoved himself to his feet, snarling, and came after the sergeant, winding up a fist for a blow that would have flattened a bear.

Dirk wasn't a bear. He leaped in close and drove his right straight up into Korgash's chin. The big man's head snapped back, but even as it did, he slammed a fist at Dirk's head. Dirk blocked it, but it landed anyway, and Dirk fell backward. But he kept hold of Korgash's wrist and pulled as he fell, both feet coming up to catch the big man in the stomach and send him somersaulting into the wall.

Dirk rolled and came up to his feet, panting and shaking his head to clear it. The crowd went wild, calling for Korgash to get up. He tried, rolling over, then pushing himself up, and stumbled to his feet.

Dirk stepped in, drove his left into Korgash's belly. The corporal doubled over, raising a fist to block, but far too slowly now, and Dirk slammed a punch into the side of his head. Korgash fell and lay still.

The crowd shut up on the instant, staring.

"Enough!" Cort stepped forward, and wondered why the floor seemed uneven. "I won't have my men killing each other!" He frowned down at Korgash, then jerked his head at a trooper. "Wake him up!"

The trooper grabbed the nearest flagon and poured it over Korgash's face. The big man spluttered, shook his head, sat up—and found himself staring up at Dirk, who stood over him, breathing heavily. Korgash blinked and looked around him. "Was I out?"

"Like a cobble," one of his fellow soldiers informed him.

Korgash turned back to look up at Dirk. Slowly, he reached up to fumble at his sleeve.

"Keep it," Dirk told him. "You just earned it back."

Korgash stared at him. Then, slowly, he grinned.

Dirk reached down. Korgash caught his arm, pulled himself to his feet, and came to attention as much as he could. "What's your order, sergeant?"

"To sit down until you recover," Dirk said, still breathing heavily, "and to have a drink."

Korgash smiled again. "Yes, sergeant!" He moved to sit down, started to fall, but two of his buddies jumped forward to catch him and ease him down on a bench.

As they gathered around him, praising and reassuring, Cort stepped over to Dirk. "Very imp . . . impreshive, Shergeant. But those . . . tricksh won't work . . . twishe."

"They don't have to," Dirk assured him. "I've got fifty more."

"The'll try t' uzhe 'em on you," Cort warned.

"They're not as easy as they look," Dirk answered.

But Cort wasn't listening; he had reached the remorseful stage of drunkenness. He turned away, shaking his head and muttering, "Shouldn't'a letcha do it. Korgash's lethal, prob'ly a changeling."

"Changeling?" Dirk frowned. "Isn't he a little big to be an elf left in somebody else's cradle?"

"Big?" Cort frowned up at Dirk, then squinted, trying to bring him into focus. " 'Course he's big! Fair Folk're bigger'n him!"

"Are they really?" Dirk said slowly.

"Ev'body knowzh 'at." Suddenly, Cort's knees gave way. He folded onto a bench, blinking.

The soldiers didn't notice; they were busy putting the chairs and tables back in order. Dirk sat down to keep Cort company.

"Ale for the officers!" A wide trooper slammed two tankards down on the table. "After a fight like that, sergeant, you need it!"

"Thanks, uh, private." Dirk managed to spot the man's single stripe as he turned away. Then he turned back to pull the ale away from Cort, but the lieutenant already had the flagon tilted to his lips, gulping thirstily, dribbles running down at each corner of his mouth. Dirk raised a cautioning hand, but Cort managed to lower the empty flagon and say, "Can't trusht women, shergeant," before his eyes closed, and he slumped forward onto the table.

A nightbird called, and the family came rushing back into the house; even the grandmother hobbled as quickly as she could.

"Nightbirds don't call in the daytime," Gar said to the ancient, tangle-haired, sack-clothed man next to him, "and the sun hasn't quite set yet. Was that their lookout?" He knew the answer, of course, but had to make it look as though he didn't.

"It was," Ralke told him. Bilar's family had brought him gypsum to whiten his hair and beard and cooking grease to make it stringy. He looked very much like any of the village grandfathers, and this house had none anymore. "Get under the straw, quickly!"

Gar dove in and held his breath. Small feet came pattering, and children heaped the mouldering, foul-smelling straw high over him. Gar wondered if they only had clean bales every fall.

The inside of the hut smelled of stale sweat and staler cooking odors; the aroma had slapped Gar in the face when he'd stepped in through the hide door. The place was dark and foul; he'd stepped to the side carefully, and waited for his eyes to adjust. Then he'd wished they hadn't.

The dwelling was a circle twenty feet across, a dugout four feet down from ground level with the haystack-thatched room starting where the earthen walls left off. The thatch, like the sleeping pallets, was of old and rotting straw—again, probably replaced only in the fall, when the harvest yielded fresh heaps. In fact, Gar doubted whether it was properly thatched indeed, or only piled on layer by layer, like the haystack it resembled. There was a wooden frame to hold it up, made of bent tree branches, but no boards to bridge the spaces between them, only a sketchy network of withes. A fire smouldered in a central pit, directly below a smokehole. The floor was earth, hardened by generations of calloused feet. There was one pitiful attempt at a rug, maybe six feet square, woven of rags. Heaps of soiled straw lay along the foot of the wall, beds for the family. Daytime living centered around the fire.

There wasn't even an attempt at privacy.

The posts that held up the roof served for hanging two pots and pans, a scythe, several hoes, and a saw. There were no weapons, of course.

"So this is how the average family lives in this land," Gar muttered.

Ralke nodded. "Now you see why everyone dreams of going to the towns. Of course, most folk there live no better than this, but there's always the chance of making enough money for a better life. Here, there's no chance at all."

Now, an hour later, Gar lay under the straw, trying not to breathe the odors of mildew and stale sweat. A sudden weight landed on his hips, then spread out from his knees to his shoulders; he grunted. A clear female voice told him, "Pardon, sair, but ah mun hide ma face—an' they'll ne'er think I'm layin' atop a man."

"Thanks for the disguise," Gar wheezed. Then both he and the girl settled into waiting in suspense for the soldiers to come stamping in. They had passed by four hours before, quick-marching through the village and roaring at the peasants to get out of their way—laughable, really, considering that everyone had disappeared into their houses the second the sentry had called, "Boots coming!" But they had trotted out of the village as quickly as they had come in, hot on what they thought was the caravan's trail—after all, the mules had to stay on the road, didn't they? They scarcely spared a glance for the fields, and didn't seem to notice that there were more field hands, and more mules, than normal.

Now, though, they must have searched everywhere the caravan could have gone in so short a time, and were coming back to double check.

"One side!" a boot bellowed as he burst through the doorway. "Let's see what you're hiding!" Then he noticed the girl lying on the straw. He laughed low and in his throat, as he strode over, reaching down. "Here now, sweetmeat! Don't hide your face from me! Turn and show me your beauty!"

"None of that!" a voice barked, and another boot came in.

The family moaned and cringed away.

"There's no time for skin-games now," the brute snapped. "Besides, if she's worth looking at any, the boss will want her!"

"Aye, but if she's only half-pretty, she's our meat," the boot protested.

"Then come back another day! We're looking for merchants now, not toys!"

"As you will, brute," the boot said with disgust. He drove his toe into the straw.

There was enough of it to weaken the impact, but Gar still felt the blow on his shin, then on his thigh, his belly, and his chest. He clamped his jaw to keep from grunting at the pain.

"Nothing there but a year's rot," the boot said in disgust. "It's packed tight from a year's sleeping. How can you live like this? You, there, boy! Remember when you grow up—boots get clean straw every month!"

"We'll recruit them later," the brute snapped. "You on the bed by the door! Why aren't you in the fields?"

"Sick," Bilar groaned.

The brute backed away, making the sign against evil. "What sickness is it, woman?" he demanded.

"Only bread that molded too much, sair," Bilar's wife whined. "I hope."

"Well, keep an eye on him, and if anyone else gets stomach pains, keep everyone inside," the brute ordered. "We don't want pestilence spreading among you cattle. Boot! Check those other three beds while I check these!"

Gar heard a succession of kicks all around the hut. Then the brute said with disgust, "Nothing. They must have hidden in the woods between here and the castle. Off with you, now!" He went out the door, bellowing, "Form up!"

"How old is she?" the boot asked Ralke. "Answer true, or you'll feel a boot's boot!" He chuckled at his own cleverness.

"Twelve," Ralke answered, his accent thicker than normal. "She'm budded early, our Else, though she'm still be but twelve."

"Then I'll be back in three years," the boot promised, and went out the door, calling, "Aye, aye, brute, I'm here."

Everyone sat, still and taut, while they listened to the brute bellowing his troops into line. Then came the heavy tread of forty feet marching. It faded and was gone.

Ralke heaved a sigh of relief and came to his feet. "Good fortune! I've never been more glad for a boot's stupidity!"

"I'm glad, too." Bilar rolled to his feet.

"I'm fifteen," the girl said indignantly as her weight lifted off Gar. He sat up, scattering straw.

"So tha art, ma lass, but if the boot had knowed it, he'd ha' come back and taken 'ee off to the woods, and brought ye back weeping," her mother said, with the air of one who knows by bitter experience. "Keep the face smudged and the locks in a tangle, as I've bade 'ee!"

"Thank 'ee for so quick a lie," Bilar said to Ralke.

"The least ah could do," Ralke said, unconsciously falling back into the villager's accent. "Thank 'ee for the hiding of us!"

"Glad, we're glad. Remember us if tha comest back this way. Dress thee, na, an' be off!"

Ralke changed clothes quickly, leaving his hair for later washing. Then he beckoned to Gar and went out the door—but he turned back to count twelve copper coins into Bilar's hand.

The earthquake hit, and Cort's eyes flew open, his heart thudding wildly with fear. "What's happening?"

The earthquake stopped abruptly, the room stopped shaking, and a strange voice said, with regret, "Sorry to have to wake you, lieutenant. You need your sleep—say, another ten hours' worth."

"Sleep?" Cort sagged back onto the bed. His stomach lurched and tried to climb up his throat. "Let me die! My head feels like an anvil with a smith forging a sword! Who stuffed their laundry into my mouth?"

"You did, only it wasn't laundry, it was a whole bottle of brandy."

Memory stirred. Cort rolled to the side, squinting against the horrid glare. "I know you from somewhere . . ."

"We met last night," the stranger said obligingly, "over a couple of civilians your soldiers had decided to use as punching bags."

"I remember." But the effort made Cort's head hurt, and he grabbed it with a groan. "An alley . . . a band of citizens . . ." He squinted up at the stranger. "You're . . . Poniard? Dagger?"

"Dirk," the stranger said helpfully, "Dulaine. Here, drink this." He held out a tin cup full of dark fluid.

Cort flinched at the smell. "Brandy? It turns my stomach now!"

"Hair of the dog that bit you," Dirk insisted. "Just a shot, lieutenant. Drink it down and you'll feel better—eventually."

Cort eyed Dirk, decided he must be ten years older than Cort himself and had presumably had more experience with toxic fluids. He accepted the tin cup gingerly, took a deep breath, and downed the liquid at one swallow. Then he dropped the cup and exhaled, feeling as though he were breathing fire.

Dirk caught the cup and set it aside. "It'll help, believe me."

Cort held his head, moaning. "What happened? I remember the alleyway, and . . ." He stared up at Dirk. "I hired you as a sergeant!"

Dirk nodded. "You were a little drunk by that time. You can change your mind, no hard feelings."

But Cort was hot on the track of memory. "You beat the changeling corporal!"

"Well, you know and I know that he's not really a changeling . . ."

"No, any man who can do that is too valuable to let go," Cort mused. "Why did you let me drink so much?"

"I'm your sergeant, not your conscience! Besides, I could tell you were in a mood to get very drunk on very little, so I figured you needed it, as long as it was safe."

"And you made sure it was safe." Cort stiffened, looking around him, realizing for the first time that he was in a bedchamber. "How did I get here?"

"I carried you," Dirk explained simply.

"And rolled me into this bed?" For the first time, Cort realized he was naked except for his loincloth. "And stripped me?"

"Your uniform needed cleaning, by that time," Dirk explained. "Excuse me—your livery."

"I couldn't keep the liquor down?" Cort blushed furiously.

"The body's little defense against alcohol poisoning, lieutenant."

"Did I . . ." Cort reddened. "Did I babble?"

"Nothing worth repeating," Dirk said firmly, "and I was the only one who heard you."

But the sympathy in his eyes told Cort that his new sergeant had heard about his broken love in detail. He reddened even more and turned away, but said, "Would you hand me my kerchief, please?"

"I'm just one of your sergeants." Dirk rummaged on the table, then came back to press the kerchief into Cort's hand. "You don't need to say 'please' to me."

"I don't usually ask my sergeants to wait on me," Cort said. He slid Violet's ring from his finger, and noticed for the first time that it was really a rather cheap gaud—surely the metal was only brass, for it had made his finger green, and the stone in it was the color of her name, yes, but it had the sheen of glass. Why had he never thought of that before? But he wrapped the ring in his kerchief and turned to hold it out to Dirk. "Would you do me one more favor? Take this to Squire Ellsworth's house, down on that broad side street where the well-to-do people live. Anyone in town can tell you where it is. Tell them . . ." His stomach suddenly bucked, and he stopped to choke it down. "Tell them it's for Violet, and that I wish her well in her future life."

"Sure, lieutenant, no problem. I mean, 'Yes, sir.' " Dirk straightened and turned to go.

"Why couldn't you have just let me sleep?" Cort moaned.

"Oh, yeah, I almost forgot!" Dirk turned back. "There's a messenger here, a very young soldier wearing your livery, who says he's from Captain Devers. Want me to let him in?"

"No!" Cort clutched the blanket about him, then remembered himself and pointed at his pack. "There's spare livery in there. Toss it to me, will you?"

"Sure." Dirk opened Cort's pack, pulled out the clean clothing, and set it on the bed. "I'll tell him you'll just be a few minutes. Want him to wait downstairs?"

Cort weighed the likelihood of his making it down the stairway without falling, and decided, "No. Tell him to have his breakfast, if he hasn't already, and to have a flagon of ale if he has, then to come back up and wait upon me here."

"Will do. Hope you feel better soon." Dirk went out, but before the door closed, Cort heard him telling the messenger, "He's a little under the weather, but if you give him a few minutes . . ."

Then the door closed, and Cort heaved his legs out of bed, then waited for his stomach to settle again. The movement had made his head start pounding worse, too. When both had slackened, he reached out for the livery and began dressing. He knew that the young soldier was indeed a messenger, and suspected what he was going to tell Cort: that they were to report back to headquarters as quickly as possible.

8

The mules began to pace faster, heads bobbing, and the drivers began to talk to one another with excitement. Then the caravan rounded a curve. The trees opened out into a broad plain cut up into small fields surrounding the walls of a city with a castle dimly seen through the morning mist. The drivers cheered, and Ralke breathed, "Home!" His eyes sparkled, his gaze fastened to his city.

Gar studied the town. Something was different about it, contrasting with Loutre, but he couldn't pin it down. "Who's your boss?"

"Ranatista has no boss, friend," Ralke said. "Legend says that when the troubles started, we were far enough from the seacoast settlements that our ancestors had time to get ready for trouble. Their sage had already taught them to fight with their open hands, for it was a discipline that taught the mind control of the body, and taught the soul to compete without hatred or anger."

Gar frowned, though it sounded very familiar. "How do you know that?"

"Because that's why our sages still teach it to us today. But the first squire, Sanahan, called our ancestors to defend themselves. He led them in learning how to use flails and scythes and staves in a kind of fighting that kept the spirit the sages taught, and quarterstaff-play turned very quickly to spear-play. They even had time to build this wall that you see glowing golden in the sunrise. When the bullies came marching to conquer us, our ancestors poured boiling water on them from the battlements, and wherever they broke through the wall or climbed over it, our ancestors made short work of their boots. One after another, the bullies advanced against us, then retired in consternation, for bullies won't stay chewing at a target that costs them too much in men or weapons."

"Most bullies pick victims they're sure they can beat," Gar said grimly.

"Indeed they do, so all our ancestors needed was to defend themselves well, and the bullies left, since none of them wished to sit down in a siege, easy meat for any other bully who came after them. Thus it is to this day, and all our young men take it in turns to serve in the home guard."

"And Sanahan's successor?"

"We choose a new squire when the old one is fifty, if he lives that long—and most of them do. Then he leads us till his turn comes to retire."

"None of them want to stay squire?"

"Most of them, surely, but they can't deny custom! Oh, they can still live in the castle with their families, and the new squires always value their council—but after fifty, they can't be squire any more, though folk still call them that out of courtesy."

"Squire, retired." Gar nodded. "A good system. Do all the merchants come from such towns as yours?"

Ralke looked sharply at him, then smiled slowly. "You reason quickly, friend. Yes, merchants always come from free towns. Every now and again a young man from a boss's town tries to break into the trade, and we give him what help we can, but the boss always takes all the profit when the youngster returns home, and he has nothing with which to begin another journey."

"Odd that the bosses don't realize they need to encourage the merchants, if they want the wealth they bring in."

"Bosses can see no further than their own comfort, friend Gar."

"Do any of the young men from bosses' towns ever escape to the free towns?"

"It happens now and again," Ralke said, amused. "I was one such."

Gar nodded. "That makes sense. Otherwise, how would you have been a peasant in a boss's domain?" He pointed at the cottages of a small village a few hundred yards from the road and the farmers who were mowing hay nearby. They wore tunics and cross-gartered hose with sandals, and though the garments weren't new, they weren't nearly worn through, either. "Your peasants seem to live a bit better than the ones who hid us."

"Be sure they do! They're citizens like the rest of us, after all, and share in the wealth of the domain as much as any other!"

"Except the squire."

Ralke shrugged. "He leads us in battle, sees that we're taught how to fight, and works far into the night overseeing the growing and storage of crops. No one begrudges him his home in the castle, nor the grand clothes he must wear when he greets the emissary of the next boss who threatens to attack us."

The guards at the gate called out a cheerful greeting, welcoming Ralke home, glad to see him well, and were saddened at the news of the man who had died. Citizens came running to welcome the caravan, cheering them as though they were a victorious army—which in some measure they were, having fought off bandits and brought home the spoils, though they were the profits of commerce, not the loot of battle.

The cheering throng accompanied them to Ralke's warehouse, and his wife came running down the outer stairs to throw herself into his arms. A teenaged boy and girl waited their turn, with two younger children dancing in impatience. "Poppa, Poppa! What did you bring us?"

Gar smiled, amused at the timeless chant, then smoothed his face into impassivity as his heart twisted, pained at the sight of the warmth he would never know.

When they had unpacked the mules and turned them over to the hostlers, Ralke called his drivers up one by one for their pay and their share of the profits. Whooping with delight, they ran out to indulge themselves in a bit of celebration—but Gar noticed that each of them stopped by the window in the big building next to the warehouse, each handing over his pay bag, keeping only a few coins for his purse. When Ralke had paid the last driver, Gar asked, "Why are they giving their money to the man in that building?"

"Why, to keep it safe, friend. They lay their money on the bank for him to count—"

"We'd call it a counter," Gar said, "and the building a bank."

Ralke shrugged, miffed that it wasn't all news to Gar. "Then you probably also know that the banker keeps accounts of how much each man has deposited, but keeps all the coins in a huge vault."

"Yes." Gar smiled. "And I suspect that he lends some of it out to merchants who want to buy more goods for their next trip."

"You know more of commerce than I'd thought," Ralke said, giving him the keen look again. "Will you ride with us on our next venture?"

"It's a very attractive offer," Gar said slowly, "and I'd love to. How soon will it be?"

"Two weeks."

Gar shook his head. "I'm too restless a man to wait that long, Master Ralke, but if I'm back this way at that time, I'll be glad to join you."

"I had thought as much," Ralke said with a sigh. "Well, friend, here's your pay. I'll write a letter like the one you showed me from the Braccalese fellow, recommending you to anyone who wants to hire you. Off with you to your next employment—but try to pick one that ends in time to join us when we next go a-venturing."

At least Cort had gotten over wishing he were going to die, and had risen to the level of being afraid that he would. Under the circumstances, it was a major improvement.

The road stretched out before him in the afternoon sunlight, filled with a double file of disgruntled and hungover soldiers. Their form was lousy, but Cort was in no condition to complain. The master sergeant was leading, being in better shape than Cort. The sergeants paced beside, careful to see that no one lagged. Cort was riding, and Dirk, being the only other soldier who had a horse, rode beside him.

"You understand you'll have to leave your mount in the company stables once we're back at headquarters, don't you?" Cort asked.

Dirk nodded. "Sure do. You hired me on as infantry, after all."

"You've been cavalry, then?"

"Anything in soldiering, lieutenant—even an officer when they were desperate."

So he'd had at least one battlefield promotion. In spite of the hangover, Cort was almost interested.

Almost. Not quite enough to think up another question. He let the conversation lapse, and turned back to watching his men straggle on before him. Dirk had given him some strange white pills that had killed the worst of his headache, but the nausea was still there, and the general feeling of sickness. It was hard to think about anything else, so he was only irritated when Dirk pointed at the huge grassy dome rising out of the fields and said, "Odd-looking hill, that. You don't often see one that looks like half a melon."

"Unh?" Cort looked up, following Dirk's pointing arm. " 'Course you do. They're all over the land, at least one in every district. Haven't you ever seen a Hollow Hill before?"

"Hollow Hill?" Dirk turned to him, interested. "Where the Little People live?"

"Little People?" Cort asked, puzzled. "Maybe they're little where you come from, but in our country, the Fair Folk are anything but little! They're taller than the biggest of us, and fair of hair and skin. Beautiful they are, men and women alike, and deadly with their magic! They may choose to help or choose to harm, and a man never knows which!"

"That last part sounds like the People of the Hollow Hills, back home," Dirk mused. "I've heard of the tall kind, of course, but I've never been in their country before."

"You *are* from far away," Cort grunted.

"And Corporal Korgash? You think the Fair Folk left him in an ordinary person's cradle?"

"He's the right coloring and size," Cort grunted, "blond and light-skinned, and more than six feet tall. Besides, he's ugly enough for the Fair Folk to have wanted to be rid of him." With that, he lapsed back into the misery of his hangover. Probably because of his stomach and his general malaise, he never thought twice about the conversation, and never remembered it, either.

It had taken the sergeants most of the morning to find all the troopers and gather them together to hear the captain's order. Cort had been awfully glad of Dirk then; he had taken word to the master sergeant, letting Cort stay in bed. Then he had helped corral the Blue Company and feed each man his "hair of the dog;" he confided later that he had put the white pills in with the beer. By that time, Cort had managed to pull himself together enough to address the men, telling them that the captain wanted them back at headquarters right away, and had found the strength to stand against the wind of their massed groan and torrent of cursing. When the worst of it had passed, he had ordered them to form up into columns, then chivvied them into moving out of the town and onto the trail. From there, he had slumped and let the sergeants take over. It was pretty routine, and any sergeant would tell you that he could manage the men better than any officer—unless the order was one he didn't want to take the blame for, of course. When Cort had needed to issue a command, he had muttered it to Dirk, who had ridden to the head of the column to relay the order to the master sergeant, letting Cort suffer through his hangover in relative peace.

But between the hangovers and a startling lack of eagerness to reach their destination, the troopers moved far more slowly than they had coming down to the town. Night caught them only halfway to the mountains and the captain, so Cort sent up the order to pitch camp.

The hangovers had worn off enough for the men to have worked up appetites, and for Cort to be able to stroll around the camp to keep up morale. Dirk stayed beside him, though, probably worried that Cort might collapse. Cort didn't scold him—he wasn't all that sure that Dirk might not be right.

"Why the plague is he calling us back?" one trooper grunted. "Only a single lousy night of liberty!"

"Just a bastard," his mate griped. "All officers are." Then he caught sight of Cort approaching and ducked his head, staring down into his cooking pot.

Cort managed a mirthless smile and walked on.

"Don't worry, I know it's not true," Dirk told him. "I also know that thinking all officers are heartless brutes helps keep soldiers in line."

"Especially the ones who *are* heartless brutes," Cort agreed. "There are always the ones who'd disobey every order and savage every civilian, if they didn't think the captain was a tougher old dog than any of them."

"What the clash could be so all-powered important to call us back so sudden?" another trooper grunted.

"Maybe the captain's got a new girlfriend he wants to impress," the other trooper guessed, "so he needs us all there to parade for her."

"Maybe you'd better tell them the real reason," Dirk said as they sauntered past the cookfire.

"Tomorrow," Cort told him, "when I'm feeling fit again."

"You can guess what it is, of course."

"What else?" Cort said, with an impatient shrug. "The captain's found another job for us, and it can't wait. Probably paying us double to come protect some slob of a boss from his neighbor, when he's too slack to keep his men in fighting trim. Oh, don't look so shocked—that's one of the good things about being a mercenary, being able to speak your mind about the bosses."

"But if a bruiser tried that, his bully would hear about it and string him up at dawn the next day, huh?"

"Why would he wait for dawn?" Cort asked. He reflected that this foreigner had a great many odd ideas.

"Ever wonder why the bosses are always fighting?" Dirk asked. "From what I see, most of their battles are about some small strip of land right on the border, which they both claim. A skirmish like that would be really easy to settle by making both men sit down and discuss it reasonably."

"True, if the quarrel were really about that strip of land," Cort agreed, "but it isn't—it's just an excuse to fight. The attacking boss actually wants the whole domain, and his rival boss as a prisoner into the bargain."

"Too bad somebody can't make 'em stop," Dirk grunted.

"What are you trying to do, ruin our business?"

Dirk shrugged. "You're telling me the bosses and their men don't really want to resolve their disputes, just want an excuse to fight every few years. There're so many of them, each lording it over a dozen square miles or so, that the warfare is constant—As soon as one battle stops, another begins a few miles away."

Cort nodded. "Tragic, isn't it? Sometimes I wish there really were some way to end it—but then I tell myself I'm a fool, that it makes good business for us."

"There is that," Dirk agreed. "So much for the only force that could make the bosses behave."

"The only force?" Cort frowned. "What do you mean?"

"If the mercenaries banded together, they could tell the bosses to stay in their own domains, and make it stick."

"Easily," Cort said, with a snort that might have been a laugh if he'd been feeling better. "Any three mercenary companies could easily beat any one boss—but why bother? That's how we make our money, after all—by fighting the bosses' battles for them."

"So the mercenaries could stop the fighting," Dirk sighed, "but they won't. They have a vested interest in warfare."

"You could put it that way," Cort agreed, "especially since every now and then, one of the captains manages to become a bully himself."

"And never thinks of pushing for boss, and conquering all the others?"

"Are you joking?" Cort asked. "All the other bosses would ally against him on the instant, and all the mercenary captains, too. No one's going to risk the rise of a boss of bosses who would be able to tell any one of them what he could and couldn't do."

"Right," Dirk said sourly. "No bully wants to be bullied, eh? But he always is."

"There's always someone stronger than a bully—and they call him boss." Cort nodded. "But there isn't a bully of bosses, and they're bound and determined that there never will be."

They had come to the edge of the camp. Cort looked out over it with a sigh. "I take first watch. If ever I didn't want it, this is the night."

"Go to bed," Dirk said. "I'll take your shift. What is it, just walking the perimeter and making sure the sentries stay awake?"

"You *have* been an officer, haven't you?" Cort asked. "Yes, you'll be officer of the watch. Thank you deeply, Dirk."

"My pleasure. Who do I wake up to take second watch, and when?"

"The master sergeant, at midnight." Cort hesitated. "He might . . ."

"Resent me a bit, because I've been hired in as a sergeant and stayed pretty close to you? Don't worry, lieutenant, I'll reason with him."

"Just make sure your reasoning doesn't leave any bruises," Cort cautioned.

Dirk grinned, shaking his head. "I wouldn't dream of assaulting a senior noncom, lieutenant. Sleep tight."

"That's what sent me into this misery," Cort groaned. "If you don't mind, I'll sleep sober."

True to his word, Dirk wandered through the camp while the men were bedding down, and even found a chance to exchange a few words with Sergeant Otto.

"Glad you joined up," the older man told him. "Young officers need watchdogs now and then, and I'm just as glad to have someone share the job."

Dirk grinned. "So you knew why I really signed up."

"Took a liking to him right away, didn't you? And you had nothing else going, at the moment. Well, it's good for young men to make friends. You've been an officer, too, though, haven't you?"

"An officer, and a sergeant major before that," Dirk confirmed, "but I started as a private."

Sergeant Otto nodded. "Then I'm glad to have someone else to help keep this crew of thugs in order. Just don't let on when we rejoin the company."

"I'll revert to the lowliest infantry sergeant," Dirk promised.

"I doubt that." Otto grinned. "But I'll settle for your taking orders."

Then Dirk went out to pace the unseen picket line, visible only as line-of-sight between sentries. They were easy enough to see, because they were on a flat meadow. He stopped by the first and said, "What of the night?"

"Quiet, sergeant." The trooper tried to hide his disdain of this disguised civilian.

Dirk decided he needed a lesson. He pointed. "See that bush?"

"Of course, sergeant," the soldier replied, with a trace of scorn.

"How far away is it?"

The soldier thought a moment, then said, "Twenty yards."

Dirk nodded. "Keep an eye on it. When I come back, tell me if it's even five yards nearer."

"Closer?" The soldier stared at him as though he were crazy. "How could a bush move?"

"By somebody cutting it off at the roots and using it to hide behind as he crept closer to you," Dirk explained.

The sentry's gaze snapped back to the bush, staring.

"Keep the watch," Dirk said, turning away.

"Yes, sergeant!" The young man's voice held a note of respect now.

Dirk made the rounds, chatting with each soldier and winning a little trust from each, if not yet respect. Then he stepped out past the picket line, strolling around it twenty yards out, ostensibly checking the ground. It wasn't the best military tactic, but it did provide some privacy. He took the medallion out of his shirt front and managed to fake a rather believable sneeze. He waited a few minutes, then sneezed again.

The medallion spoke in Gar's voice. "Receiving."

9

Are you someplace where you can talk without being overheard?" Dirk asked.

"I've just signed off as a caravan guard, and I'm out on my own, camping in a cave for the night," Gar answered. "Where are you?"

"Patrolling the perimeter as officer of the watch for a mercenary company," Dirk answered. "I bummed around for a bit, learning the language, until I found the town they were visiting for R and R. Stayed overnight in a peasant hovel, took a short courier job for a boss, that kind of thing. How about you?"

"We fought off some mercenaries moonlighting as bandits," Gar told him, "and I pumped the caravan merchant for every bit of information I could get about trade and the political setup, or lack of it. Then we outwitted a translator who was trying to make a profit out of swindling both his boss and us, and he sicced some off-duty boots on us—that's . . ."

"Boss's soldiers, I know," Dirk said. "Just offhand, I'd say that between the two of us we've seen a pretty good cross section of the population."

"I've picked up enough legends to work out the history of the planet after Terra cut them off," Gar told him.

"Me, too," Dirk said. "The folktales make it pretty clear the people remember their ancestors being anarchists."

"From what I've heard, they really thought they could live with no government, imitating the virtue of their sages," Gar agreed. "The first generation managed to live by their ideals, but some of their children didn't feel obligated. A few of them liked to throw their weight around, and decided to steal as much as they could by brute force. They bullied other tough guys into taking orders, gathered gangs, and started beating up their neighbors, enslaving them, and taking all their food except the bare minimum to keep them alive and reproducing."

Dirk nodded, forgetting that Gar couldn't see him. "Then one bully started conquering another, two allied against one, the one allied with two more, and the situation turned into perpetual warfare. Finally one bully managed to conquer three or four others and declared himself boss. Word got out, the idea caught on, and other bullies started fighting it out to see who could become boss."

"Which worked fine to make a boss over several bullies," Gar agreed, "but by the time one boss started trying to conquer another one, some enterprising soul had already invented mercenary companies, and with each side hiring mercenaries to help out, the battles only ended in futility and bloodshed."

Dirk added, "And nobody noticed that it wasn't exactly ethical."

"They seem to have the idea that morality is only for weaklings," Gar said, "and there's no religion to make them rethink the point."

"Yes, you noticed that, too?" Dirk frowned. "No religion at all. I gather the original colonists were trying very hard to be good philosophers and better atheists."

"Well, they succeeded," Gar said grimly, "and the bosses finished the job. They did their best to kill off all the philosophers."

"Yeah, I picked up traces of that, too," Dirk agreed. "The

sages told their people not to try to defend them, but the people tried to fight for them anyway, and were slaughtered. So ended all the philosophers."

"Except for the ones who were willing to come up with logical excuses for bosses to exist, and be used as mouthpieces," Gar said, "and willing to concoct a philosophy that said bosses were right to be bosses, and the common people should stay in their places."

"I get the impression that a very few sages survived by going so far out into the wilderness that the bosses didn't care about them," Dirk said. "Anyway, each district seems to have at least one sage, and he's keeping the basic ideas of Taoism alive, to comfort the people when they're on the verge of despair."

"So philosophy becomes the opiate of the masses," Gar said, with irony. "I also found out that after Terra cut the colony off and manufactured goods became scarce, the second generation reinvented capitalism. Since there was no government to force it to stop, it caught on."

"Interesting that you've found a merchant," Dirk commented. "All I've seen are mercenaries."

"That does seem to be the most widespread form of capitalism," Gar agreed. "Most of the bosses' money goes into hiring free companies. The wars between bosses quickly became a matter of seeing who could hire the most and the best mercenaries, and the ordinary people were ground down to pay for them."

"I've found out that mercenary officers can become rich enough to retire in comfort," Dirk said, "complete with big houses and dowries for their daughters—and captains can actually make enough money to buy their way into bossdom. How do any merchants manage to stay in business, with all this fighting?"

"Most of them come from free towns," Gar told him.

"Free towns?" Dirk frowned. "I haven't heard of those. The only towns without castles that I've seen are securely within the domain of one boss or another. I've heard a legend that some independent villages hired a bully to protect them, but after he had fought off the enemy, he wound up enslaving the people who had hired him."

"Some villages were far enough from the center of the troubles so that they had some warning, and were doubly blessed in having a sage who taught martial arts as part of his philosophy," Gar explained. "They elected a leader who figured out how to use weapons, so when a bully came to conquer, they fought him off long enough to make the price in men and arms more than he wanted to pay. Apparently, the secret of staying in the bully business was a quick win. By the time the bosses came marching, the mercenaries were available for hire, and the free cities became some of their best customers. I don't doubt that the occasional enlightened boss lets his merchants keep enough of their profits to stay in business, but most of the entrepreneurs are from the free towns."

"I expect they have to learn a lot of different dialects," Dirk mused.

"Have any communication troubles?" Gar asked.

"Only for the first twenty-four hours or so. If I listen long enough, I can track down the vowel shifts and guess the occasional home-grown word. They've all evolved out of Galactic Standard, of course, so I don't have too much trouble figuring them out. The locals don't know the original Galactic pronunciation, though, so most of them can't understand the people from the next county. It does open up work for interpreters, huh?"

"That seems to be one of the tasks of the bosses' stewards," Gar told him. "That's all the government there is—the bosses and their servants—and within each domain, the boss's whim is law. There's no central government to stop him from doing anything he wants to the people." His voice hardened. "They live like animals, Dirk—no, worse. The local bully takes any girl he wants for a night's pleasure, then turns her over to his officers, and when they're done with her, they turn her over to the boots.

I've seen a lot of poor people on a lot of planets, but I don't think I've ever seen any ground down worse than these."

"The end result of anarchy," Dirk agreed. "It works only as long as nobody gets greedy, but when somebody does, there's nothing to stop him. Didn't the original anarchists have some idea about assassinating anyone who tried to bully his neighbors?"

"Not that I've ever read," Gar replied. "Good idea, I suppose, if you don't find it unethical to kill somebody without a trial, or without his being there to be tried. But who's going to keep the assassin from becoming a bully himself?"

"The old problem." Dirk sighed. " 'Who will police the police?' Or, you might say, who will govern the government?"

"The people," Gar answered, "but that means you've developed some form of democracy."

"In which everyone's a soldier when he's needed," Dirk concurred. "Well, there are advantages to military life: a guaranteed place to live, steady pay if you ever find a place to spend it, regular meals, free clothing . . ."

"The clothes tend to be a bit monotonous," Gar reminded him, "but yes, it's a secure life, apart from the chance of being killed in battle every now and then. Take it to the extreme of everyday life, and you have Sparta, where everyone's a soldier all the time."

"Except for the slaves," Dirk reminded.

"But the Spartans didn't count them as people," Gar pointed out. "From what else I hear about them, it was a nice place to have on your side, but you wouldn't want to visit."

"And definitely not live there," Dirk agreed. "But let's not lose sight of the fact that there are one or two good things about this sort of anarchy."

"I must have missed them," Gar said, voice dripping sarcasm. "Remind me."

"High social mobility, for one," Dirk said. "You can be born a peasant, but end up the captain of a Free Company, or maybe even a boss."

"But more likely in an early grave," Gar pointed out.

"The risks are very high," Dirk conceded. "Of course, if you live in one of the free towns you've told me about, there are probably all sorts of opportunities, such as becoming a merchant. How high is their death rate?"

"Fairly high, from what I saw on this journey," Gar told him, "and it probably would have been worse, if they hadn't had a telepath along to tell them when the enemy was coming. But you're right about the free cities being a decent existence—they even have enough extra food and money to support an artist or two. Of course, everybody has to drill every week, and the men march off to war every year or so, but as long as they can keep from being conquered, they live fairly well."

"Government?" Dirk asked.

"Town council," Gar answered. "I'm sure there are power blocs and influence peddlers, but I wasn't there long enough to study the details. So life is all right here, if you're a soldier or a citizen of a free town—but for the serfs it's miserable."

"Yes," Dirk said, "and they're the vast majority. Aside from near-starvation and back-breaking work, life in a hole in the ground isn't too bad, if you don't mind sacks for clothes and freezing toes. Of course, there's the little problem of constant warfare, with women being raped and people killed, villages burned, and crops trampled . . ."

"Which leads to *complete* starvation," Gar said, his voice tight with pain. "Do you have any doubts that we have to destroy this system?"

"None at all," Dirk said with full conviction. "But what is there to destroy? We're professionals at overthrowing governments, Gar. Where's the government to overthrow?"

"I'm very much afraid that this time, we'll actually have to set up a government," Gar sighed, "but it does go against the grain. We'll have to start by establishing a lasting peace."

"I thought we were going to have to cobble together some sort of government, in order to see that peace declared," Dirk countered. "These people are so miserable that they'd even cheer for a dictator—at least it would be some protection, some order."

"They'd be ground down just as badly," Gar said, his voice hard. "Think of the last planet we visited, of our friends Miles and Orgoru and the dictator who ruled them. What about the torture, and the stunted lives, his people endured?" Then he remembered, and his voice lightened. "Miles! How's about that, Dirk? Think you can start a minstrel movement, and introduce songs with the underlying idea that peasants are fully human?"

"It's a start, anyway," Dirk sighed. "I do think it's time for us to get back together, though."

"I agree. Herkimer, where is Dirk relative to me?" Gar asked.

The computer answered instantly, obviously eavesdropping. "His signal originates from a district approximately twenty miles south by southwest of you, Magnus."

"We're in the foothills of a mountain range," Dirk told him, "on our way back to the Blue Company's headquarters. I'm sure they'll love having you as a recruit. We've just come out of a forest, and we're in a meadow, but we'll be going back into forest as we start upslope tomorrow."

"I'll see you in the trees, then."

"Right." But Dirk hesitated a second, then said, "Gar? Did you ever wonder what right we have to do this? To just burst into somebody else's planet, and try to change their governmental system?"

"We probably don't have any right at all," Gar admitted, "but we do have a duty. Personally, I couldn't live with myself if I knew I could have done something to ease the suffering of a million individuals, but sat by and did nothing."

"Yeah, well, that's okay if you bump into them—but we go out looking!"

"Yes," Gar said, "because we know there are people suffering out there, and we know we have the duty to help them. After all, we're free to do it—we don't have any other responsibilities at this point in our lives—so we'd be less than ourselves if we didn't search. When the day comes that we go through all the computer records, visit every planet whose people might be oppressed, and come to the conclusion that on all of them, the government is doing the best it can and that no other government would do any better for its people—then we can very seriously ask if we have any right to interfere."

"Then we can retire," Dirk grunted.

Gar rode in silence for a while, then said, "Don't let my obsession rule your life, my friend. If you're lucky enough to find your destiny, to find a woman you love and a place where you belong, don't feel you have to forsake them all for me or my dream."

Dirk stared at the medallion, amazed, and wondered if he should feel rejected.

"If the woman and the place are your destiny," Gar said, "then your duty to them is greater than your duty to the suffering millions on dozens of planets you've never heard of. We each have to try to make life better in the corner of reality that's revealed to each of us; we can't do more."

"I never knew you were religious," Dirk said softly.

"Oh, yes, you did." Gar smiled sardonically. "But that kind of talk doesn't have to be religious. It might only mean that I'm beginning to understand my father."

It was the first time Gar had ever mentioned anyone related to him. Dirk stared, thunderstruck by the realization that Gar didn't exist in a vacuum.

Cort was his old self the next morning, at least to outward appearances, alert and energetic, issuing his orders quietly to the master sergeant, who bawled them out to the other sergeants, who ordered the men into columns and set them moving onto the road.

It was an uphill climb, and though the men were no longer hungover, they weren't happy about having their leave cut short, so they still went slowly. They were just coming to the first plateau when a rider came out of the trees before them. Discipline kept the soldiers marching, but without it, they would have stopped dead, for the stranger was huge, seven feet tall and broad to match, astride a horse that stood five hands taller than most.

He started to ride toward them. Then brown-clothed soldiers burst from the trees by the roadside with shrill, ear-splitting cries.

Their first charge mowed down a dozen men, but the sergeants were already bawling, "Stand to! Fight!" and the soldiers, out of sheer reflex, turned on their ambushers.

There were at least forty of them to the platoon's thirty, well armed and armored, with boiled-leather breastplates and iron skullcaps. They wielded their spears as both quarterstaves and cutting blades, still skirling their battlecry. But the Blue Company, now braced for battle and over their first surprise, fought back with equal skill, and with the ferocity of outrage. Spearheads rang on bucklers, shafts rattled against shafts. Sergeants bellowed as they ran back and forth, knocking the attackers off their men.

Cort rode through the battleline, shouting in anger and hewing about him with his sword. A brown-coated soldier leaped to catch his horse's reins as a second stabbed upward at him and a third jammed his spearbutt between Cort and his saddle. Cort caught the spear on his buckler, then whirled to chop at the lever-man, but the spear came back and grazed his ribs even as the third soldier fell away. Cort roared in rage and pain and slammed his shield into the second soldier's face. He turned to the front just as a spearhead came stabbing up at his face.

Another sword leaped in from the side, knocking the spear up, and Dirk kicked its bearer in the head. The first soldier fell, letting go of the reins.

"Thanks," Cort called. "Where's their officer?"

"Only a lieutenant, as far as I can see," Dirk shouted back.

"He's mine!" Cort turned and charged at a brown-coat with brass epaulets, but even as he did, a brown-clad rider burst out of the trees at the roadside, howling and riding straight toward him, sword slashing.

A huge roar sounded. The brown-coat turned and whirled his sword frantically, trying to protect himself—as well he might, for the man who thrust and slashed at him was the giant, wielding a blade more than three feet long. He bellowed like a bear and hacked and chopped at the brown-coat officer, then suddenly spun his horse away and charged down the battleline, bellowing.

The brown-coats took one look and leaped away—but so did the Blue Company, in sheer terror. The giant turned on the brown soldiers, though, slashing at them with his huge sword. Soldiers jumped aside, for they could see his swings coming a mile away—and a mile wide they seemed. But none wanted to stay for another slash, so they turned and fled, leaving half their number groaning and writhing in the road.

Still roaring, the giant chased them back into the woods.

"Rally!" the brown-coat officer cried, turning on the Blue Company alone.

His sword rang on Cort's blade, and both men went silent, slashing in quick and desperate strokes.

10

The two were about the same age and size, Cort a little younger, his enemy a little older. They were so well matched that they stayed where they were, neither advancing or giving ground, their horses dancing around and about one another.

The Blue Company stared at the duel, fascinated.

"You're all alone, you know," Dirk called.

Startled, the officer spun his horse, still facing Cort and parrying madly, but looking past his foe to see that there wasn't a single brown-coat left in sight. Suddenly he broke away with a high, shrill cry and spurred his mount toward the trees.

Cort started to chase him, but the man reached the trees first, and Cort pulled up, cursing, knowing the man might have left a rearguard in ambush. He turned back to his own troops.

Sergeant Otto had already bullied the unwounded men back into a battleline, spears outward, while the other sergeants went from wounded man to wounded man, doing what they could for first aid; so did Dirk. The huge stranger was off his horse and down with them, tending to the fallen brown-coats.

Cort rode up to Sergeant Otto. "What's the tally?"

"Two of ours dead and ten wounded, sir," Sergeant Otto answered. "Too soon to tell who can walk, but my guess is that six of them won't fight again for months."

Cort nodded grimly and glanced at the giant. "Detail men to guard him. I don't know who he is, but he helped us, and I don't want some wounded Hawk killing him with a lucky stroke."

"Yes, sir." The master sergeant turned to bawl orders, then turned back to Cort. "Why would the Hawk Company attack us when neither of us is hired to fight, sir?"

"Just because the Blue Company hasn't been hired, doesn't mean the Hawks haven't," Cort told him, "and for all we know, Captain Devers may have already signed on with some boss or squire who has a war coming up. My guess is that the Hawks are fighting for the enemies of whoever has just hired the Blue Company, and the more of us they can kill before the battle, the fewer they'll have to face on the field."

"That's against all the rules in the Free Companies' Code," the master sergeant said grimly.

"It certainly is." Cort's words rang like those of a judge pronouncing sentence.

"When the captains hear of this, they'll turn on the Hawk Company in a body," Otto predicted.

"They will indeed," Cort agreed. "That's why the Hawks don't dare let us live to tell of it."

The master sergeant's eyes widened. "You're right, sir, of course! They'll be back with three times their number!"

"And they won't be surprised by a giant this time," Cort said grimly. "Form up the men as soon as you can, sergeant! We have to march." He turned away. "Sergeant Dulaine!"

"One more stitch, sir." Incredibly, Dirk was sewing a man's wound shut. He tied off the thread, broke it, and came over to Cort, tucking his needle away in a little wooden case that he slipped into his tunic. "Who the hell were *they*?"

"Two platoons from the Hawk Company, ambushing us before the battle begins," Cort told him. "How long before our wounded are fit to travel?"

"Now, sir, if you carry them in litters," Dirk said. "Seven of them can walk, but they can't fight."

"You and I will have to carry the dead on our horses until we can bury them," Cort told him. "There's no time now; the Hawks will be back with three times our number, maybe with their whole company. Set up litters."

Dirk nodded. "Yes, sir." He turned away and called, "How many of those brown-coats will live until their friends come back, Gar?"

"They all will, if their buddies stay to take care of them," the giant answered.

Cort stared. "You know each other?"

"Old friends," Dirk told him. "He was supposed to meet me back in town, but he was late, so I left a note at the inn, telling him which road to take, and that there might be work for him at the end of it."

"Oh, there surely is," Cort said softly, "and he doesn't even have to wait till he reaches headquarters."

It made sense that they should know each other—the huge man's accent was even worse than Dirk's. Cort raised his voice. "You there! Giant!"

The big man's head snapped up; he scowled. "Yes, little man?"

Cort stiffened, and Dirk said quickly, "He doesn't like to be called names any more than any of us do."

"My apologies," Cort called stiffly.

"Accepted." Gar stood and came over to the officer; his head was as high as the horse's. "I'm Gar Pike at your service, sometime officer and sometime sergeant."

"I'm only a lieutenant, so I can only hire you as a sergeant," Cort told him, then turned to call. "Sergeant Otto?"

"Yes, sir?" the noncom called as he came over.

"Will you accept yet one more sergeant?"

"Him?" The master sergeant stared. "Be sure I will, sir, and I won't be surprised if the captain promotes him over me!" He held out a hand. "I'm Master Sergeant Otto. You fought well."

"Gar Pike." The giant shook his hand. "It's easy, when you can scare your opponents just by standing up."

"No, I watched how you handled your sword," the master sergeant said. "You're damn good—but so was that Hawk lieutenant."

"Yes, he was," Gar said, frowning. "I hope they sent their best, because if the rest of their officers are that good, we're in trouble."

"You know they'll come back, then?" Cort asked, surprised.

"I would," Gar explained, "no matter why they attacked us. They weren't just after loot, or they wouldn't have picked on professional soldiers. No, we were their assignment, and they're not going to leave it unfinished."

"Wise insight," Cort approved. "We have to march to some kind of stronghold." He looked around at his makeshift cadre. "Any ideas?"

Gar pointed to the northeast. "I passed a town with a small castle on my way here. The peasants in the fields were well dressed, so I'd guess it's a free town."

"A good guess!" Cort's spirits lifted. "Free towns always want to keep mercenaries on their side—they never know when they'll need us." Then he frowned. "Of course, they could be the ones who hired the Hawk Company."

"I didn't see anyone in that uniform around there," Gar told him, "and if the peasants were out hoeing, they weren't expecting a battle. Besides, if these Hawks had been there and *had* expected a fight, they would have challenged me or tried to recruit me, not just let me ride through."

"True." Cort nodded. "Will you carry a dead man across your horse's rump, Sergeant Pike?"

Gar smiled slowly. "I like an officer who won't leave his dead if he doesn't have to. Of course I'll carry a dead man, sir, and a live one too, if I have to."

"It may come to that," Cort admitted. "How far away is this castle?"

"A dozen miles." Gar pointed northeast again, off to the side of the road. "I came overland."

"Then you found a route that doesn't need a road, and won't leave trampled crops to show where we've gone?"

Gar nodded. "Yes, sir."

"Then lead us!" Cort ordered, and turned back to Sergeant Otto. "Load up! We march!"

They marched for the rest of the day, slowly because of their walking wounded, and when the sun set, Cort had to call a halt. The wounded men sat down heavily right where they stood, but the others set to pitching camp and warming dinner.

"We can't rest long, sir," the master sergeant said.

"I know," Cort said, frowning. "I wish I had some notion how far behind us the Hawks are."

"A day's march," Gar said with certainty. "I followed them in until I had to cut off to find the village."

"A day?" Cort said with relief. "Then we can rest for a few hours." It occurred to him to wonder how Gar could have followed so many soldiers and still have seen peasants hoeing without fear, but he had other things to worry about.

"How long do we rest, sir?" Sergeant Otto asked.

"Six hours at the most," Cort told him. "Then we'll move out."

"Marching at midnight?" The sergeant major paled. "But the Fair Folk, sir!"

"We'll have to chance it. After all, I haven't seen a Hollow Hill anywhere along the route."

"There might be one farther ahead, sir," the master sergeant protested.

"Hollow Hill? Fair Folk?" Gar frowned. "Why should we fear them?"

Cort turned to him in surprise, then remembered. "That's right, you're a foreigner."

"I'll tell him while we pitch camp," Dirk said, and led Gar away, talking in low tones, but Cort did catch the phrase, "gas domes." He wondered what Dirk was saying—and Gar, for that matter. He overheard the big man telling Dirk something about doing as the Romans do. He had heard of Romans, of course, but they were just legends, tales that grandmothers told as the winter nights drew in. What did Romans have to do with Fair Folk?

He dismissed the thought—he had worse worries at the moment. He wondered just how far away the Hawk Company camp was, and hoped Gar was right.

The very beautiful girl started to unlace her bodice, then reached down to shake Cort's shoulder. "Wake up, lieutenant!" she insisted.

Cort wanted to do anything but wake up. Actually, he had something very definite he wanted to do, but the girl said "Wake up!" again, and this time she had a deep basso voice. Cort shoved himself up on one elbow as the girl faded to nothing, and forced his eyes open to see the banked and glowing campfire. Alarm jolted through him; he sat up, staring around, and saw Gar.

"Good, you're awake," the big man said. "I made a mistake about the Hawks, lieutenant."

Cort scrambled to his feet. "Are they here?"

"No, and their camp is where I thought it was, but they sent cavalry. I can hear hooves, way out there." Gar pointed off toward the west.

Cort froze, listening, but all he could hear was the breeze. "You've good ears, sergeant."

"It was just a minute's sound blown on a breeze," Gar told him, "a freak echo from the far side of the valley, and of course I can't be sure it's the Hawk Company . . ."

"But farmers don't usually drive that many horses on their wagons," Cort said with sarcasm. "Wake Sergeant Otto and get the company on the march."

The men weren't happy about marching at night—they muttered constantly, and fearfully, about the Fair Folk and other night-spirits.

"Stop worrying about something you *might* run into," Dirk told them, "and pay attention to the danger you can be sure will jump you, if you don't keep moving—the Hawk Company!"

The muttering didn't stop, but the men did march faster.

Even without the wounded men and the corpses, they would have gone far more slowly than the horsemen who were chasing them. With them, progress seemed to be a crawl. Gar kept listening, though, and claimed to be able to hear the Hawks. They were approaching, but were having trouble finding the Blue Company's trail—they had expected them to stay on the roads. So they weren't following directly—they were going at an angle, cutting across the Blue Company's line of march, then turning to search and cutting across the line again. "They'll find us sooner or later, lieutenant, but it'll be dawn before they can see our signs well enough to catch up fast."

"With any luck, we'll have found a stronghold by then, or been able to talk the free town into sheltering us," Cort said, but his stomach was hollow with dread.

The world paled with predawn light, and finally, on the crisp breeze that blew through the clear air of early morning, Cort heard it, too: the distant thudding of hooves, almost felt rather than heard, horses at the trot.

The soldiers heard it as well. They glanced over their shoulders and muttered with dread, but the hooves faded again.

"Still cutting our trail," Gar reported, "but it won't be long before they see our footprints, and follow directly."

"Faster!" Cort barked. "I know you're dog tired, but march faster, blast it! Or you'll have a worse lash than mine on your backs!"

"There!" Dirk pointed uphill, at a towering mass of stone pierced here and there by holes. "Better than nothing, lieutenant!"

"I'll take it! There, men—march for that wall, quickstep!"

The soldiers needed no urging. Exhausted but on the verge of panic, they picked up the pace to a double march.

As they came up to the wall, they heard the sound of hooves come back, faint with distance, but it didn't fade this time.

"They've found our trail!" Gar snapped. "Quickly, lieutenant! Fort up!"

They rode around behind the wall—and stared. "Thank all our lucky stars," Cort breathed. "Shelter!"

There was no roof and maybe never had been, but the wall extended around them in a circle, only fifty feet across, and was pierced here and there with tall, narrow holes. "It *is* a stronghold," Cort cried, "or the ruins of one! Thanks be to whatever ancestors built it!"

One of the soldiers let out a cry, pointing upward. Cort whirled to look, and saw a man in green clothing slide down a slope of the wall and leap to the ground.

"Bring him down!" Sergeant Otto called, and two soldiers ran for the gateway, hefting their spears.

"No!" Cort bellowed. "We're guests, and we want their hospitality! Let them bring all the troopers they have! Maybe they'll fight the Hawks for us!"

"And maybe they'll spit us like pheasants for roasting," Otto grumbled. "But you're right, lieutenant, they're probably more interested in making friends with a Free Company, as long as it doesn't have enough men to threaten them."

The sentry appeared again through the gateway, running flat out across the fields toward a walled town with a small castle that appeared through the morning mist as a sunbeam struck it, turning it golden. The soldiers lowered their spears reluctantly; the man was running in a straight line, and was a tempting target. Even as they watched, though, he veered, then veered again.

"Smart," Otto approved. "Ran straight just long enough to draw our fire, then swerved in time to avoid it."

"It might be that we're not dealing with amateurs," Cort said.

Then he realized that the drum of hooves had become louder. "Into the arrow slits, quickly! A ruin is better protection than none! One man to each aperture, hurry!"

Sergeants bawled orders, and the soldiers set down their wounded comrades behind the walls. Dirk, Gar, and Cort tied their horses to large rocks, then scrambled upward. Even the walking wounded climbed up to the embrasures. Loose rock slipped under foot, and men went sliding, but their comrades caught them and pulled them up.

"Stay out of sight unless they charge us!" Cort called.

All the men flattened themselves against the wall beside the arrow slits, watching the grassy courtyard below, waiting for the sound of the Hawks' horses on the outside of the wall.

Finally it came, drumming closer and closer, then slowing to a walk, and a disgusted voice cried, "A fortress! And they've gone in!"

"Then we'll have to go in after them," a heavier voice growled. "Follow their track around! Ready your crossbows!"

Several of the Blue Company blanched—they only had one spear each, and two javelins across their backs. But Cort grinned with delight and hefted a rock half the size of his head, nodding to his men. The sergeants nodded and turned to the men, pantomiming javelin throwing. The soldiers took their short spears from their backs and lifted them.

The horses suddenly leaped into a gallop and burst into the courtyard below. Eighteen arms swung, filling the air with javelins. Even as they did, bowstrings twanged. The Blue Company threw themselves to the ground. One or two shouted oaths as crossbow bolts caught them in buttock or leg, whichever was too slow in falling. Then Cort leaped up, and the men who could, imitated him, their second javelins in their hands. They saw half a dozen Hawk horses with empty saddles, their riders writhing on the ground.

The crossbows would take too long to crank. The Hawk commander shouted "Charge!" and spurred his horse. His men pounded after him.

"The idiots!" Cort called, to hearten his men. "Charging stone walls! Wait for sure targets!"

But as they came close, the horses suddenly swerved, galloping in zigzags, almost colliding but never quite, and always coming closer and closer to the walls.

"Choose your target and stay with him!" Cort bawled. The soldiers did as he told them, then threw their spears. Some struck home, and a few more Hawks fell from their saddles. Most missed their targets by scant inches. The Hawks shouted triumph and pulled up by the walls, climbing onto their saddles, then leaping for handholds and footholds to take them up to their quarry.

The Blue Company braced their spears and waited, thin-lipped. They were still outnumbered two to one.

Then more hooves thundered, and sixty horsemen rode into the ruined courtyard with a slender officer at their fore who cried, "Loose high!" in a clear tenor, and bowstrings thrummed. A storm of arrows rattled on the walls. A few ricocheted and struck Hawk men; others struck flakes that fell into their eyes. The Hawks let go with an oath and leaped down to the ground, turning with naked swords—to face sixty drawn bows, the archers crowding their horses forward around their officer.

"Leave this place at once!" the tenor cried. "Mount and ride back beyond the river, for everything between it and this ruin is part of the territory of Quilichen!"

The Hawks stood, truculent and reluctant. Then one man mounted, and the others, grumbling, followed suit, but the first rider snatched his crossbow from his saddle, slapped a bolt in it, and started winding.

"I forbid!" the tenor cried, and an arrow struck the man's shoulder. He dropped the crossbow with a howl of pain.

"Let no man else try to load," the Quilichen officer ordered.

"All our bows are bent, and be sure we can loose three rounds for every one of yours!"

The shaft in the soldier's shoulder had pierced boiled-leather armor, with bit enough left to lodge itself in the muscle. The Hawks slowly lifted their hands from their weapons.

"None may come to this domain without our leave!" the Quilichen officer cried. "Be off with you!"

"What of our enemies?" the Hawk officer retorted. "Will you let them stay?"

"I shall deal with them when you are gone," the Quilichen officer replied.

The Hawk officer said, in a threatening tone, "Your town may need us someday. Do you dare court our ill will?"

"Do I dare court the ill will of the Blue Company?" the tenor returned.

"So, then," the Hawk officer said, with a smile of cold malice, "it comes down to a question of which company you trust."

"I trust that neither of you will let sentiment get in the way of business."

The Hawk officer lost his smile.

"We shall have to take that chance, though," the Quilichen officer said. "In the meantime, you must leave, or be turned into pincushions. Besides the archers you see, there are many more behind and to each side of you, who have crept up into the ruins while we've been talking."

"You could be lying," the Hawk officer said through stiff lips.

"I could also be telling the truth. Do you dare take the chance?" The Quilichen officer went right on without giving him the chance to embarrass himself by having to reply. "There are even more of my archers hidden flanking the path through the woods to the river. Again, I request that you leave, and don't come back into Quilichen's territory unless we hire you."

"Or your enemies do!"

"That's as may be, and the future shall show it," the Quilichen officer replied. "Now go, and don't stop till you've crossed the river, for you may be sure that archers of mine will watch you every step of the way. You won't see them, but they'll be there!"

Slow and surly, the Hawk officer moved his horse forward. His men fell into line behind him, grumbling, and the Quilichen riders stepped aside, opening a lane for them to exit.

When the last of them had ridden out of the courtyard, the officer spurred forward. "You on the walls! I see you are Blue Company by your livery! Why have you come to Quilichen?"

"To ask sanctuary of you," Cort replied. "These Hawks ambushed my platoon on our way back to headquarters, when we were not yet at war. They have killed or wounded a quarter of my force, and would have slain all the rest. Quilichen was the nearest stronghold that might take pity on poor fugitives who were so vastly outnumbered."

The officer turned aside for a quick conference with a sergeant, then turned back and cried, "You have chosen well and wisely! We have no great wish to make enemies of the Hawk Company, but we don't have it in us to send you to certain doom! Lay down your weapons and come with us to our town, to heal your wounded and recover yourselves! We shall give you back your weapons when you leave!"

Without hesitation, Cort slid his sword back into the scabbard, unbuckled his sword belt, and laid it down on the rock. Slowly, Gar, Dirk, and Otto imitated him. Then, with great reluctance (for a spearman's spear is his life), so did the rest of the men.

"Come down and be our guests!" the officer called.

Cort led the way, as was his right—led the way into possible death, but also into possible life. His only security was the hope that no free town would willingly bring down the wrath of the Blue Company upon itself by slaying soldiers to whom they'd promised sanctuary.

But the Quilichen archers cheered as Cort strode among them, and the officer dismounted to clasp his hand. "You fought valiantly even outnumbered and facing sure death! Any of us will honor you highly for that!"

"I thank you," Cort said, feeling dazed.

"We, too." Gar, Dirk, and Otto came up behind Cort. "We thank you for our very lives."

"Have I the honor of addressing the Squire of Quilichen?" Cort asked.

"No, you have met the castellan, his sister." The officer removed her helmet, and a wealth of chestnut hair tumbled down around her shoulders.

11

All four men stared at large, dark-brown eyes, a finely chiseled face, and wide, full lips that were red without any aid of paint. The lovely, gentle face seemed incongruous above the chain mail and surcoat with the town's emblem appliqued on it, but the companions couldn't deny her effectiveness.

"I am Magda, castellan in my brother's absence," the officer explained.

"I have heard of women having to hold the castle while their husbands were away at war," Cort said slowly, "but I have never met one."

"I won't be the last, I'm sure," Magda told him. "My brother, Wilhelm, has taken service with the Achilles Company for a while, to see if he can hear rumors of any threats to us while we are still at peace."

"That," Gar said, "has more the sound of a restless young man who is eager for glory and finds little chance of it at home."

"I'm afraid you read Wilhelm aright," Magda admitted, then turned to smile at Dirk. "Have you never seen a woman warrior before, sir?"

"Uh . . . yes!" Dirk snapped out of a staring trance. "But never so many at once. A third of your archers are women, if I guess rightly."

"You have sharp eyes." Magda should have known, because those eyes were fastened on her, and hers on him, even though she spoke of others. "A man of our village invented a way of stringing a compound bow with pulleys, so that it takes a fair amount of strength to bend it, but very little to hold it ready. My women may not draw bows quite so powerful as those of my men, but they are quite strong enough to drive an arrow that will pierce armor."

"I don't doubt it," Dirk said, with a tone of awe.

Cort had a notion that the awe wasn't for the wonderful bow. Gar was thinking that Dirk must have noticed the genders of the archers during the parlay, because he certainly hadn't been looking at them since Magda took off her helmet.

She turned her horse toward the gateway from the ruins. "Come, let's go back to Quilichen Town. You have men who must be buried, I see, and my footmen will dig their graves quickly."

"I fear the Hawk Company were better fighters than we hoped," Gar admitted. He fell in beside Magda, gaining a look of resentment from Dirk, but knew that his friend wasn't quite up to the rudeness of asking what he was dying to know. "I'm surprised that your brother would risk his sister in the leading of your troops."

Magda shrugged. "We're at peace now, and there's little danger. Besides, I've no one to leave bereft of care if I'm slain."

Dirk stared, horrified.

"I'm sure your brother would be desolate," Gar demurred, "and all your people."

"I think they would grieve," Magda agreed, with a trace of a smile, "but it's not as though I would leave a husband to pine in melancholy, or children with no one to care for them."

Gar could fairly hear Dirk's pulse accelerate. "I'm amazed that you're not married."

"Because I'm too old, or because I'm attractive?" Magda's smile was a little bitter. "Men often think that a beautiful woman unmarried is a waste, but women only think that a life is a waste without love."

Gar's face suddenly became an unreadable mask. "I would agree to that last."

Magda noticed, and relented. "I was married, though, for ten months, and my husband was very dear to me, the more so because he was away fighting for a month at a time, then home only for a week before he was off again. There was no help for it—his city was at war—but he was slain, and I left a widow."

"I'm sorry to hear it," Dirk said slowly. "Is that why you're commanding your home domain?"

There was a brief and awkward silence. Dirk realized he'd made a social mistake, tripped up by a custom he didn't know.

"They're foreigners," Cort explained to Magda, "from very far away. They don't understand our ways."

"Of course," Magda said, relieved.

"It's quite true," Gar said. "Tell me, since I'm so ignorant of your ways, how do I address you? Castellan?"

"Yes, castellan, though my brother is a squire," Magda said. "No other title is really necessary."

"Her people probably call her 'my lady,' though," Cort told them.

"They do," Magda admitted, then turned the tables. "And how do I address you, gentlemen?"

"Oh! Forgive my rudeness!" Cort exclaimed. "I'm Lieutenant Cort of Molerpa. This is my sergeant major, Otto, and these are two of my staff sergeants, Dirk Dulaine and Gar Pike."

"Gar Pike?" Magda looked Gar up and down and bit back a laugh.

"You're very polite," Gar said gravely.

"Thank you." Magda had the laugh under control, but her eyes were merry. "My brother and I aren't bullies, after all, nor any sort of tyrants—we're squires, chosen by our people to lead them, not to rule them."

"Who does rule you?" Gar asked.

"The town council, sergeant, and my brother only enforces such measures as they issue—and oversees their military training, and leads them in war, of course."

Privately, Dirk thought the young man must have done very well to stay alive so long. He shuddered at the thought of this delicate, beautiful creature having to stand against the lances of a whole army.

"Who taught your people to fight?" Gar asked.

"The sages, sir, and ours still do teach the young in that fashion. Our ancestor-farmers were farther from the cauldron of conquests and bloody battles than most, and their sages had always taught them arts such as T'ai Chi and Yoga, to help them teach the mind to control the body, and Kung Fu and Karate to those who wished to become sages themselves. When they began to hear rumors of bullies riding forth to conquer, they and their advanced students taught the arts martial to all the people. That encouraged the headmen of the villages in this domain, making them think that they might actually defend themselves, so they joined together in discovering ways to use their farming tools as weapons—fighting with long poles and shovels, battling with flails and scythes. Thus our ancestors studied war, and when the bullies came, they fought them off. True, there were dead, but there would have been even if the people had bowed in submission to the bullies without a fight—that they had learned from the news about other villages."

"But once they had saved themselves," Gar guessed, "they found they had to stay organized?"

"Yes, for the bosses came when the bullies had failed, and still do. The villages banded together and looked to the largest, Quilichen, to lead them. Thus my ancestors reared their children to war, and became squires from generation to generation who led troops of yeomen, not gangs of slaves in soldiers' livery."

"I take it your people live better than the serfs of the bosses."

"Look about you," Magda said with a broad gesture. They had come out into the open plain, a patchwork of fields circling all about Quilichen. The farmers straightened to wave, watching them as they passed, alert and ready.

"At her slightest sign, they would charge us with those hoes," Cort confided to Dirk, "and they could do great damage with them, believe me! Even with spears and swords, we would be hard-pressed to come out of it alive!"

"They wear good clothing," Dirk commented, "stout broadcloth, dyed in bright colors."

Cort nodded. "Proper breeches and smocks, not the sacks of the bosses' peasants. Oh, they have much to fight for, these yeomen of the free cities."

Dirk saw a bit more of that later, as they rode through a village. The elders and mothers were watchful, but didn't run for cover at the sound of hooves; indeed, they surveyed the newcomers with curiosity, and waved to the archers with smiles. The children ran and shouted, and looked to be well fed and healthy. The women wore skirts and blouses in jewel tones, with kerchiefs for the grandmothers and white aprons for everyone. Their houses were proper cottages, single story but all of it above ground, built of fieldstone with windows and thatched roofs, and chimneys that bespoke proper fireplaces.

"Your form of governing works well," Gar commented.

"I thank you," Magda said.

"But the office of squire passes from father to son?"

Magda nodded. "And the daughters grow up to become castellans. We have to stand for the acclamation of all the yeomen, mind you, but there have only been three squires' children who were not acclaimed in all the history of this village, and that's more than four hundred years."

"An enviable record," Gar said with approval. "I gather that not all the free villages fared so well."

Magda looked up at him in surprise. "No, they didn't. Many squires gathered the best of their fighters into a standing army, then used them to enslave their own people, becoming bullies. My ancestors did not, though, nor shall my brother and I."

They came to the gates of the town, and the guards hailed them, calling, "Bravely won, my lady!"

"Overawed, at least," she answered, smiling. "There was little enough fighting to do, thank our stars."

They rode through the gates into the midst of a cheering throng. Magda smiled and waved to her people, but confided to her guests, "It doesn't take much of a victory to make them happy."

"Don't underestimate it." Dirk came riding up on her other side, green with envy of Gar. "You faced down a mercenary officer. That took a lot of courage."

She flashed him a grateful smile, but said only, "We do what we must, Sergeant Dirk. Greet my people, please, for you're their guests as much as mine."

So Cort and his sergeants rode beside their hostess, waving and smiling, up winding streets between stone houses, higher and higher on the hillside until the houses ended abruptly, giving way to a long slope of well-tended lawn, dotted with grazing sheep and a few cows.

"No army is going to be able to sneak up on your castle through the back alleys," Cort observed.

"Indeed they won't," Magda said, "and during peacetime, the people enjoy this lawn for exercise and pleasure—and, of course, grazing."

"So that's how you keep it so neatly trimmed," Dirk said, smiling.

Magda returned the smile, and did he imagine it, or were her eyes showing more than amusement? But she only said, "Indeed so, sergeant, but we must limit the numbers of the sheep and cows quite strictly."

"Still, it gives you a valuable asset during a siege."

"It does indeed," she replied, and Dirk was seeing definite interest in her gaze now. He hoped it was really there, not just in his mind.

Through the castle gates they rode, with the sentries cheering as loudly as any of the townspeople, then into the courtyard, where a groom sprang to hold Magda's horse. She slipped from the saddle onto a mounting block, then stepped down. "My steward will show you where you may bathe and refresh yourselves, sirs, while I change my garb. I'd far rather have the freedom of skirts than these clumsy trousers—but they're better for riding, I fear."

"Only reason anybody ever invented them, I think," Dirk agreed, and bowed as a maid stepped up to take Magda's helmet. "In an hour, then, my lady?"

"An hour will do," she agreed. "Till then, my guests."

She turned away, and a footman stepped up to lead the men to the tub. They followed him, Gar muttering, "She *is* pretty, isn't she?"

"Hm?" Dirk looked up at him, startled. "Sorry—I wasn't listening. What did you say?"

"Nothing worth hearing. Do you suppose they'll have clean clothes for us?"

"I sure hope so!" Dirk said. Then his gaze drifted.

Cort smiled and said, "If they don't give us fresh clothing, there's not much point in our bathing, is there?"

"Oh, Dirk won't mind." Gar glanced at his friend with a smile. "Right now, I don't think he'd even notice."

The conversation during dinner was quite lively, Cort and Dirk trying to outdo one other in wit and sparkle. Magda simply sat back and enjoyed it with the air of a woman to whom this was familiar, but who hadn't experienced it in a long time. After dinner, though, she offered her guests a tour of the gardens.

"Why, that sounds—" Cort broke off, gritting his teeth; Gar's boot had caught him on the shins.

Gar said, "I thank you, but I'm rather weary from the day's events—and the night's."

Cort forced a smile. "Yes, that sounds just the way I feel! If you'll excuse me, my lady, I'll retire." He dug an elbow into Sergeant Otto's ribs.

The sergeant said a bright "Oof!" then, "I'm afraid I'm tired, too, my lady. Will you excuse me?"

"Of course," Magda said graciously, and rose.

The men shoved themselves to their feet, too.

"Who wouldn't be tired, after a day of fighting and retreating?" their hostess asked. "But you, Sergeant Dirk, will you see my gardens?"

"I'd love to, my lady."

"Thank you, sergeant. Then good night, gentlemen."

The other three chorused "Good night," inclining their heads in bows, then turned away to follow a footman back to their rooms. Magda led Dirk through the screens passage. "You flatter me in choosing my company over that of Sleep, sergeant, when you must be as tired as your companions."

"Oddly, I don't feel the weariness when I'm in your company." After all, if she already knew he was flattering her, why not lay it on thicker?

Magda gave a low, musical laugh and led him out into the garden. Moonlight made it a magical place, old trees bending low over glittering flower beds, pale marble benches standing beside a glimmering pool. Roses filled the night with perfume. She led him toward the water, then sat on the bench. Dirk stood beside her, looking about him, enthralled by the moment of peace and enchantment in which he had suddenly become embedded, then realized that the garden's illusion of serenity and beauty was Magda's doing. He opened himself to the enchantment, letting the thrill build within him, partly the beauty of the garden, but more the beauty of the woman.

"You are silent," she murmured.

"Only enjoying one of the rare moments of bliss that life brings, my lady," Dirk said, "a moment that comes from beauty twice experienced."

Magda let out an audible breath, but before she could tell him his flattery was too thick, he changed topics. "I'm very impressed with the quality of life you give your people, my lady."

"Do you criticize my hospitality, sergeant?" she asked, but there was a teasing note in her voice.

"Not at all, though I notice you don't live in anywhere nearly as much luxury as you could. Instead, you seem to be doing all you can to improve the lot of your yeomen and their families."

Magda nodded. "It isn't enough simply to live as rightly as we can, doing our best to be in harmony with the living world about us, and expect our people to imitate us. We must help them to live as closely to our standard as we can, hoping that the more prosperous they become, the more rightly they shall live, for they'll have less reason to do otherwise."

Dirk turned back to her, frowning. "I thought it was the job of your sages to teach right living."

"It's everyone's job, each doing as much as he or she can. Squires must try to follow the sages in selflessness and not needing things. We enjoy such luxuries as we have, but try not to depend on them, the proof of that being that we're willing to share them with our people—and most of them seem to do the same." But the teasing note was gone, and her brows puckered.

"You seem worried," Dirk ventured.

Magda sighed. "There's always the problem of explaining the well-being of the yeomen to my brother, whenever he returns home. I tell him that our strength is the love and loyalty of our people, who will be our shield against our enemies, but he sees only a waste of money. He has been out among the bullies and the bosses, and in his mind, if the yeomen have decent clothing and even sandals instead of wads of rags, they are no doubt using money that could be spent on a new suit of armor."

"Well, taking the statement literally, it's true," Dirk said, "but you have to ask if the new armor is really needed."

"I wouldn't dare!"

Dirk smiled, unable to imagine even a brother managing to

be angry with this woman—at least, not for long. "One must also ask if the yeomen produce more when they're happier."

"Why, that's true!" Magda turned to him, eyes wide. "They do raise more grain and fruit than the bosses' slaves, don't they? Surely more than they spend, with something left over toward that new suit of armor!"

"Probably," Dirk qualified. "You'd have to sit down and compare the production of your fields against those of an equal number of common people on a boss's estate, then subtract the cost of living of your yeomen and their families—but I think you'd find that there's almost as much left toward, shall we say, improvements in the war budget your way, as with gouging the serfs for every copper you can get."

" 'Gouging'—a very vivid term indeed!" Magda smiled. "What a font of ideas you are, Sergeant Dirk! Might I guess that you haven't always been a sergeant?"

"If you're asking if I've been an officer, the answer is yes," Dirk said. "Whenever I travel a long distance, though, I have to start all over again and work my way up through the ranks."

"Surely." Magda frowned. "Why do you travel so often and so far?"

"Looking for the right woman," Dirk said, gazing straight into her eyes.

She stared back at him, paling, frozen for a moment.

Then she turned away, blushing. "I wish you joy of your search, sir. My own is done, my goal both gained and failed."

Dirk realized he was being given a warning. He sat beside her, asking, "How could it be both?"

"I'm a widow," she said simply. "You are quite valiant to seek my company, sir."

"When the widow is as beautiful as yourself, there's no valor about it, only self-indulgence."

She smiled, lips trembling, and her eyes glistened with moisture as she leaned toward him. For a moment, he hoped those lips would part for a kiss—but she only said, her voice low, "My husband died without an heir. I hadn't borne him a baby, and wasn't with child, either."

She said it with such a tragic tone that Dirk's heart went out to her; he had to stifle the impulse to take her in his arms and comfort her. "How desolate! To have nothing left of him!"

"Yes," she said slowly, but frowned a little, searching his face. "This is another one of our ways that you don't know, I see. Learn, sir, that by the customs of our people, I can't remarry."

"What?" Dirk exclaimed, then bit his tongue.

"You're a foreigner," she said gently, "from very far away. You don't understand our ways."

"No, not at all," Dirk said, frowning, "and this one seems quite wrong."

"Wrong or right, it's the custom," Magda said, her voice hard. "I didn't have children, so I can't have children, so no man will want to marry me—and I'm not about to become any man's concubine, either, so I came home. If motherhood is denied me, I can at least devote myself to my people, to those among whom I grew up—but you'll see now, sir, why I don't mind risking my life in battle."

Dirk caught the note of despair in her voice, and had to stifle the impulse to reach out to her again—but he did take her hand, and she seemed not at all reluctant. "Forgive me," Dirk said, "but there's no sense in that custom. Maybe for a woman who'd been married ten years or so, and still hadn't borne a child, but certainly not for a lady who'd only been with her mate for a few weeks. You probably are very likely to have a child, my lady, if you're only given enough time with another husband." Then he realized how he had sounded, and dropped her hands. "Forgive me . . . I hadn't meant . . ."

But her eyes filled with tears, and she said only, "You meant well, sir, very well, and have given me more hope in a few minutes than all my people in four years." She leaned closer, eyes bright and lips parting.

Heart hammering, Dirk took his courage in both hands and

her in his arms, kissing her lips, and never in his life had anything felt so wonderful or tasted so sweet.

He came back to the bedchamber he shared with Gar perhaps an hour later, though to him it might have been only minutes.

He drifted in, closing the door quietly, but Gar woke anyway and said, "You saw the lady to her room, then?"

"No, only to her ladies in waiting." Dirk sat on his bed. "She's the most wonderful woman I've ever met, Gar."

"Lucky man." Gar's voice was keen with envy. "No, I don't fancy her myself—but I wish I could feel as you feel now. Enjoy your sleep, Dirk, and may you have heavenly dreams."

Dirk slept well indeed, and if his dreams weren't quite heavenly, they were certainly intoxicating.

12

Some things the colonists had held onto from old Earth, as curiosities if nothing else, and their descendants had taken them up again—among them military titles, ranks, organization, and the bugle. They had also held onto "Taps," presumably because of the sheer beauty of its simple melody. The Blue Company soldiers stood in the midst of their hosts, all with helmets off, as the bugle played the haunting farewell over the two new graves in the Quilichen churchyard.

The bugler lowered his instrument, the sextons took up theirs, and the soldiers turned away, mercenaries mixing with yeomen in muttered thanks and good-byes.

"I shall care well for your wounded," Magda promised Cort, "and send them back to you when they are healed."

"Thank you, my lady." Cort bowed over her hand, but didn't kiss it. "Your hospitality to them shall allow us to fare much better in evading our enemies."

Magda turned to Dirk. "I trust you are no worse wounded than when you came, sergeant."

"More filled with life than ever I have been, my lady." Dirk bowed over her hand, too—but he did kiss it, and a bit longer than was really polite.

He straightened, and Magda retrieved her hand, reddening somewhat. "I think you had better go now. You have far to travel, after all."

"Even so." Gar nudged Dirk aside and bowed over Magda's hand, the very picture of punctilious politeness. "I thank you for your hospitality, my lady, and hope that some day I may return your generosity."

"Then I shall send for you when next we are besieged," Magda said, smiling with relief. "Good day to you, gentlemen, and safe journeying."

They mounted, waved with a chorus of farewells, and rode off without a backward glance—except for Dirk, who kept turning around for one more look. His heart leaped each time, to discover that Magda still stood, hand raised, eyes haunted.

They went into the woods, and Dirk sighed with regret, turning to look ahead, knowing that he couldn't see the beautiful castellan again.

He was riding at the tail end of the dozen men, so he didn't hear Gar say to Cort, "A very bad case, I think."

Cort glanced back. "You're right; he's already sunken in gloom." He frowned, turning somber himself.

"I wouldn't think that to be a problem," Gar replied, "in view of the looks she gave him."

"Yes," Cort said thoughtfully, "assuming she doesn't give such glances to every man who comes within her sphere."

Gar looked up, eyebrows raised. "You think she may be one of the ones who delights in winning the heart of every man she can?"

"There is that," Cort said slowly, "especially if she's truly devoted to her people and as much aware of her beauty as I think she is. She might try to sway every stranger to her, to help protect her town."

"That could be," Gar admitted, "but from the way she looked at him as we rode away, I think she may be having as much sadness now as our friend Dirk."

"Maybe," Cort allowed. "I'd certainly like to think so." His face darkened even more. "For his sake, I hope so indeed." He shrugged, his face clearing. "It really doesn't matter, though—she'd have better sense than to marry him when she knows she's barren."

"What? Unable to have children?" Gar looked up, startled. "How do you know that?"

"It's plain, isn't it? She was married for most of a year, but when her husband died, she was still without child."

Gar answered with a smile tight with irony. "Considering that they probably had fewer than thirty nights together, I scarcely think that proves much. She barely had time to conceive."

"There is that," Cort admitted. "Still, it's the custom."

"You mean there have been thousands of women down the centuries who might have had loving families, but were denied the chance because they hadn't managed to conceive with their first husbands?" Gar stared, horrified.

"Well, there are always some whores who do bear children," Cort admitted, "though never many."

"That's because prostitutes learn ways to prevent conception, lieutenant!" Gar shuddered. "Those poor women! You mean if a man dies without leaving his wife pregnant, she has to become a prostitute?"

"Usually, yes." Cort eyed Gar warily, wondering why the man was so upset. "Of course, there're always those beautiful enough to become bullies' mistresses or bosses' concubines. Then, too, gentlewomen, like the Lady Magda, may have fathers or brothers who're willing to take them back into their homes."

"I don't suppose the wife could inherit her husband's property."

Cort shrugged. "How would she hold it? The neighboring bullies would attack her in an instant, and if she proved unable to lead her boots in battle, she would be captured and made to serve her conqueror."

"And there's no law to stop him," Gar said, anger gathering in his face. "This is what anarchy comes to!"

"Of course, a woman of enough beauty might be able to persuade men to fight for her, and to lead her troops," Cort offered. "In fact, that may be why the Lady Magda made her way into Sergeant Dirk's heart."

Gar shook his head. "If that had been her reason, she would have gone after the lieutenant, not the sergeant—and she certainly wouldn't have sent him on his way so easily; she would have tried to hold him."

"There is that," Cort admitted. "Still, a barren woman is a poor wife for any man who wants heirs."

"I'm not sure that Dirk does." Gar remembered a few of his friend's more bitter comments about the nature of human life. "It could very easily be that he wouldn't care about that little problem."

"Let him leave this world with none to come after him?" Cort exclaimed, scandalized. "No, my friend! If you care for your companion at all, you'll try to keep him out of a marriage where he would be so woefully used!"

Gar turned to him with a frown. "Not too fond of women, are you?"

Cort turned away, face turning thunderous. "Let's just say that I've finally come to realize how treacherous they are."

"Very recently, too, by the intensity of your emotions." Gar's tone was sympathetic. "Either that, or you've been jilted more than once."

"Only the one time," Cort growled, glaring at the road ahead, "but that was enough. I'll not give it the chance of happening again."

"The hurt is *very* recent, then," Gar said softly.

Cort gave him a short nod.

"I know it's too soon to be saying much about it, lieutenant," Gar went on, "but I will remind you that one goose in a flock of swans doesn't lessen the beauty of the rest."

Cort frowned up at him. "What's that supposed to mean?"

"That one woman who's too young to know her own heart is no proof that you won't find other women who are mature enough to be true," Gar said. "It would be a shame to deprive yourself of joy only because of the risk of pain."

Cort's eyes narrowed into a glare. "And yourself? I didn't notice you making overtures to the beauty!"

"Touché." Gar nodded, mouth a grim line. "I've taken hurts enough in my time, lieutenant, but they don't drown the hope that some day I'll meet a woman who will make me forget all the pain, make me think only of the joy of her presence."

"A child's tale," Cort scoffed, "one that the old wives tell to beguile young boys into yearning to grow up to be husbands. After all, why should a healthy young man go to waste when he might be earning a living for a woman?"

Gar sighed, lifting his head. "I know it seems so to us now, lieutenant, when grief makes us bitter. We have to try to remember that a woman has a right to change her mind, though—a right, and a duty, too, to us as well as to herself, because no heartbreak can be so bad as being condemned to be bound for life to a person you don't love, who will gradually come to despise you."

Cort felt anger surge, the more because he recognized the truth in Gar's words. He demanded, "Why haven't you married, then, if you have so high an opinion of women?"

Gar shrugged, his face bleak. "I'm still waiting for the right one, of course, lieutenant: the one with whom I fall in love, and who falls in love with me—and I'll wait for her half my life, or all of it, rather than marry the wrong one."

Empathy stirred in Cort's breast, and the anger faded. He studied his new sergeant's profile, brooding on the senselessness of feelings. "What if she never comes, sergeant? What if you never find her?"

Gar shrugged. "Then I'll take what joy I can from life, lieutenant: the solid satisfaction of seeing the few people I can help better off than when I met them; the delight of watching children play; the inspiration of a sunrise on a clear, chill day."

"Is that all?"

Gar shrugged. "Measured against the lifetime of grief I'd receive from the wrong woman, and the constant pain of knowing I'd made her miserable? I'd count the small, quiet joys to be quite a lot, yes."

"What of roistering?" Cort demanded. "Most men count their lives rich if they can swill and whore to their heart's content."

"I've already learned that physical pleasure doesn't bring joy," Gar told him, "or bring happiness that lasts any longer than the pleasure itself. I don't intend to spend my life running from one sensation to another to try to forget my sorrow. I've seen people who did that. They became bored with their pleasures, and had to search more and more frantically, for ever more extreme sensations. As each pleasure lost its ability to distract them, they had to rush after the next, until some of them were actually amusing themselves with pain." He shuddered. "None of that for me, thank you. The quiet pleasures last, and lead you steadily to greater and greater delights."

"If you say so," Cort said, rather doubtfully. "If I understand you rightly, you're saying that the pleasures of women never pall, as long as you don't touch their bodies."

"Unless you're in love with one, yes." Gar nodded. "They're wonderful, charming creatures, and just being near them can be a pleasure."

"You're too much the sage for me," Cort sighed, and wondered why the big man laughed, and why his laughter was so sardonic.

At noon they had come down from the slopes into flat land, and came near the river that marked the boundary of Quilichen. Cort halted their little column. "The Hawks have probably had the good sense to withdraw," he told his sergeants, "but they're still between us and our headquarters, and if I were them, I'd be waiting in ambush not very far past the stream—just far enough to lull our suspicions."

Sergeant Otto nodded in approval of his pupil. "Very likely, lieutenant. Shall I scout out the territory?"

"No, let's leave that to our newest recruits." Cort turned to Gar and Dirk. "Sergeants, it's your turn. Reconnoiter."

"Huh?" Dirk came out of a brown study. "Oh. Yeah, sure, lieutenant. I mean, yes, sir!"

"We should be back in an hour or two," Gar promised. He gestured at the meadow across the river. "After all, it's so flat over there that there isn't much place to hide."

"They could be crafty," Cort warned. "Think like a sneak."

Gar grinned. "That should be easy enough. Come on, Dirk."

The two rode away.

"Why them, lieutenant?" Otto asked, frowning.

"Because they're used to faring on their own," Cort explained, "and they don't have Blue Company livery yet. Besides, if they only joined us out of expediency, this gives them their chance to get away from our danger."

The other reason, of course, was to give Gar a chance to talk with Dirk alone. Love was all well and good, but a man moping about like a sick cow wasn't going to be any use to Cort when his unit was in such danger.

Gar wasted no time. Even as he and Dirk rode across the bridge, he said, "I thought love made a man feel better, Dirk, not sunk in gloom."

"Huh?" Dirk looked up, startled, then frowned, thinking it over. "Yeah, I guess I am in love."

"Worst case I've ever seen," Gar assured him. "So why aren't you happy?"

Dirk heaved a sigh. "Because I can't see her, Gar, and probably won't, ever again."

"Stuff and nonsense! As soon as peace breaks out, you can

ride back there for a visit. You aren't put off by this nonsense about her being barren, are you?"

"Barren? No. I've got it too bad for that to worry me much." Dirk smiled suddenly, a sardonic contraction. "Besides, there's no chance I could marry her, anyway."

"Why not?" Gar asked, frowning. "I admit I usually think of you as an ugly young cuss, but she obviously doesn't. In fact, judging from the number of women who have flirted with you on four planets now, I'd have to say you were reasonably handsome."

"Thanks for small praise," Dirk said sourly. "But a wonderful, beautiful, intelligent woman like that? A born leader, a natural philanthropist, a . . . "

"Spare me the list." Gar held up a hand. "It's good to see you start looking lively again, but I have a feeling you could go on for an hour. I'll grant she's beautiful and wonderful. All the more reason why you should court her."

"All the more reason why she'd turn me down! I could never win Magda's love, and even if I did, I wouldn't have a chance of a successful marriage!"

"Any particular reason why?" Gar asked, frown deepening to a scowl.

"I'm a churl, man! Born as low as any of these bullies' serfs, and she's a gentlewoman by birth, a squire's daughter, the equal of a baron on any world where they remember the old aristocratic titles! How could I possibly make a solid marriage with a woman so far above my station?"

Gar stared at him in disbelief. At last he said, "You may have been born a churl, Dirk Dulaine, but you have grown into something far more."

"I am what I am," Dirk said stubbornly.

"Yes, but that means you're also what you have become. The rebels of your home planet took you offworld and gave you a modern education, for starters."

"Well, yeah, but I don't know the manners of her people, the social graces."

"No, you know the social graces of the galaxy! You're quite well schooled in etiquette, and if they don't have as many pieces of silverware as you know how to use, that certainly doesn't leave you deficient!"

"But I don't know the *local* manners."

"You'll learn them," Gar said, with full assurance. "That's the biggest gain from having an education: you've learned how to learn. Besides, the spirit of etiquette is far more important than its details."

"Yes, to avoid giving offense, and that's mostly a matter of consideration and respect for the people about you," Dirk said, frowning. "You're right—I could learn the local details."

"Of course!" Gar began to feel that he was making some progress. "There's not a shred of doubt that you're far better educated than she, and at least as cultured."

"Well, yeah, but what good does that do? I don't know *her* culture, do I?"

Gar sighed. "Even if you count all the local lore she knows as being equal to the best works of the Terran Sphere, you're still very sophisticated in critical standards, and you'll learn the local arts quickly enough. As to their history, we've already guessed most of it—you just need it confirmed. Certainly you're way ahead of any of the local men in both."

"Nice of you to say so, but if you'll pardon the observation, we haven't really had enough local experience to judge."

"We've both managed to get to know a pretty good cross section of the people here. Believe me, I've met one of the local bosses, and all he knows is war. In fact, I'd say you're more than a match for Lady Magda in learning and culture—and social station. After all, you're both a knight and a wizard, in local terms."

"I haven't seen any wizards," Dirk retorted.

"Neither have I, but I've heard enough about their sages."

"I don't know Taoism *that* well," Dirk protested.

"But you know enough science to be able to work the wonders they dream about."

"That doesn't make me a sage. As to being a knight, you know I've never been knighted."

"But I have been." Gar dismounted and turned to Dirk, drawing his sword. "Kneel down."

Dirk eyed him warily. "Is this supposed to be some sort of a joke?"

"I don't joke about knighthood," Gar snapped. "I've seen you in action, in war and in peace, and I know full well that you're an expert in fighting, and live the code of chivalry far better than most men who profess it. Kneel down!"

He actually seemed to be getting angry, and that was rare for Gar. Dirk decided to humor him. Slowly, he dismounted, then dropped to one knee, facing Gar.

"Do you swear to defend the weak against the strong and wicked?" Gar demanded.

"I do." Dirk was seized with a moment of dizziness, a feeling of unreality.

"Do you swear to defend the Right and prosecute the Wrong?"

"I do." After all, how could he refuse, when Gar phrased it so broadly?

"Will you defend the root ethical principles of all humanity that allow them to exist as social units, instead of trying to tear one another apart?"

"I will." Dirk wondered how Gar had developed that oath.

The sword lowered, touching his right shoulder. "Then I hereby dub thee knight!" The sword crossed to touch his left shoulder, then drew away. Gar stepped in and, with great calmness and precision, clouted Dirk on the side of the head.

Dirk went sprawling, and anger roared up in him. He started

to scramble up, then heard Gar saying, without the slightest trace of humor, "Arise, Sir Dirk Dulaine."

The anger fell away as suddenly as it had come; Dirk realized that his friend was actually trying to do something good for him. "I don't remember that punch from the stories."

"It's the older form of the accolade, and I choose to use it with the newer, to remind you of the trials you'll have to endure in the name of chivalry," Gar said sternly, then thawed and admitted, "I may have overdone it a bit. Your pardon, Sir Dirk—I was carried away with zeal." He reached down and caught his friend by the arm, hauling him to his feet. "I assure you, it's real. I was knighted by a king. You really are a knight, and entitled to all the rights and privileges of that rank—as long as you fulfill its duties."

"From what you say, I've been doing that already." Dirk frowned, then looked his friend in the eyes. "Have I really?"

"You have," Gar assured him. "Why else would you keep throwing yourself into the middle of a fight that could get you killed, just to help a lot of people you don't even know and never will?"

"Well, when you put it that way . . ."

"I do," Gar said firmly. "I should have done this long ago—as soon as we left your home planet, in fact. But you're so patently my equal that it frankly never occurred to me."

Dirk felt a warm glow spreading through him. "I don't know if I can ever be that, Gar, but I'll work on it."

"Don't," Gar told him, "because you're there already. From now on, just work on being as good as Lady Magda."

"Thought you told me I already was."

"Yes, but that doesn't mean you believed me." Gar turned to his horse. "Mount up, Sir Dirk—we still have a hidden enemy to find."

Dirk mounted, then rode beside Gar across the plain and into the forest. He didn't even notice that he scarcely said anything, and Gar wisely didn't interrupt his meditation, for Dirk was still glowing, intensely excited at the idea of being worthy of Magda, of being able to win her.

And, of course, since he wasn't really very alert, he was slow coming out of his rosy haze when Gar snapped, "Ambush!"

13

Fortunately, the road stayed still and empty under the leafy canopy. It gave Dirk a few minutes to return to the here and now and brace himself for battle. "Where are they?"

"To either side of that big oak, with two of them on the branch overhead. If you look carefully, you can just make out their livery."

Dirk reflected that a telepath could be a very useful traveling companion. "They're planning to jump us? Why not just wait until the whole platoon is marching by?"

"They were only set on sentry duty, to watch for the platoon coming," Gar told him, "so they were going to stay out of sight, but when they saw me, their pulses roared, and they sprinted into position."

"You mean it's us they want, not the Blue Company?"

"They're certainly not thinking about Cort and his men right now," Gar said. "Is your buckler on your arm?"

"Not yet." Dirk lifted the small shield from the hook on his saddle, slipped his arm through the straps, and tightened them. "Okay now."

"Draw your sword when they jump us, and spur your horse so we jump forward past that limb as they drop from it. Then we'll turn and cut them down. Remember, we need one for questioning."

"Kill, not stun?" Dirk frowned. "That doesn't sound like you. How many of them are there?"

"Eight."

"Can't you put them to sleep?"

"Too much adrenaline. Yes, by all means, wound if you can, but don't pull your strokes—there's too great a chance you'll wind up dead. Ready, now?" He forced a laugh. Dirk joined in. They rode under the bough, laughing; then Dirk said, "Remember the one about . . ."

Gar drew his sword, Dirk was only a split second behind him. Then the Hawk squad burst from the trees, screaming like birds of prey.

Dirk and Gar yelled and spurred their horses. Dirk's beast stumbled as a heavy weight struck its rump; two bodies thumped onto the ground behind. Dirk and Gar pulled back on the reins, and their mounts reared, screaming and turning. The Hawks scrambled to their feet and jumped out of the way, but not quickly enough; the horses landed, striking glancing blows to two heads. Soldiers came riding; Dirk caught a sword thrust on his buckler, chopped through a lance shaft on his right, kicked the swordsman in the jaw, then stabbed down at the lancer. The Hawk swerved his horse out of the way, though, and another thrust his spear, scoring Dirk's arm and stabbing deep into his saddle. Dirk shouted in anger as pain flared, but struck down. The saddle held the lance a second too long, and his sword chopped the shaft. The lancer went stumbling backward, tripped over a fallen comrade, and fell.

The comrade had fallen because Gar had seen him coming. The big man had leaned aside from the sword thrust and clouted the man in the jaw with the knuckle-guard of his own weapon. The man dropped in satisfactory style, and Gar decided he rather liked the effect. He turned, swinging his buckler arm to knock a lance aside, then brought his sword over to stab. The lancer danced away from it, then darted in, lance thrusting. Gar leaned back to let the lancehead pass, then leaned in to swing the buckler, clouting the man on the side of the head. He dropped like a stone, too, off his horse and stretched out.

Dirk whirled to take a sword thrust on his buckler, then stabbed overhand into the man's shoulder. The soldier fell back with a howl of pain.

A bellow of anger erupted, and Dirk turned to see that the lancer had caught up his fallen comrade's weapon and scrambled to his feet. He charged, lance leveled at the chest of Dirk's horse.

A lance came stabbing at Gar, too, and he chopped off its head. The resourceful lancer turned and jabbed the shaft under Gar's bottom, then heaved. Gar bellowed in anger as he went over. He fell, but rolled quickly, and two lances stabbed the ground where he'd been. He leaped up and thrust at the nearest man's thigh; the rider fell off his horse with a howl, and Gar dove out of the way of thundering hooves, rolling again, then shoved himself up just in time to meet the second lancer's charge. He caught the weapon on his buckler, then sprang high, slamming his knuckle-guard into the man's jaw. The lancer's eyes rolled up; he fell.

Dirk pivoted his mount aside and swung a light, bouncing stroke as the charging lancer thundered past. The man screamed as a bright line of blood streaked the backs of his shoulders.

But Dirk had turned his horse completely in the maneuver, and saw two more troopers charging from the trees beside the road. He danced his mount aside and thrust, stabbing one in the thigh. The man fell, bellowing in pain. His mate reared his horse, turning with a snarl, and struck.

Dirk had leaned too low, was too slow rising. He chopped frantically; the lancehead flew, but the shaft struck his ribs, knocking the breath out of him. He ground his teeth and counterthrust. The lancer screamed, reeling in his saddle and clutching his shoulder; scarlet spread over his fingers.

Gar spun on general principles, and saw the principal soldier, or at least the sergeant, swinging his sword up for a slash. Gar stepped in, parrying, and exchanged a mad few strokes before he caught the man's belt, yanked him off his horse, and swung the buckler cracking into the side of the man's head. The sergeant blundered forward a step or two; Gar obligingly stepped aside to let him fall.

Dirk shoved himself upright, trying to ignore the ache in his side, looking about in quick glances—but all the Hawk horses were galloping away down the forest road, and the only one standing was Gar's horse, who stood trembling at the side of the road. The giant himself stood on the ground, feet spread wide, two rivulets of blood running down his face and his arm, dripping sword in hand, grinning like a gargoyle.

Well, there was also one last, poor lancer who took one appalled look at his seven fallen comrades, then took off galloping for the trees.

Without an instant's hesitation, Gar threw his sword after the man. It went spinning through the air until the hilt cracked down on the trooper's head. His horse kept going another paceor two before he fell. The sword landed quivering in the ground.

"Nice throw." Dirk rode over, yanked the sword out of the ground, and brought it back to Gar. "How did you know it wasn't going to hit him point first?"

"Practice," Gar assured him.

Dirk nodded, wondering exactly what kind of practice his big friend had in mind. He had a brief mental vision of Gar standing perfectly still, with various swords, daggers, poniards, and broken bottles leaping from the ground in front of him and sailing toward a target fifty feet away, each striking the bull's eye, then leaping back out just in time for the next one to land. He shook his head to clear the image and turned to look around him instead. "Eleven men down and groaning. Why don't I feel guilty?"

"Well," Gar said thoughtfully, "it could be because they were trying to kill you—or it could be because they tried to kill our whole platoon."

"Yeah, that might have something to do with it," Dirk conceded. "Anyone dying?"

Gar shook his head. "Careless of us, that. While we were calling our shots to keep from killing them, they might have skewered us."

"There wasn't really time to be merciful," Dirk admitted. "Getting to be too much of a habit, I suppose."

"You'll have to work on that," Gar agreed.

"So what do we do with them?" Dirk demanded. "Just leave them here?"

"Have you a better place in mind?" Gar returned. "I do want a souvenir, though. Watch them and make sure none of them does anything foolish, like trying to throw a lance, will you?"

"Sure." Dirk began a routine of scanning, turning his head slowly, but with quick glances at Gar.

The big man walked over to the sergeant, checked to make sure he was unconscious, then heaved him up on one shoulder in a fireman's carry. He brought the burden back to his own horse, slung him over the rump, tied hands and feet to keep him from slipping off, then mounted up. "All right. Back to the platoon, or what's left of it."

The sentry called, and Cort came hurrying over to see Gar and Dirk riding in. "At last! We thought the Hawks had ambushed you."

"They did." Gar nodded at his horse's burden, awake and cursing now. "We brought one of them back for you. Don't worry, the rest of his squad are hurt too badly to fight. Besides, their horses ran away."

Cort stared at the sergeant, then nodded slowly. "All that from just the two of you, eh? Well, well!" He turned and started back toward the campfire. "Bring him over here."

Gar followed, dismounted, and untied the man. As soon as one hand was free, the sergeant swung at him. Gar dodged easily. "That's stupid. Your muscles are stiff from being bound. You couldn't hit hard enough to do any damage, anyway." But when he untied a foot, the man lashed out a kick that caught Gar in the jaw and sent him stumbling. When he came striding back, fighting down his temper, he saw Dirk and Sergeant Otto hauling the limp body down between them. "I decided he needed another nap," Dirk explained.

"I didn't even know you carried that little stick," Cort said to Dirk.

"Neither did he." Dirk stretched the Hawk sergeant on the ground in front of Cort.

"Tie down his wrists and ankles," Cort directed, and soldiers stepped up to drive pegs into the ground, then bind the Hawk's joints. They weren't very gentle about it, but considering the ambush they'd lived through and their comrades who hadn't, that wasn't much of a surprise.

Gar took a canteen from the nearest soldier and sloshed water into the Hawk's face. The sergeant spluttered, coming to.

Cort glared down at the man. "Torturing another mercenary is against the code of the Free Companies, fellow, but I'm minded to try it, anyway. After all, your band have broken the rules of war already."

"No, we haven't!" the sergeant protested.

"Oh, really? When did the code change to allow one band to ambush another before they've begun to march?"

"Uh, by your leave, lieutenant." Gar stepped away from the captive. "Could I have a word with you?"

Cort frowned. "What is it that you don't want this Hawk to hear?" But he stepped aside with Gar anyway.

"Breaking rules is a bad business," Gar explained, "especially if you don't know for sure that the other side has broken them first."

"But we do!"

"No, lieutenant, we've only guessed it. Besides, even if they broke a rule, then if you break another rule to get back at them, they'll break a third rule, and the first thing you know, everyone will be breaking every rule, and every code will be broken."

"We wouldn't want that." Cort scowled. "The Free Companies would kill each other off in a fortnight."

"Exactly. May I offer an alternative?"

"Speak," Cort allowed.

"Instead of torture or execution, let's capture the Hawk captain and bring him before a tribunal of other mercenary captains. If they think he's broken the rules, let them decide what to do with him."

Cort's eyes lit, intrigued. "A fascinating idea! But how do you suggest we capture a captain in the midst of his company?"

"Watch and catch him when he's *away* from his company. Is there anything in the code against that?"

"No, but only because no one's ever thought of it, I suspect." Cort grinned. "That might do, indeed. I'll ask Captain Devers about it when we get back, and if he allows it, we'll send out a reconnaissance party. You'll volunteer, of course."

"It will be an honor." Gar inclined his head. "In the meantime, tell me what you want to know, and I'll see if I can't persuade this sergeant to tell us without the thumbscrews. I might threaten them, you understand . . ."

Cort's grin widened. "Go right ahead. If you can trick him into telling us why they attacked us and who hired their company to do it, I'll be very happy to let him go unscathed."

"No ransom?"

Cort shrugged. "You can't get much for a sergeant."

"Very flattering," Sergeant Gar Pike said with a wry grimace. "Well, we'll see what we can do with the man."

They went back to the staked-out sergeant. Dirk was standing over him, loudly arguing with Sergeant Otto. "Look, we're civilized soldiers! Let's not be crude about this! Tie him under a drip of water so that it hits him square on the head, and watch him go crazy!"

Otto shook his head, truculent and stubborn. "We haven't got that kind of time. A good old-fashioned beating's best, I say. Quick and clean, it is."

"Yeah, but he can't talk with his jaw broken and his mouth all—"

"Gentlemen, if you don't mind?" Gar said, with withering sarcasm.

"Huh?" Dirk looked up, frowning. "Oh, you want a shot at him? Well, go ahead—we can't agree on where to start."

"If you'd stand a little farther off?" Gar suggested. "I do need room to sit down by him, after all."

"Oh, all right." Dirk huffed, and stepped a few yards away, saying, "Now, I've heard of a technique that's supposed to work a lot faster. We take Gar's camp cot and put the sergeant on it, and if he doesn't fit . . ."

"Pay no attention to them," Gar said as he knelt by the captive sergeant. "Dirk always thinks torture is the fastest way to get information out of a prisoner. Myself, I'd prefer to ask him first."

Dirk took his cue. "Torture him! Okay, we'll let Sergeant Otto beat him up a little bit for starters. Then you can have my pair of monogrammed thumbscrews, and I'll take out the cat-o'-nine-tails."

"He's so hasty," Gar sighed, "just because your infantry jumped our platoon, and when we fought them off, sent you and your cavalry to hunt us down. I have to admit that wasn't very sporting of you, but you're just taking orders, aren't you? It scarcely deserves torture."

"No, it doesn't." The Hawk sergeant was sweating now, glancing at Dirk.

"Myself, I maintain that you had to do your best to carry out your orders, so it was nothing personal. Would I be right?"

"Oh, yes!" The sergeant nodded vigorously. "Just doing my job, that's all."

"As we were only doing ours," Gar agreed. "But my friend says you've broken the mercenary's code, attacking us before we met on the battlefield, simply because you knew our company had been hired to fight yours."

"The iron boot," Dirk called.

"Not a word of truth in it!" the sergeant said. "We were hired to kill you, that's all! Open and aboveboard, nothing against the rules at all."

Gar exchanged a startled glance with Dirk, then turned back. "No, just doing the job your company was hired for," he said slowly, "and certainly nothing wrong for you in telling us that. There's nothing secret about it, is there?"

"Not after our first attack, no."

"Of course not. Tell me, since it's open knowledge now—when you say you were hired to kill us, did that mean our whole platoon?"

"Oh, no! Just you, the big one! Not even your friend there." The sergeant took a deep breath. "How did the two of you manage to beat the whole lot of us, anyway?"

"Magic," Gar told him.

Cort stared at him.

The sergeant scowled. "No such thing as magic."

Gar nodded with approval. "An educated man, I see. What if I told you I was a sage with great powers stemming from meditation?"

"I've heard of it," the sergeant allowed. "Never believed a word of it, myself."

"I suppose not," Gar sighed. "Well, then, you'll have to put it down to practice, constant practice."

"We always need new targets to practice on," Cort added.

The sergeant's eyes bulged.

"Tell me," Gar said softly, "who hired you."

"It was the steward!" the sergeant said. "The steward of the Boss of Loutre! Why his boss wants you dead, I don't know, but he paid for the whole company to kill you."

Gar knelt very still. Dirk, not knowing what the sergeant had said, called out, "Can I light the fire for the branding iron now?"

"Not just yet, I think," Gar called back. Then, to the sergeant, "That must have cost a great deal of money—a compliment, in its way. Are you paid by the day, or for the job?"

"For the job—five hundred golden marks for proof you're dead. We thought it would only take a day or so, but you look as though you're going to make it expensive."

"Yes. You might lose on this one." Gar sighed. "Nothing personal, of course."

"Right," the sergeant agreed, eyeing him very strangely. "Nothing personal."

"Pincers?" Dirk called.

"If you can find her," Gar called back absently. "So, sergeant, you attacked our whole platoon, just to get me?"

"You wouldn't go away from them long enough," the sergeant explained. "The lieutenant who took the infantry platoon out found your trail a mile away, and was going to jump you at nightfall—but he realized you were about to join up with this Blue Company platoon, so he jumped you all."

"Yes, why wait until you can attack one man alone, when you could assault a dozen?" Gar's nod was tight with irony. "I hope he isn't your shrewdest man."

"He's an officer," the sergeant said simply, and left the rest unspoken—that wars would be a lot simpler, less bloody, and shorter, if they just left things up to the noncoms.

"I suppose it's become a matter of honor now," Gar sighed. "Your captain feels he has to kill me, no matter what it takes—even if he has to kill the rest of my companions, or even the whole Blue Company."

"I expect so," the sergeant agreed. "Captains don't tell us noncoms, though."

"No, of course not. By the way, did you see the steward?"

"Yes. He was a lean man, about as tall as your master sergeant, black hair . . ."

"Torgi." Gar nodded, then rose and turned to Cort. "Lieutenant, I hereby volunteer to give myself up."

"We don't desert comrades," Cort said stiffly.

"Don't be silly," Dirk added.

"You stood by us; we'll stand by you." But Sergeant Otto was looking grim at the news that Gar had brought the attack down on them all.

"Then let me offer an alternative," Gar said slowly. "Dirk and I will travel by ourselves. Now that we know they're after us, we'll make sure they never find us, and you and your men will be safe from attack."

Otto shook his head. "The Hawks are looking for our platoon now."

"Then send this sergeant back with news that we're going on by ourselves. The Hawks will know there's no need to attack Blue Company soldiers then."

"You're sergeants of the Blue Company now," Otto snapped. "We don't desert our own."

"No, we don't," Cort said slowly, "but we can use your plan, with one slight change." He turned to Otto. "Sergeant, take the platoon back to headquarters. I'll go on with Dirk and Gar."

"No, lieutenant!" Otto cried, and Gar said, "Really, lieutenant, it's not necessary."

"But it is." Cort turned to look up at him, fists on hips. "It satisfies the Blue Company's honor, and it keeps the rest of the platoon safe. Besides, even if you're as good at stealth as you say, it's much easier to hide only three of us than the whole platoon."

Gar stood, frowning down at him, thinking.

"If, by some fluke, they do find us," Dirk said, "a third sword could be handy."

"And a man who knows the territory could be even handier." Gar nodded slowly. "All right, lieutenant. We'll take you up on your offer."

Sergeant Otto groaned.

* * *

"Honor," in the chaos of a society dominated by warlords, turned out to have a very solid meaning. If a mercenary didn't fulfill a commission, no one else would hire him. If a captain didn't stand by his men, or the men stand by one another, the company would break up and dissolve.

Gar and Dirk learned that much from Cort as they searched for a hiding place. They rode away from Quilichen, and if now and again Dirk turned and looked back when there was nothing to see but trees and leaves or, later, meadowland stretching away from hills, who could blame him? After all, he didn't do it so often that it might become irritating.

They rode down a shallow stream until it ended in a pond fed by a dozen springs, then found a deer trail and followed it. Dirk brought out handfuls of grain and scattered it behind them, so that birds would flutter down and disturb their tracks while pecking for the seeds. Then, in the evening, the deer would cover even those traces as they came down to the water.

They came to a shelf of shale and rode along it for a hundred feet, till it buried itself in the earth again. A little farther on, they found a stand of pines and rode through it; the slippery needles underfoot didn't hold tracks very well.

So they went, taking advantage of every chance to hide their trail, riding at a canter when they could, a trot when the way was open, a walk when it wasn't, putting as much distance as possible between themselves and the Hawk cavalry.

In the middle of the afternoon, though, Gar suddenly reined in and sat, listening, for a minute.

"What is it?" Cort asked.

"Horses," Gar said. "That sergeant made quick time going back to camp. The rest of the platoon is out after us."

"They'll have a jolly time trying to follow, with all the ways we broke our trail," Dirk said, grinning.

"They surely will," Cort agreed. "By the way, Gar, what did you do to anger the Boss of Loutre so?"

"I didn't," Gar answered. "I doubt he even knows about it. But I tripped up his steward badly, when he was translating for the boss with a merchant I was guarding—mistranslating, I should say. He was trying to get the boss to pay more than the merchant was asking."

"He would have pocketed the difference!" Cort exclaimed. "No wonder he wants to kill you—if you tell his boss about it, the boss will kill *him*!"

"That does lend him some reason," Gar admitted. "Myself, I think he's just piqued at having someone catch him at his game."

"But to hire a whole company to murder you! Where did the steward get that much money?"

"That is an interesting question, isn't it?" Gar asked, with a hard little smile. "I think I'll ask his boss about that." He halted suddenly, losing his smile, cocking his head. "We'd better find shelter, quickly! The Hawks will find our trail after all!"

"How do you know?" Cort asked, frowning.

"Because I hear hounds! They've bought themselves dogs someplace! Ride!"

Gar whipped his mount into a canter. Dirk followed with Cort right behind him, marveling at the big man's hearing.

By nightfall, though, Cort could hear the hounds himself. Worse, they had come out of the woods into a flat plain, too dry for any life but grass and the multitude of living things that grazed. Cattle roamed here and there, sheep grazed by the roadside, but there were few people, and virtually nowhere to hide.

"We have to find somewhere!" Cort said. "The horses can't keep going much longer."

"I know," Gar said, thin-lipped, "and I keep looking for a haystack to hide in, but all I see is the hay without the stack!"

The moon's first sliver bulged over the horizon, showing the silhouette of the hill before it.

Gar stiffened, staring ahead. "What's that?"

He knew darned well, Dirk thought. "Looks like one of those half-dome hills."

"Stay away!" Cort reined in his horse, dread of the supernatural striking ten times stronger in the night. "The Fair Folk will kill us if they find us near their hill—or take us captive for twenty years, if they're feeling merciful!"

"Old stories," Dirk said with scorn.

"They're much more than stories!" Cort reddened with anger. "I talked with a gaffer myself who'd been in one of their hills! Gone in a young man, he had, and come out an old one, and couldn't remember more than one night among them!"

"What was his name?" Dirk asked. "Rip Van Winkle?"

"Wh . . . ? No! His name was Katz!"

Dirk frowned, unsure suddenly, but Gar said, "If those Hawks catch us, I'll be losing a great deal more than twenty years. I hope you two will have the sense to surrender, but I'm very much afraid that you'll fight, and the Hawks will kill us a great deal more surely than your Fair Folk."

"Well," Cort admitted, "they don't *always* kill trespassers. Sometimes they don't even take them captive, just toy with them for a bit, then let them go. They've even sent some peasants away with riches. You never can tell with the Fair Folk."

"Then at least we'll have a chance on their hill," Dirk pointed out, "and if dread of it would have kept you away, it might keep the Hawks away, too, at least until morning."

"And by dawn, our horses will be rested," Gar agreed. "I say it's a chance worth taking!"

"What other chance do we have?" Cort sighed, and followed them as they galloped toward the hill.

Halfway there, the baying of the hounds suddenly grew louder. Turning, Cort could see they had come over the horizon and were there on the road behind, a blot in the moonlight. He turned back to the front, calling, "Faster!"

They rode faster indeed. The horses ran flat out with their last spurt of energy, fleeing from the belling and barking behind them, though their breath came hard with exhaustion. The hounds were far fresher—most of their afternoon had been spent at the walk, with their noses to the ground. They ran easily, and the horsemen behind them kept pace. Then they passed the hounds, riding for the trio whom they could see now, fifty men on horses, leaving the dogs to their peasant handlers.

But the hill was close now, so close. Finally the companions' horses thudded up twenty feet on the hillside, and Gar reined in, leaping off his horse and drawing his sword. "Surrender, gentlemen! It's for me to die, not you!"

"Sometimes you can be a real pain, you know?" Dirk sprang down and drew his sword, taking his stance back to back with Gar.

Cort felt his death coming upon him, and was only sorry there would be no gleeman to see it and sing his saga to Violet. He dismounted and took station by his companions, sword and dagger drawn. "Let them come down!"

They came up, though, with thundering hooves and yells of triumph, swords flashing in the air, swinging high for the death strokes.

Then the earth groaned and shook. A glare of light split the night, throwing the companions' shadows long before them, and a vast, cavernous voice echoed all about them:

"Who disturbs the home of the Fair Folk? Who dares come near the Hollow Hill with Cold Iron in hand?"

14

The Hawks screamed, their horses reared and turned, and the enemy line boiled in confusion for a minute.

Cort ached to turn and see, but held his eyes on the enemy. The Hawks did look, though, and froze.

Lances of light sprang out, spearing Hawk soldiers, searing through their ranks like scythes. The Hawks screamed and fled.

"Lasers!" Dirk stared at the carnage.

The light rays pursued the Hawks relentlessly, but the voice called again, echoing with the hollowness of a tomb: "Let some escape, to tell the tale!"

"Amplified," Dirk said.

Gar nodded. "Digital reverb."

The rays shifted downward to score the horses' hooves. In two minutes the whole squadron was gone, leaving half a dozen dead behind. The survivors galloped away, back down the road, as far from the Hollow Hill as they could get. Even the hounds turned tail and ran with fading howls of terror.

Cort went limp. "Thank our lucky stars! Your gamble worked, Gar!"

"Maybe not." Dirk glanced over his shoulder. "Take a look behind you."

Slowly, dread rising like a giant in the night, Cort turned to look, and cried out in terror.

Gar turned too, and stood staring.

An oblong door in the side of the hill had opened like an eye, filled with glaring light. Tall men stood silhouetted against that glare. They were more than six feet in height, much more, almost as tall as Gar, and the weapons in their hands weren't swords.

As the three comrades stared, the light dimmed to little more than the moonlight itself. Cort blinked, trying to see through dazzled eyes. He could make out other lights floating in midair, of a gentle brightness and delicate color, some rose, some lavender, some the shade of new straw.

Beneath those lights came the most beautiful women he had ever seen. He gasped, amazed at their slenderness, their tallness, their delicate grace, their perfect straightness—and the equally perfect curvature of their figures. Their hair fell long and wild about their shoulders, some pale as new straw, some rich as red gold, some even perfectly white. Their skin too was pale, delicate as the petals of new rose blooms. Their eyes were huge, lustrous in the night; their cheekbones were high, their lips full and wide. They wore the simplest of gowns of gauzy cloth, fabric that shimmered and clung as they moved, more becoming than any confection a boss's wife might wear—gowns that left rounded, soft arms bare in the moonlight, gowns that swept down to their ankles, revealing slender, graceful feet in gilded sandals, gowns that scooped low from their necks, to hint at voluptuous curves beneath. They were easily as tall as Dirk and Cort, perhaps taller.

Cort caught his breath, feeling himself go weak.

The men were much like the women, fair-haired and lean, with high cheekbones, large eyes that seemed to glow in the reflected light of the floating lamps, hollow cheeks, and long, straight-nosed faces. Their hair hung long, below their collars, and they were dressed in doublet and hose with cloaks of rich, heavy fabric. Each wore a baldric holding a rapier and a dagger, but the weapons sheened with the golden tone of bronze. In their hands, though, they held things like crossbow stocks, though strangely elongated, squarish and bulky.

"These also bear weapons!" the sepulchral voice thundered. "Slay them, too!"

But, "Hold!" one of the women cried, raising a hand. Bold and daring, she stepped toward Gar, swaying, and held up a hand to stroke his cheek. "This one is as tall as we, and taller! Could he be a son of the Fair Folk?"

"With that black hair? Come, Maora!" one of the men said with scorn. His voice wasn't amplified.

"Who knows what a changeling might grow into, Daripon?" Maora smiled languorously, and Cort could see Gar brace himself. "After all," she went on, "we have given our babes to Milesian women for no better reason than having such hair as his."

"Or for having such ugliness," Daripon sneered. "Speak, intruder! Are you of the blood of the Fair Folk?"

"No changeling would know that," Cort objected.

"Silence, small man!"

Blood boiled, and Cort laid a hand on his sword. The crossbow stocks swung toward him, and he froze, having seen what those light lances could do.

Another of the women swung toward him, too, though—shorter than the others, no taller than Cort himself. Her eyes were even wilder than those of the other women, and her face was a dream of loveliness, with delicate brows arching over violet eyes, a retroussé nose, and full ruby lips that smiled lazily in a broad invitation. "Hold your fire, Lavere," she said, and placed a hand on Cort's sword.

At her touch, he felt himself go weak, but the look in her eyes brought all his strength raging back, making the blood pound through his veins. How could he have ever counted Violet beautiful, when there was a face such as this in the world?

Except, of course, that she wasn't really of his world . . .

"I shall keep this one," she said. "He might prove amusing."

"Don't be a fool, Desirée!" Lavere said, reddening, and raised his rifle, sighting along the barrel. Cort yanked at his sword, but the woman's hand tightened on his, holding it still with amazing strength for one so delicate in appearance.

"Hold!" the sepulchral voice snapped. "We need his blood for our pool!"

Lavere froze, then ever so slowly, ever so reluctantly, lowered his weapon.

"Do they speak of human sacrifice?" Cort demanded.

"Only the kind that you would die for," Gar reassured him.

Cort relaxed a little, for Desirée was a woman he would die for indeed. He looked back into her eyes . . .

And was lost. He gazed into violet pools, felt all go dark about him save their glow, felt them envelop him, felt himself floating adrift in their coolness . . .

"Come back!" Gar commanded, and all at once the woman's eyes were only eyes, he was aware of her face around those eyes again, and saw the Fair Folk behind her amid their glowing lights—but all dimly; only she seemed bright.

Dirk's voice came to him distantly: "There's some of this spell you can't break."

"Yes," Gar agreed, "but that's entirely natural."

"He has the weirding way!" exclaimed another man of the Fair Folk. "He must be of our blood!"

"I can't be," Gar returned, "for I'm from a different world than yours. But I am a wizard, and so is my friend, though he's a wizard of another kind, from yet another world."

"That's overstating the case," Dirk objected.

"Not if you know the words for our weapons and voice," another Fair Man said, thin-lipped.

"All the more reason to slay them out of hand, Aldor," Lavere said bitterly, his gaze still on Cort.

"No, Lavere," said Desirée, eyes all but devouring the lieutenant. "There is too much strange about them, too much we must learn of what they know. My lord duke, bring them in to question."

"Yes, bring them in," the sepulchral voice commanded. "We can always slay them there."

The Fair Folk men stepped downhill to surround the companions, weapons trained on them.

"Our horses," Gar reminded.

"Let them wander," Lavere replied. "If you are fortunate, they will still be near in the morning. If you are even more fortunate, you may come forth to join them."

"Enter!" the sepulchral voice commanded, and the Fair Folk stood aside from the still-glowing doorway.

Gar and Dirk hesitated, but Cort, gaze still rapt on his fairy, said, "You must always do what the Fair Folk command."

"You must indeed," she agreed, her voice throaty. She lifted a hand to touch his cheek, and his own hand darted to catch hers, but the feather-light palm was already gone, leaving a print behind that seemed to burn with gentle fire.

"I never argue with laser rifles," Dirk said.

"Especially when they're pointed at me," Gar agreed. "All right, then. Thank you, Fair Folk. We'll be your guests for the night."

"I just hope it's a short one," Dirk said, and followed Gar into the hill.

Cort was almost unaware of their going; he only went with his fairy, by her side, gaze still joined with hers, the blood in his veins singing with hope and desire.

Metal grated on metal. He whirled, hand on his sword, but only saw the door closing—though how strangely it closed! A huge, curved panel slid down from above while another slid upward from below, both flattening as they went until they met in a straight line with a metallic clash.

The touch that stung his blood was light on his hand, and he turned to gaze into Desirée's face again. "There are many strange and wonderful things in this hill," she said, her eyes mischievous. "You must not draw your sword at each new encounter."

"If you say it, lady." Cort took his hand away. "Only speak to me, and I will notice nothing else."

She laughed, a sound like a springtime brook. "How gallant, sir! Where did you gain such a silver tongue?"

Cort wondered about that, himself. He'd never been much of a man for the ladies before—but then, this wasn't flirting. He meant every word.

The oldest of the Fair Folk, a man, took a medallion from about his neck and hung it on a velvet-lined circular pad, as though it were a diamond on a tray. They were in a vestibule, magical in its decoration. The walls were smoothly curved and intricately patterned in the light of the floating lamps. The floor was carpeted, no design, but thicker and softer than any Cort had ever seen. The chamber was about eight feet square with an eight-foot ceiling.

Something whined behind him. Cort glanced back, marveling as metal spun outward to form a circular door opposite the outer portal. He smiled, the wonder of it all heightening the euphoria he felt as he glanced back at Desirée. She returned his smile, then followed the others through the door and on into the Hill, which meant Cort did, too, behind Dirk and Gar.

The Fair Folk men had to stoop as they came through the inner portal. Desirée followed the rest of the band through the inner door. Cort stepped through too, and heard the whining again. Turning, he saw metal sliding in from the sides, making the doorway smaller and smaller, like the pupil of an eye in bright light. He shook his head in amazement, then turned to follow Desirée, and stepped into Fairyland indeed. Cort looked about him and caught his breath.

They were surrounded by marble buildings, none more than a story tall, with green grass forming broad lawns about them. The stone was pastel in its swirling patterns, and each house's walls were pierced with broad windows glinting with glass. Cort had never known panes could be made so large, for not a single window was subdivided. The doorways were intricately carved, the panels bulging in bas-relief sculptures.

Gar and Dirk were tossing meaningless phrases at one another.

"How old is that style of hatch?" Dirk asked.

"Iris doors went out of use three hundred years ago," Gar said, "though my family archives said they were very popular for two centuries before that. I'm amazed it still works."

"You know too much," Lavere said sternly, but the duke commanded, his voice no longer sepulchral, "Let them speak. We must know how much they know."

Dazed, Cort looked about him as they strolled down the street that led from the plaza. Now that his eyes were accustomed to it, he could see that the light really wasn't as bright as it had seemed at first, but was soft and rosy, from lamps that rose from the roofs of all the houses. Garlands of flowers grew from the lawns, the roofs, the windows, the vines that climbed the corners of the dwellings. The air was warm, and sweet with the perfume of many blossoms. It invited a man to relax, to rest, to dally in love . . .

His gaze strayed to Desirée again. With a start, he saw she was watching him with a smile of amusement. "What think you of our hill, sir?"

"Wondrous," Cort told her, "and everywhere beautiful—but nothing so beautiful as yourself."

She lowered her gaze demurely. "I think you praise me overmuch."

"I speak only truth," Cort breathed.

She looked up at him, a calculating, weighing gaze, but with a smile that was inviting nonetheless. Then she tossed her head and turned away. "Come, sir! We must attend the duke!"

They went on down the lane, and Cort wondered where the rest of the people were. But he followed Gar and Dirk steadily, even though they were making more of their meaningless noises.

"A domed city," Dirk was saying, "left over from the colony days. Didn't the history say the first colonists lived in domes while they were Terraforming the planet?"

"It did," Gar confirmed. "Apparently not all of them felt the urge for the great outdoors."

Dirk eyed one of the lamps at the top corner of a house. "Lighted by electricity, and I'll bet there's a nuclear generator busily breeding more reaction mass for itself. I hope it's far underground."

"It must be," Gar said, "or the people would show a lot more mutation than they have."

"Everything we're seeing could be explained by genetic drift and good nutrition," Dirk agreed. "I'll bet each house has a vegetable garden and robots to till it, and the lamps emit imitation sunlight while the people sleep."

"They wouldn't want it while they're awake, with those fair skins," Gar agreed.

"Where did you learn these words, sir?" Maora asked, frowning.

"In school," Dirk told her. "We're from very far away."

"In space or time? For you speak as good a Galactic Standard as we, though with a slight accent."

"Do I really?" Dirk asked, looking up with interest. "Say, can you tell the difference between my accent and my friend's?"

"It is noticeable," Maora said, with an odd frostiness to her words. Her glance was concerned.

Dirk decided to relieve her mind. "If only Magda were here to see these wonders with me!" he sighed, and promptly fell despondent.

"He loves a lady, then?" the woman asked, interested.

"Totally smitten," Gar told her.

"That explains it, Maora," another woman said, and to Gar, "No Milesian man can resist a woman of the Fair Folk. Therefore we know you for one of us."

"Really?" Gar asked, amused. "How do you know I'm not just in love with the girl I left behind me?"

"If you were, your young friend's state would make you sad, reminding you of your love," Maora said, nodding toward Cort.

"I fear there's some truth to that," Gar sighed, glancing at the lieutenant. "What am I going to do with *two* lovesick comrades? Have pity, ladies! Tell your friend Desirée to free my companion from her spell!"

"She cannot," Maora said simply. "His heart is hers; he is past her control in that."

"But only in that," Gar qualified.

Maora smiled, relaxing, almost gloating. "In all else, he will gladly do as she bids."

Gar knew there were limits to that, but wasn't about to bet on what they were.

As they came toward the center of the dome, the buildings grew taller, having more headroom. They began to hear music, reeds and strings, with an odd beat from softened drums that seemed to invade Cort's head and work itself into his blood, until his heart beat to its rhythm. Finally they came to a palace that towered three stories high in the very center of the town. It was brightly lit both inside and out, and in the wide plaza before it, the Fair Folk were dancing—stately, courtly measures that were somehow also completely voluptuous.

"What make you of that, my friend?" Gar nudged Dirk.

"Hnnh?" Dirk tore an envious gaze away from Cort's infatuated face and looked about him. "Hey! It's the town square of the colony dome. And the courthouse, probably, or at least City Hall." He inhaled deeply. "I don't know what they're serving for refreshments, but it smells delectable!"

Cort snapped out of his daze, turning to stare at them, appalled. "Don't eat or drink anything! If you do, you'll be in their power, and they can keep you as a slave or companion for twenty years!"

Amused, Desirée assured him, "Do not flatter yourself, mortal man. We would scarcely want you for so long a period."

Cort turned to her, dismayed. She laughed at the look on his face, then, instantly contrite, touched his cheek and told him, "But if I did, be sure that you would want to stay, and we would have no need of enchanted food or drink."

Cort let himself drift into her eyes and knew her words for truth.

"Indeed, you are far more likely to want to stay than we are to desire your presence," Maora said, though the measuring look and sultry smile she gave Gar belied her words.

"Come, hero of daring." Desirée turned, holding out her hands and making an invitation somehow into a challenge. "Are you bold enough to dance with a woman of the Sidhe?"

She pronounced it "shee," and Cort grinned, taking her hands. "Bold enough for a she indeed!"

Then they were off, whirling and turning as though they were thistledown in the wind, instantly lost in a world of their own, in which nothing existed except the music, and each other.

Maora smiled, taking Gar's hand. "Will you dance, too, sir?"

"I thank you, but shanks so long as mine are clumsy in such giddy measures. . . . Trouble breathing, friend?"

Dirk's whole body shook, as though strangling a coughing spasm. "Yes, you might say I had trouble swallowing something," he wheezed.

A golden-haired boy as tall as Dirk's shoulder came twisting through the crowd and bowed to them. He was already broad in the shoulder. "My lady, the duke wishes to speak with these Milesians."

15

"'Milesians?' " Dirk frowned, turning to Maora.

"Mortals," she explained, "who are not of the Fair Folk. Go with the lad; he will lead you to the duke." She turned away to a tall, handsome man who stepped up to take her hand. She laughed gaily as he swept her off into the dance.

Gar followed her with his gaze.

"Regrets?" Dirk jibed.

"Yes, but not about her specifically." Gar turned back to the youth. "We shall be honored by an audience with His Grace."

"You are courteous, for Milesians," the boy said in surprise. "Follow, then." He turned and went.

" 'Milesians,' " Dirk mused as they followed. "I think there's an awful lot of Celtic influence here."

"Not my area of study," Gar said. "What are the signs?"

"The Irish called their last wave of prehistoric invaders Milesians," Dirk explained. "The scholars think they were the ancestors of the modern Irish. They drove the earlier invaders, the Tuatha de Danaan, 'the people of Danu,' before them, until finally the Old People withdrew into the Hollow Hills in disgust. The medieval Irish referred to them as the Daonine Sidhe." He pronounced it "Theena Shee." "They lived inside the green hills or in a land under the waters."

"Let's hope these people see themselves as Daonine Sidhe, then," Gar said grimly. "Put on your happy face—here's the duke."

Their young guide led them up to a high dais, where the oldest of the Fair Folk sat alone, in a gilded, high-backed, intricately carved armchair that gleamed with the look of neither wood nor metal, but of some sort of synthetic. The boy bowed. "My lord duke, here are the Milesians."

"Bravely done," the duke said, and waved him away. "Go now to the dancing, Riban."

"I thank Your Grace." The boy bowed again, and went.

Dirk gazed after him. "How old is he? Fourteen?"

"Ten," the duke snapped. "The Fair Folk grow tall from childhood—and you are most lacking in courtesy, Milesian!"

"Oh, sorry." Dirk turned and bowed. "Thank you for your hospitality, Your Grace."

"Better," the duke said, mollified. He turned to Gar, who bowed and said, "You are gracious, Lord Duke."

"This one, at least, knows manners." The duke looked him up and down. "I might almost think you were of noble birth."

"I am the grandson of a count, Your Grace, and the son of a lord."

"Then you are no man of this world of Durvie!"

"Your insight is excellent," Gar confirmed. "We have come from off-world."

"I might have known it, from the things you've said! Have you laser rifles of your own, then?"

"Not with us, my lord, but we have both fired them in battle, yes."

Dirk stared at him in alarm—he was giving too much away.

"How much else have you recognized?" the duke demanded.

Dirk sighed. If the cat was out of the bag, it might as well yowl. "This Hollow Hill is a colonists' atmosphere dome, the portal into the hill is an airlock that's no longer used for keeping the breathable air in, and your medallion is a wireless audio pickup that feeds loudspeakers high up on the hill. Its amplifier has a digital reverberation unit, a frequency equalizer, and a basso enhancer."

The duke sat rigid, his eyes smoldering. At last he said, "You are as knowledgeable as I had feared." He turned to Gar. "And you? What one of you knows, both must!"

"We have different areas of expertise," Gar temporized. "For myself, I conjecture that, like those you call Milesians, you're descended from the original colonists, but your ancestors chose to stay in the domes, rather than go out into the world and farm. Tell me, are all the Hollow Hills inhabited by tribes of Fair Folk?"

"All," the duke confirmed. "Those whose people abandoned them were taken as homes by those who grew to be too many for one single hill. They scorned the ancestors of the Milesians for being so uncouth as to grub in the ground, and the Milesians scorned them for choosing prison over freedom." He smiled vindictively. "The more fools they! As they found when the famines came and they had foolishly spawned as many brats as each of them wished! They came against our ancestors in their hordes, trying to batter a way into the hills—but our ancestors had never forgotten the magic of their textbooks and learning programs, and to add to the power of the nuclear generators, had learned how to tap enough geothermal energy, and to harness wind and water with turbines that charged storage batteries, so that they kept the machines working. Our ancestors took up the laser rifles they had learned to repair, and mowed down the Milesians by the hundreds. Oh, some of them died in those wars, but each took a hundred Milesians with him, and another of the Fair Folk rose up in his place!"

"Giving rise to the rumor that you couldn't be killed." Dirk suppressed a shudder.

"So your people all still learn how to repair the machines, and operate them?" Gar asked.

"All indeed! Some even become obsessed with such learning, and ferret out new knowledge, inventing new devices!"

"A rather solitary occupation," Gar noted.

"There are some solitary Fair Folk, yes," the duke agreed, "but there were always leprechauns and their like among the Old People. Most, though, fulfill their assigned hours at the consoles and the repair benches, then pass the rest of their time in cultivating the arts, and in the delights of conversation."

Dirk suspected that "the arts" included martial arts, and that "conversation" covered a lot of flirtation, dalliance, social maneuvering, and jockeying for status, but he was wise enough not to say so.

"Now we live in luxury," the duke went on, "with leisure for learning and revelry, while the descendants of those who yearned for the freedom of the plains and forests must toil and sweat for scraps of bread, and strive against one another in ceaseless combat while we live in harmony."

"Do you really?" Gar asked, interested. "How do you manage that?"

"We meet to discuss such issues as might cause friction—"

"All of you together?"

"Of course." The duke frowned. "There are not so many of us that the town square cannot hold us all."

"And if one of you is angry at another?"

"We hear their arguments at the assembly, and all decide together who is right to what degree, and wherein each should be blamed."

"A time-consuming but effective way of governing," Gar said. "However, you have plenty of spare time, don't you?"

"That is our privilege," the duke agreed, his voice guarded.

"Bought at the price of being able to roam freely, or to do as you damn well please even if it doesn't suit the others—but the Milesians have little enough of such freedom, either."

"Much less, for most of them," the duke said darkly.

"But you also choose leaders," Gar pressed. "How did you come to be duke? Simply by living long? Or by birth?"

"By long life and acclamation," the duke replied. "There are many of my generation still living, but I was the one for whom the most applause rose when the old duke died. As to leading, I preside at the assemblies, and speak for us all in dealings with other hills. That is all."

"And command if you need to fight the Milesians," Gar inferred. "I assume, though, that you ride to one another's hills now and again, probably at each equinox and solstice . . ."

"And woe to the peasants who cross our paths." The duke smiled, eyes glowing. "I congratulate you on having discerned how we use the legend of the Wild Hunt, and the solstices and equinoxes as well, to add to our mystical aura."

Dirk frowned; the duke was being entirely too open.

"I am sure it keeps you safe, and prevents your having to burn down more than a few Milesians," Gar said diplomatically. "I would further conjecture that the festivals you hold on those occasions center on the exchanging of genes."

"The festivals are also chances for athletic contests, which inspire our men to strive to perfect themselves in body and in skill at fighting," the duke said sharply.

"And of course, the winner finds himself more attractive to the women of the neighboring Hill," Gar interpreted.

The duke's smile was brittle. "A tactful way of saying that we make no bar to the young, and not so young, who wish to taste and revel in one another's joys."

"An excellent safeguard against inbreeding," Gar agreed. "Still, you must need the occasional influx of genes from completely outside the Fair Folk community; your gene pool can't be very large."

"You guess rightly, which is why we tolerate Desirée's desire to amuse herself with your friend," the duke said with a hard smile. "In fact, every now and again a Milesian proves so diverting that we allow him to remain among us all his days."

"Or until you tire of him?" Gar smiled, and recited,

> "He has taken a coat of the even cloth,
> And a pair of shoes of velvet green,
> And till seven years were past and gone,
> True Thomas on Earth was never seen."

"Even so," the duke said, "and those whom we find diverting, we keep until they start to age and lose their beauty. Those who cease to be diverting, we keep in other ways—those who cease amusing, or learn too much."

"Learn what?" Gar asked. "That you're only human, and can be slain like anyone else?"

Anger sparked from the duke's eyes. "Yes, that and more," he hissed. "But we are not 'merely human,' like these Milesians, these clod-poll folk among whom you've been wandering!"

"They're not all clods!" Dirk spoke in anger, the vision of Magda bright before him. "Some are beautiful, some highly skilled, many excellent soldiers! The rigors of their lives have made them hardy and strong, clever and skillful! Some are even as wonderful as any of your Fair Folk!"

"Ridiculous!" the duke snapped. "Are any Milesians as tall as we, as graceful or as handsome?"

Dirk frowned. "So you think that your inbreeding has made you superior to the people of the outside world."

"Not inbreeding—selective breeding! The Hill can support only so many! Each woman may bear only two children during her lifetime, and if one is born dark-haired, ugly, or maimed, we give him to the Milesians!"

Dirk remembered the tall "changeling" in Cort's platoon. "But only if you can trade it for a good-looking Milesian. So that's why you continually steal Milesian babies and leave Fair Folk infants in their places—as you say, you need the genes, but you take only the prettiest and the strongest!"

"And have been doing so for four hundred years," the duke confirmed. "After all that time, surely we have all the best genes, and the Milesians all the worst!"

"Not at all," Gar said, "for the babies you trade away have all your genes within them, even if they're recessive. If you gain the strengths of the Milesians, so do they gain yours!"

"What strengths have they that we would wish?" the duke scoffed. His eyes glittered as he looked from Dirk to Gar and back. "Does it not worry you that I am so free to confirm your guesses, so open as to tell you facts you did not know?"

"Well, now that you mention it," Dirk said, swallowing hard, "yes."

The duke laughed, gloating. "You fear that we will keep you inside the hill all your lives, for committing the crime of knowing too much—and you fear rightly. We cannot let you walk abroad, to tell the Milesians we are only mortal, as they are, but with more powerful weapons."

"You're planning to hold onto us," Dirk said, his mouth dry. He thought of Magda, and his heart twisted.

"Your friend already wishes to stay." The duke nodded at a smaller building off to the side of the plaza. "Look where he comes!"

Turning, Dirk and Gar saw Desirée coming out the door, holding the hand of a very besotted Cort. He moved like a sleepwalker, letting her touch guide him, never taking his gaze from her face. She beamed back into his eyes, face radiant with triumph.

Dirk felt his heart sink. "He's lost to us."

"And to all the outer world," the duke agreed. "He is a good fighter and a strong, tall, handsome man, for a Milesian. His genes will protect us against the inbreeding you cite, without introducing too many unpleasant traits."

"Can he stay as anything but a servant?" Gar asked.

"We do, very rarely, allow a Milesian to marry one of us," the duke hedged, "as much as any of us marry."

"Which means that the only vows they exchange are that they love each other right then, at that moment?" Dirk asked.

"Something like that, yes." The duke seemed disgruntled that Dirk had guessed.

"But no one expects it to last longer than a few years," Gar suggested.

"None," the duke agreed. "When they decide their marriage is done, he who has married one Fair Lady may marry another. He need not be a slave all his days."

"Meaning that you think he or she is a superior enough specimen that you want to spread their genes widely through the pool," Dirk said drily.

"And of sufficient interest to help dispel ennui, the perpetual restless boredom that is our bane," the duke said.

"Will you decide to so honor our friend?" Gar asked.

"Perhaps," the duke answered. "If a man of such grace and beauty survived long enough in the chaotic world outside, he may be worth keeping as something other than a bondsman—though mind you, even our slaves wish to remain here, where they are safe, and all is laughter and music."

"But you are definitely keeping him," Dirk inferred.

The duke watched the couple, brooding, as Desirée dropped Cort's hand, tossed her head, and turned away. He stared after her, dumbfounded.

The duke smiled. "I see that Desirée has had her fill of him for the time being. She may decide to reclaim him some day. For now, though, dawn is coming, and he is free to go."

He turned to a side table, filled with fruit and decanters. "Eat and drink! The night has been long, the way longer, and you are surely hungry."

Dirk glanced at the fruit; his mouth watered and his stomach rumbled. But Gar caught his eye and gave the slightest shake of the head. Dirk remembered Cort's warning not to eat or drink, and ground out, "I thank you, Your Grace, but on a mission such as we follow now, we must eat only journey rations." He wondered what malice Gar had overheard in the man's thoughts.

The duke's face darkened. "I urge you to taste and sip! It is quite pleasant—far more pleasant than it is without."

"It's drugged, isn't it?" Gar asked. "Your ancestors read the old legends, and liked the irony. You feed sedatives to the Milesians you don't want to keep around, but don't want to let go, either—the ones who know too much. Then you store them away somehow, for twenty years. When you let them out, the world is a generation older, and though people believe they've spent a night in Hollow Hill, they also believe the experience has left them mad, and don't believe anything they say about you!"

The duke flushed with anger. "You see far too much, far too quickly! I warn you, it will be far more pleasant for you if you eat or drink!"

"I thank you." Gar inclined his head. "But we must decline the invitation."

The duke snapped his fingers, and Fair Folk men whirled from the dance and fell on Dirk and Gar, drawing their swords.

The companions leaped back, whipping out their blades, and met the onslaught, parrying frantically. "Try not to injure them!" Gar called.

"Look, I have some idea of good manners!" Dirk called back.

Then a shout split the air, and Cort barreled between two of the tall men. They leaped aside in sheer surprise as he turned, rapier and dagger drawn and whirling. "If you fight my friends, you fight me!"

"Cort, no!" Desirée wailed.

"Game's over, lady," Dirk snapped, parrying a blade that ripped his sleeve. Blood welled, but he ignored it and caught another sword on his dagger.

"Spare him!" Desirée cried. "I have more games to play!"

If anything, that made the Fair Men fight harder. They piled on the trio ten to one and bore them down by the weight of sheer numbers. Gar felt his blade cut flesh; a tall man cried out in pain, and Gar felt blades pierce his shoulder, his thigh. Then a blow rocked his head, and he went limp.

He could still see and hear, though everything seemed distant. He felt his body heaved up high, saw Cort and Dirk borne up on the shoulders of tall men, heard Desirée wailing, and saw the floating lights slide by overhead, then the lintel of the palace portal. Its ceiling reeled past, painted in beautiful, ornate designs; then the roof closed in, they passed under a low lintel, his head tilted downward, and they went jolting down and down into gloom.

Then, suddenly, the ride leveled, and the roof rose again. Gar felt control of his limbs returning as the daze faded, leaving a splitting headache. He looked about him and saw a domed ceiling painted a cold blue. The light was cold, too, and glaring white—mercury vapor, at a guess.

Then they lowered his legs, and Gar saw that he stood in an underground chamber filled with clear glass doors. Behind a dozen of those doors stood Milesians, men and women of Cort's kind, who had come into the Hill by chance or the caprice of a Fair Person, but who now stood frozen and rigid, eyes closed in cryogenic sleep.

16

The Fair Men lowered Dirk's and Cort's feet, too, but kept hold of their arms. Cort and Gar managed to stand, but Dirk sagged, as though all the stiffening had been taken out of him. "All right, I can't fight against odds like these! And I have to admit you boys can fight. What the hell, it isn't death—and whatever I'm planning to do with my life can wait twenty years."

Gar stared at him, and Cort gaped, scandalized—but it became worse instantly, for Gar's knees weakened, too, and his head bowed. "He's right. There's no point in fighting it."

"Are you mad?" Cort cried. "You'll lose twenty years with the people you've grown with! When you come out of this place, you'll still be twenty-five, but they'll be forty-five! You'll be bachelors, but they'll have grown children!"

"Not much loss, in my case," Gar grunted. "There's no lady love waiting for me to find her."

"I know the feeling," Dirk said, totally despondent—and Cort stiffened, suddenly sure that Dirk was lying.

Dirk looked up, frowning, gaining the energy of outrage, glaring at the duke. "But you were going to kick our buddy Cort out of the hill. He shouldn't have to lose twenty years of his life just because he was loyal enough to fight for his friends!"

"Indeed he should not!" Desirée cried, unseen behind the wall of men, but a dozen women's voices clamored in agreement.

The duke scowled, glancing to the side, probably at the women, then nodded reluctantly. "He shall go. After all, he knows very little."

Desirée's voice cried out with delight, and the other women cheered with her. Cort felt massive relief, then remembered and frowned at Dirk and Gar. What had they hidden from him?

Nothing, he realized. He had heard them talking openly about the Hollow Hill, but hadn't understood a word of it.

"Thank heaven for that," Dirk sighed. "You wouldn't mind if we go as far as the portal to tell him good-bye, would you?"

The duke eyed him suspiciously, but said, "I see no harm in that—though I warn you, it will only delay your long sleep for the half of an hour."

"I'll take every minute I can get!" Dirk said.

"Up, then, and out!" the duke slashed an arm toward the stairway.

Desirée ran up to take Cort's arm, babbling with excitement. "You are saved, then! Luck is with us! You would find me not at all attractive in twenty years, for you would still be as young as you are now!"

"I will always find you to be beautiful," Cort said fervently.

Desirée blushed and lowered her gaze. "In twenty years I will be . . . more bulky, and my face will have its first few faint lines."

"You'll still be graceful, and as beautiful as all the songbirds of the skies together—no, far more beautiful!"

They went up the stairs, with Cort heaping compliments on Desirée, and with her drinking them in, flashing him occasional looks that heated his blood. When they came to the airlock, and the duke pressed the patch that made the outer hatch swing open, Desirée pulled back on Cort's arm, pleading with the duke. "May I not keep him an hour longer?" The glance she gave Cort made it clear what she wanted to do with that hour, and weakened his knees.

"If this coil with his friends had not risen, I would have said yes," the duke said severely, "but since it has, we must bid him good-bye on the instant!"

"But when shall I hold him again?" Desirée wailed.

"On Midsummer's Eve. You may catch him up in our rout, as we journey to Rondel's Hill," the duke snapped.

Desirée cried out with delight and flung her arms around Cort's neck. He folded her in his arms, savoring the feel of her body against his for a minute, before she stepped away and said, "On Midsummer's Eve, be waiting in this meadow, near the pathway into the wood!"

"I shall," Cort promised with all his heart.

"He must go now," the duke said testily.

Desirée held tight to Cort's arm, protesting, "But he should not go alone!"

"No, he certainly shouldn't," Dirk said, and stamped on the foot of the man holding his right arm.

The Fair Man howled, hopping back and letting go. Dirk drove his left elbow into the belly of the man holding his left arm, then spun away, lashing out a kick at the Fair Man who sprang to bar his way.

Gar leaped backward and swung his arms forward, slamming his two captors into one another. He kicked their feet out from under them.

The duke roared with anger and drew his sword.

Dirk's foot caught his opponent in the belly, and he leaped over the falling body, sprinting toward the portal. "Out, Cort! Quickly!"

The duke's sword flicked out at Dirk, but he was too late, only managing to rip the back of his tunic as he dove out the door. Cursing, the duke spun to lunge at Gar. The big man twisted aside, grunting as the swordpoint grazed his hip, then swung a backhanded fist at the duke's hand. Something cracked; the duke howled, dropping his sword. Gar caught it as he plunged through the portal.

He landed rolling and came to his feet to see Dirk and Cort sprinting for the woods ten yards ahead of him. He started after them, thundering down the slope of the hill.

Cort's heart raced as he ran, wondering why he was in such a hurry to leave the hill that held all he had ever desired. But loyalty won over love; Desirée was safe, after all, but Dirk and Gar were not.

A thunderclap split the air behind him. He ran all the harder, not daring to look back. What magic were the Fair Folk using against them now? He dodged and weaved frantically, trying to be completely unpredictable—and must have succeeded, for a bright ray sizzled past him on his right, setting the grass afire. Shouts of rage echoed behind him with more flashes of light.

Then, somehow, he was in among the trees with Dirk still beside him. Dirk dropped behind, and Cort led the way, pelting down the path until the trees grew so thick that he couldn't see ahead anymore and had to halt, leaning against a tree and breathing like a bellows.

Something light and bright flitted between the trees. Cort straightened, hand on his sword, but a warm body flung itself into his arms, and moist full lips found his. He stood stiff a moment in sheer surprise, then melted to wrap his arms around her, for it was Desirée whom he held.

Finally he had to breathe. He leaned away from her, still gazing down into those wondrous, lustrous eyes—and saw Gar looming over them. His gaze leaped up to the giant. "How did you manage to come here so quickly?"

"Long legs," Gar answered, but Cort wondered why he wasn't panting as Dirk was. Of course, Cort was breathing hard, too, but for a different reason.

"You are safe for a few moments here," Desirée told them. "They won't use their light rays within the wood for fear of fire, and they'll go slowly for fear of ambush."

"You ran past them all to guard me!"

Desirée lowered her gaze. "They wouldn't have dared shoot if I had stepped between you and them, but I had other reasons in mind." She turned her face up again, but Gar coughed discreetly, and Dirk said, "I don't think we have quite that long."

Cort's military sense came to the fore. He stepped away from Desirée, but held tightly to her hand. "I can't believe we won a fight against Fair Folk—but that means our lives are forfeit, for they can't have us going about among our fellow mortals bragging!"

"I fear he speaks truth," Desirée said, huge eyes glowing in the gloom. "The Fair Folk will never rest now until they have tracked you down and slain you." She spun, throwing her arms around Cort and pressing her head to his chest. "O my love, I am so horribly afraid for you! I shall plead on your behalf, but the duke is so enraged, and the Fair Men so jealous, that I doubt they shall heed me at all!"

Cort lifted her chin and gazed into her eyes. "Even if they slay me for this night's joy, it'll have been worth it ten times over."

Desirée seemed to melt in his arms at the same time that she covered his mouth with her own for a long, long kiss—so long, in fact, that Gar finally had to lay a hand on the shoulder of each and part them, saying, "Enough, or the Fair Folk will be upon us before you two come up for air."

"Don't worry," Cort told him, "I've just learned how to breathe while I kiss." He started to lower his head again.

But Gar hauled him bodily away from Desirée. "You know, they're not going to be terribly pleased with her, either, if they catch her kissing you just now."

But Desirée lifted her head, looked about her, and said, "The gloom has lightened!"

Gar glanced around, realizing that he could actually make out individual tree trunks. "Is that good?"

"Yes! The false dawn is always our signal to go back inside the Hill! The Fair Folk have no liking for daylight."

"That sounds like the beautiful people of my own ancestral asteroid," Gar said, "though I suspect the reasons differ. Your folk aren't afraid the sun will burn them, are they?"

"In fact, they are," Desirée said. "Our skins are so fair that any sunlight at all will give us a painful burn in less than an hour. We only dare go abroad in daylight liberally smeared with an ointment that defeats the sun's rays, and even then with broad-brimmed hats and full clothing."

"Summer is a good time for you to stay in your hills, then," Gar agreed, "and fortunately, it's summer now."

"But you must go back quickly, my love!" Cort protested. "I don't want to see you burned!"

"Worse," Dirk said, "they might close the door to the Hill."

"They will not be overly quick about it," Desirée said, "seeing that they have come out hunting. Nevertheless, even as you say, I must go quickly." She still held Cort's hand, though, and turned back to him with longing. "Wait for me, my love! It will be long months before they let you come to me again, and I fear we must not look to Midsummer's Eve as I had hoped—but Harvest Home should see us reunited. Wait by the little brook that runs through this wood every night for a week before that festival, and I'll come as soon as I can, to tell you where I may meet you!"

"So long as that?" Cort said mournfully. "But it's better than never being with you again at all!"

"Farewell, then," Desirée said softly, and their farewell lasted so long that Gar had to separate them again. Then Desirée drifted off into the woods with many a backward glance until she seemed only a wraith of morning mist that faded, and was gone.

Cort stood looking after her, his face stark with loss.

Finally Dirk clapped him on the shoulder. "I know how it feels, my friend—in fact, I'm still feeling the same way myself! But if she's worth having, she's worth waiting for."

"And working for," Gar agreed, "but if you have any hope of seeing her again, you'll have to stay alive. Come on, let's run—the sun isn't up yet, and the Fair Folk might be pushing their luck and searching the woods for us."

"Even as you say!" Cort turned and plunged down the trail. "Indeed, I have reason enough to live now!"

"You sure do," Dirk said, and followed him, thinking, *Violet who?*

But a dozen steps later, Cort suddenly turned back, crying, "If I give myself up to them, they'll let me stay with her!"

Dirk caught one arm and Gar the other, lifting and carrying Cort backward. "Oh, they'll let her see you, all right," Dirk said, "through the crystal door of one of their upright coffins! She can come down and gaze on your frozen form any time she wants!"

"I know there are some women who like to keep a spare man around in case they need him," Gar told him, "but I don't think she's one of them—at least, not in quite that fashion."

"I'll take the chance!" Cort cried.

"No, you won't," Dirk said firmly. "Look, it's hard, yes, believe me, I know how you feel."

"No you don't!" Cort cried. "You didn't spend the night with her!"

Dirk's step faltered, but he kept going. "As long as I hear the occasional hunter's cry behind me, we keep walking!"

"I don't hear anything," Cort protested.

They halted, Dirk and Gar cocking their heads to listen. As they did, a ray of sunlight lanced down between leaves, rosy with dawn.

"He's right," Dirk said. "The Hollow Hill is still."

"The door is shut," Gar agreed. As one, they dropped Cort.

He sank to his knees, buried his face in his hands, and wept.

* * *

Cort recovered enough to start walking a few minutes later. Dirk and Gar let him lead the way, talking rather grimly as they went.

"At least the Fair Folk came out of this ahead by three horses," Dirk said. "Do you still have some gold to buy new ones?"

"Yes," Gar said, "but if I didn't, we could always have Herkimer drop us some more."

"Careful what you say." Dirk nodded at Cort.

Gar glanced up at their friend, smiling sadly. "I doubt he's hearing anything right now. I'm afraid he's lost in his own misery."

"Yeah, 'fraid so," Dirk said from hard experience. "It will wear off to the point where he can function again, though."

"She may some day be only another folktale," Gar sighed, "even to him."

Dirk nodded. "Say, do you really believe the duke's version of his people's history?"

"Accurate as far as it goes," Gar said slowly, "but I suspect it's somewhat one-sided. Subtracting the duke's bias and trying to read between the lines, I would guess that some of the original colonists refused to leave the comfort of the domes, just as he said, but he only hinted that they were willing to accept a very low birth rate in order to have comfort and luxury."

"Sounds kind of selfish," Dirk said, frowning.

"Does it? Remember that on overpopulated planets, the people who want large families are the ones accused of selfishness—and since those domes were built for a very limited number of people, overpopulation would be a very real concern."

"Still, wanting to stay in the domes would select for self-centered people. Having children makes you become other-centered."

"I'd prefer to say that other-centered people make *better* parents," Gar said sharply. "I've seen too many children emotionally butchered by self-centered parents."

"How many is too many?" Dirk challenged.

"One," Gar replied, "but I've seen a lot more than that."

"It does explain their vanity and preoccupation with pleasure," Dirk admitted. "How about we say that the domes selected the most worldly?"

"Of the first generation, true. Of the second, I'd say the more worldly, selfish types became bullies."

"Meanwhile," Dirk said, "the dead grass and leaves piled up, and buried the domes."

"Over a hundred years or so, yes. Since the colonists erected their domes in flatlands, I suspect they were silted over by windblown soil."

"More or less," Dirk agreed. "So they became hills—Hollow Hills, with arrogant inhabitants who kept their knowledge of technology and culture—and kept it to themselves."

"Which made them view their fellow colonists with disdain," Gar agreed. "They learned the old fairy tales from their computerized library, invited minstrels in for the night and taught them the stories, then kicked them out to spread the word among the outdoor colonists."

"So they planted the seeds of superstitions, nourished them, then exploited the superstitious fears that grew among the peasants?"

"I would guess so," Gar agreed. "What sort of exploitation did you have in mind?"

Dirk shrugged. "They had to limit population, right? And they only wanted beautiful children—so if a child was born ugly, they fed sleeping gas into a peasant hut where there'd been a baby born, went in and traded their ugly child for the pretty Milesian infant, and let the grieving parents declare they'd had a changeling dumped on them."

"And if the villagers killed the changeling as a sign of evil, the Fair Folk didn't have to feel guilty about it," Gar said grimly.

"I hadn't thought of that," Dirk admitted, "but after a while,

I suspect they were so much afraid of the legends of the Fair Folk that they didn't dare kill the changelings—just raised them with scorn and blame."

"Poor things," Gar muttered, "but it did supply the next generation of bullies."

"And the human babies supplied the Fair Folk with a few servants, and a large enough gene pool to avoid the worst effects of inbreeding," Dirk guessed.

Gar nodded. "Of course, they kept the children who were good-looking, but had to keep the total number of people at the limit of what the dome would hold."

"Right," Dirk said, "and if the birthrate fell too low—people more interested in having fun than babies—the Fair Folk could always kidnap some peasants, babies or full-grown. In fact, there's a tradition of Wee Folk kidnapping new mothers whose babies have died, so that the fairy mothers wouldn't have to nurse their own babies."

"Nurses conveniently supplied by the mothers of changelings whom the villagers have killed," Gar grunted. "The Fair Folk are looking more and more unsavory by the minute."

"Hey, these are just guesses! We might be doing them an injustice."

"I'll try to remember that," Gar sighed. "As the centuries passed, I suspect the Fair Folk began to half believe they really were fairies, or some sort of superior being."

"They certainly do seem to have a condescending attitude," Dirk agreed. "On the other hand, they can't believe in their own superiority too much, or they wouldn't be so careful to make sure the outside world doesn't hear the truth about their mortality and their 'magic.' "

"They certainly are exploiting the Milesians as thoroughly as they can," Gar said grimly. "They have rejected their responsibility toward their fellow beings, indulging themselves in leisure and pleasure, and are paying the price: inbreeding, decadence, and a diminishing population."

Dirk nodded. "Given another few centuries of such living, they'll die out."

"I'd hate to see that," Gar said, frowning. "After all, the Fair Folk have a lot to recommend them."

"Yes. Culture and education, something resembling a legal code, and a minimal form of government, not to mention connection to the rest of human history. The Milesians have forgotten all that."

"Including technology," Gar reminded.

"Yeah, but that includes more than weapons: food synthesizers and medical diagnostic systems, things the rest of the people on this planet really need. Can't we find some way to save them from themselves?"

"Of course," Gar said. "Persuade them to save the rest of their world."

"I think I see what you mean," Dirk said slowly. "They could provide the absolute bare minimum of government and law, and enforce it with their high-tech weapons."

Gar nodded. "They could also look up modern agricultural methods, and boost production of food a hundred times in one generation."

"Malthus' Law," Dirk warned. "Population increases much faster than food supply."

"No matter how fast you increase the food supply," Gar said grimly. "But I think the Fair Folk are past masters of population control."

"Yes, I expect they have that kind of technology, too," Dirk agreed. "You're right—they could save their world from this incessant warfare and the pestilence and starvation that go with it, couldn't they?"

"Yes," Gar agreed, "if we could persuade them to come out of their hills and involve themselves in the lives of the Milesians."

"There is that little problem," Dirk sighed. "How do we solve it?"

Gar stiffened, head cocked as though he were listening. "No time to think about it any more. The Hawks haven't given up. They're still quartering the area, in case we do come out of the Hill!"

17

Dirk grabbed the lieutenant's shoulder and gave it a shake. "Cort! Enemies coming!"

"The Fair Folk?" Cort asked, jarred rudely from his reverie of huge eyes and graceful movements.

"No, the Hawks!"

"You two run to the north," Gar said, frowning. "I'll go south. They won't bother you if I'm not there."

"I've told you before, don't be ridiculous," Dirk snapped.

Cort nodded, glowering. "We don't desert friends."

Gar opened his mouth to argue, but Dirk said, "Besides, they've seen us with you, and they'd probably beat us until we told them where you are—and since we won't know, they just might keep beating until we're dead."

"All right, we all flee together." Gar flashed them a smile that momentarily lit his face with a warmth Cort had never seen. "I'm blessed with such firm friends."

"Your life is our life," Cort quoted. "That's the motto of my company. Where do we run to?"

"Quilichen!" Dirk's eyes lit. "It's the only stronghold that could take us, it's only a day away, and I know Magda wouldn't turn us out!"

Cort glanced at him through transformed eyes, the eyes of a lover, and knew that Magda would indeed not send Dirk away, for he'd seen the same glow in her eyes that he saw in Dirk's.

But not, he realized, the same that he'd seen in Desirée's.

"I hate to bring the Hawk Company down on her head," Gar said, scowling, "but we don't have much choice, do we?"

"Hey, I didn't think of that!" Dirk said, alarmed. "This is a grudge match now, and the Hawks won't rest until they get you! They'll lay siege to Quilichen!"

"They may not break it, but they'll wreak a deal of misery in trying," Cort said grimly. "I can send for the Blue Company to come fetch me out, but I hate to put them all at risk just for my skin."

"Now do you understand why I want you two to leave me?" Gar challenged.

"Yeah, and I understand why we still won't," Dirk said, jaw setting. "Would you have Herkimer pick you up if we did?"

Gar hesitated, then said, "I'm not quite ready to give up on this planet yet, and if Herkimer set me down fifty miles away, the Hawks would find me sooner or later. Better to finish it while we're here."

"Who's Herkimer?" Cort asked.

"A very strange-looking friend," Dirk answered, "who would start a whole set of folktales going on his own."

"He could be a major disruption to your culture," Gar agreed, "and I don't think the Fair Folk would thank us for the ideas he might send running rampant through your world."

Cort frowned, not sure he liked the implication that Gar knew what was good for this world of Durvie and what was not.

"No, we'll try to face them out, but lead them away from Quilichen," Gar said with decision, and turned to forge ahead through the woods.

His big body did at least shove the underbrush out of the way, and Cort followed, doing his best to navigate the uneven ground with horseman's boots. They plowed through a hundred yards of dense undergrowth before Gar stopped suddenly, head raised.

"Worse trouble?" Dirk asked.

"Yes. They've struck our trail," Gar said. "After all, we haven't been trying terribly hard to hide it, have we?"

"Go faster," Dirk urged.

Gar shook his head. "They're ahead of us, closing in from the east—and from the west, too."

"Back the way we came!" Cort cried, a vision of Desirée dancing before him.

But Gar shook his head again. "They closed ranks behind us, too, as soon as the sun was up. I think they watched through the night in case we came out of the hill."

"Just how sharp is your hearing?" Cort asked in frustration.

"Most amazingly sharp," Gar told him. "We're boxed in on three sides. The only way open is the mountainside, where it's too steep for horses."

"And on the other side of that mountain, is Quilichen." Dirk was ashamed of himself; he was feeling jubilant again. After all, if he was thrown on Magda's doorstep through no fault of his own . . .

"Time to climb, gentlemen—if we can reach the mountainside before they do. Let's march!" Gar turned at right angles and plunged off through the underbrush again.

They were in too much of a rush to try to hide their trail, though when they came to a stream, Gar pulled off his boots and waded its length as far as he could without going in the wrong direction. It took a few minutes to dry his feet and pull stockings and boots on again, but in a matter of minutes, they were across the stream and forging uphill.

"Have we reached the mountainside yet?" Dirk asked.

"The grade's not steep enough," Cort told him, then stiffened. "Listen!"

They did. Faint on the breeze came the belling of hounds.

Gar cursed. "I'd hoped they'd left those blasted nuisances

with the farmer they bought them from. Wading that stream won't slow them by more than fifteen minutes now."

"That should be time enough," Cort said. "We're almost to the mountainside."

"You're the one who knows the territory," Dirk grunted.

They toiled uphill, the ground rising more and more steeply, the hounds howling closer and closer. Finally they halted to rest and breathe at the uphill edge of a mountain meadow, turning back to look out over the countryside. The tall trees of the forest lay below them now, the smaller trees of the mountainside around them. The Hollow Hill lay below, too, past the edge of the forest and almost on the horizon.

"Yes, I'd say we're on the mountainside," Dirk said.

Then half a dozen men rode out of the trees at the other side of the meadow, following a peasant who held the leashes of five hounds. The beasts saw the companions and leaped against the leashes, baying eagerly. The horsemen shouted and spurred their horses, leveling their lances.

"Back behind the trees!" Gar snapped. "Climb if you can! If you can't, trip the horses!" He didn't need to say what to do after that.

Cort managed to find a low limb and scrambled up to hide among the leaves. Gar caught up a fallen branch and hid behind a tree. Dirk disappeared.

The horsemen came thundering in. Cort jumped down onto the back of the first, howling as though he were demented, and threw an arm around the man's neck. He wrenched back, and they both fell off to the side, away from the path. Cort twisted as they fell and landed on top. He drew his dagger and struck with the hilt, as he'd seen Gar and Dirk do. Then he scrambled up and spun about, just in time to see Gar leap out and brace one end of the branch against a tree trunk, the other aimed for the midriff of the horseman. He parried the lance with his dagger, and his makeshift staff caught the rider square in the stomach. The Hawk fell, retching.

Then another rider was galloping down on Cort, yelling, his lance pointed squarely at the lieutenant's chest. Cort leaped aside, but the horse's shoulder caught him and sent him spinning against a tree trunk. His head cracked against the wood, and the world went wobbly. He clung to consciousness desperately, working his way back to his feet by clutching the trunk, then turned, shaking his head, to see the lance shooting toward him again. With his last faint hope, he shoved the lancehead aside. It thudded into the tree trunk, and its butt whipped out of the rider's hands. He cursed, turning, and drew his sword.

Cort reversed the spear, braced the butt against the tree, and aimed it at the rider's torso. It caught him on the hip; he screamed, falling, and bright blood stained his livery. Cort yanked the lancehead free and stepped out onto the trail, ready for the next man.

They were all down, and the horses were turning to run back, shying away from the dogs, but sending them into a confused mass. Gar stood over two men, blood streaming from the wound on his hip, but with their lances in his hands, and Dirk had somehow managed to knock out his pair, too, though the side of his face was already swelling.

Then Gar strode back down the path, face contorted with rage. He raised the two spears and roared.

The dogs howled and turned to run, their handler hard on their heels.

"The Hawks will . . . catch them and . . . turn them back on us," Cort panted.

"No doubt." Gar came striding back, grinning. "But it will take time."

"I thought this mountainside was too steep for horses," Dirk said.

"It is," Gar told him. "As you see, the steeds did them absolutely no good. Come, gentlemen—onward and upward."

"Excelsior," Dirk muttered.

"What's that?" Cort asked.

"A strange device, and Heaven knows we've been seeing enough of them lately. Which way is up?"

They plowed on toward the top of the mountain, and though they heard the hounds coming closer after an hour, they weren't moving very rapidly. The Hawks couldn't make any better time on horseback than the companions could on foot, and night fell before they reached the top of the mountain.

When they did reach the peak, Dirk stopped to rest, but Gar said, "You're a very clear silhouette against the stars. Just a few more yards, my friend, to put the mountaintop between us and them."

They climbed over the ridge and started down. When they had made another dozen feet, Gar called a halt. He asked Cort, "What are the odds the Hawks will keep after us even though it's night?"

"No question about it," Cort said. "They'll keep chasing. They'll go slowly, though."

"Especially since they'll be leading their horses," Gar said. "We can go faster than they, for a change. Cort, how far to Quilichen?"

"Four hours' travel," Cort said, "since we've come over the mountain this time, instead of around it."

"But that's when we're fresh," Gar said grimly. "We're tired already. If we're lucky, we'll make it before dawn."

"Only if we can find some way to stall the Hawks," Dirk said. "They're bringing their horses with them, remember?"

"They will go faster than we will once the ground levels out," Gar admitted, "but still no faster than a walk, in the dark and with no road." He handed Cort one of his captured lances. "Use it as a staff. Let's go."

It was a long night, with the Hawks coming closer and closer behind them. They laid false trails, breaking them with streams and rock slides. Time and again they hid, and let a squadron of horse soldiers pass them by. As dawn neared, they were plodding along the bottom of a gully, both because it would hide them and because it might slow the hunters a little. They began to hear the belling of the hounds once more.

"What did they do?" Dirk groaned. "Let them sleep?"

"I suspect they had difficulty driving them back onto our trail, after their fright," Gar said, shoulders slumped with exhaustion.

In spite of his weariness, Dirk looked up at him sharply. "I'll just bet they did! Come on, Cort."

The lieutenant felt as though each foot was made of lead, but forced himself onward sternly, not complaining. "Have we gone far enough along this dry streambed?"

"I'll take a peek and see," Dirk answered, then gritted his teeth and forced each foot up the slope.

Cort took advantage of the opportunity to rest, but knew better than to sit or lie down; he simply leaned against the nearest boulder.

"They'll be on us soon," Gar told him. "If I go off away from you . . ."

"I'll be amazed if you can put one foot in front of the other, let alone outrun me," Cort said though his teeth.

"Is he volunteering for martyrdom again?" Dirk called down.

"I don't know what martyrdom is," Cort called back, "but I think he'd volunteer for anything right now."

"So would I, if it got me out of here." Dirk forced himself up the last foot and gave a cry of delight.

"Can you see it?" Cort stood bolt upright.

"Quilichen's wall!" Dirk called back. "Just enough light to see it by!"

Hope pumped new energy through the other two; they plowed up the side of the slope. Sure enough, there stood the city, looming above the morning mist in the distance.

"Let's go!" Dirk scrambled out, visions of Magda dancing in his head.

Cort put out a hand to stop him, looking back at Gar. "Why are you so slow? We need speed!"

"We need to stop our hunters even more," Gar grunted as he rolled a small boulder into place.

Cort's eyes widened. "No man can move a stone that heavy!"

"There's a trick to it," Gar wheezed.

"There sure is," Dirk said darkly.

Gar grunted again as he pushed the stone over the edge. It rolled downhill faster and faster, landing with a dull thud.

"Rolled halfway up the other side and rolled down again," Gar panted with satisfaction as he came up to them. "It wiped out our tracks on the way down—and should cause them a little trouble getting past it."

"Yes, if no one there is smart enough to realize we pushed it!" Dirk snapped.

Cort nodded. "It will show them where we left the gully."

Gar looked surprised, then crestfallen.

"At least the hounds won't have a trail to follow," Dirk sighed. "Come on! If you can run, do. If you can't, jog!"

They set off toward the city while the sky reddened behind them. They were halfway there before the belling began.

"Boulder didn't fool 'em for long," Dirk grunted. "Run!"

The hounds grew louder, and hooves drummed, oddly muffled by the mist. The three fugitives stumbled wearily on, eyes fixed on the wall ahead, none able to spare breath to cheer the others on. The hoofbeats grew louder and louder. Glancing back, Cort saw riders coming out of the mist a hundred yards behind. "Run!" he shouted, and sprinted hard.

The hoofbeats came faster.

"Hello the wall!" Dirk cried. "Sanctuary! Help! Save us!"

"We were your guests!" Cort shouted.

"These riders are the men you banished!" Gar bellowed.

Figures appeared atop the wall, staring, then raising bows. One sprinted off along the battlements. The others weighed the sight, then pointed their arrows upward and loosed. Cort cried out in despair—but the arrows arced over their heads and down, thudding into the earth in a line between hunters and hunted.

"They recognized us!" Dirk cried in jubilation.

The Hawks reined in, shouting in alarm. On the wall, a voice barked orders, and the gate swung open. The companions cried out in relief and thanks and forced themselves into one final, stumbling run. The Hawks shouted again, but in anger now, and spurred their horses.

Another line of arrows fell, these right beside them and in front of their mounts. Horses reared, shying from the swift points, and horsemen bellowed.

The companions pounded through the gate. A voice shouted atop the wall, and the great panels began to shut. The Hawks howled in rage and frustration and galloped toward the gate, their spears high.

Another volley of arrows stitched a line in front of them.

This time they took the warning; they sheered off and rode away, turning back to shake their fists with angry shouts.

The gates shut with a boom, and the great bar dropped across them. The three companions fell to the ground and lay or knelt, heaving great gulps of air. The officer of the day came down from the wall and knelt by Gar. "They were waiting for you, hey?"

Gar could only wheeze and nod.

"What of the rest of your men?" the officer asked, his face somber.

"I sent them back by another route," Cort gasped.

The officer turned to him, surprised. "Won't they have been slain?"

"No," Gar panted, "because . . . we found out . . . they're only after me."

The officer stared at him in alarm, and Dirk didn't need to be a mind reader to see the unspoken exclamation: *Throw him out!* But he didn't say so, for which Dirk was unreasonably grateful.

Then his reason arrived with a flurry of hooves and a cry from the heart.

18

Looking up, Dirk saw an escort of soldiers surrounding Magda, all reining in. She swung down from her horse and ran to him, hair disheveled, gown very obviously the first thing that came to hand. Dirk could only think, *So this is what she looks like first thing in the morning,* and found himself wishing he could be there to see the sight for years to come. He shoved himself to his feet, arms wide to catch her.

Magda threw herself into his arms and planted a long, delirious kiss on his lips. When she shoved herself away, she demanded, "Have they hurt you?"

"Nothing that won't heal in a few days." Dirk panted. After all, he hadn't caught his breath the first time.

"If they had slain you, I would have warred on the Hawk Company!" Magda told him, her voice hinting at massacres. "If they dare come against you again, I will slay them all, even if it means my death!"

"No!" Dirk pressed both her hands between his own. "I don't want your death, I want your life! With mine!"

She stared, suddenly trembling. "I don't think you meant that as it sounded, sir."

"I think I did," Dirk said slowly.

She swayed toward him, eyelids drooping, and their kiss was even longer. When it ended, Dirk held her at arm's length and said, very seriously, "No matter what happens, *you* have to live!"

"Then *I* must go."

Turning, they saw Gar looming over them like Fate, his face somber.

"Not a word of it!" Magda snapped. "The friend of my friend is mine, too! You shall stay, and we shall fight to the last for you!"

"I will not have the deaths of a whole city on my conscience," Gar told her, "nor of you and Dirk, when you might be beginning a whole life of joy. I'll only ask that you give me a horse, preferably your biggest."

Dirk turned to her, his heart wrenching. "Please understand. I have to go with him, no matter how much I want to stay with you. I can't let him face them alone."

"Nor can I," she said, chin firming with stubbornness. She turned back to Gar. "I will not risk this man for your noble wish of death! You must stay and live!"

"And how many of your people will die?" Gar demanded.

"Few or none!" Magda looked around at her officers and saw the same resolve on their faces. She turned back to Gar. "It's too late in any event. If we give you up now, the Hawk Company will think us weak, and ripe for the taking—and like as not, they'll league with several other mercenary companies. All their captains dream of becoming bosses in their own right, and will see Quilichen as their chance!"

"That's true," Cort said grimly. Breath caught, he came to his feet and confronted Gar. "If you wish to save them, my friend, you had better think up a way to give them a quick victory."

Four days later, a caravan appeared, heralded by the hoarse cries of the drivers as they urged their exhausted donkeys to one last effort. Their leader rode ahead of them, waving to the guards and crying, "Sanctuary!"

Gar was taking his turn as officer of the watch at the time, and trying to ignore the resentment of some of the troopers—not that he could blame them for it. The merchant was a welcome diversion. He looked down from the wall, then stared. "Master Ralke?"

"Gar Pike!" The merchant stared back, completely amazed. "So this is why you didn't return to guard us again!"

"Let him in," Gar called to the gate guards. "I know him; he's an honest man."

Ralke rode in, dismounted, and hurried up to the wall as his caravan entered the city. Once inside, the donkeys slowed, stopped, and dug in their heels in sheer exhaustion. Ralke bustled up to Gar. "Beware, sergeant! There are two companies of mercenaries riding toward you, and a boss with all his bullies!"

"Two companies?" Gar stared. "The Hawks I know of—but who else?"

Ralke shook his head. "I saw them from the top of a ridge, and rode for the nearest town; I couldn't tell who they were."

"Serves me right for not listening," Gar muttered. "I should be more suspicious." Then, to Ralke, "So the Hawks have managed an alliance." He made a mental note to investigate telepathicially when he could find a few minutes alone. "Thank you for the news, merchant. I believe the castellan will welcome you and your men, but you'll have to help in the defense."

"Our chances are far better inside this wall than outside it," Ralke said fervently.

"I will give you warning," Gar said slowly. "It's I the soldiers are chasing—or at least the Hawks are."

"The Hawks?" Ralke stared. "What did you do to offend them?"

"Caught Torgi out in his mistranslating scheme. He hired the Hawks to assassinate me."

Ralke grinned. "They haven't done very well, have they?" Then he realized the implications. "But if Torgi sent them after you, he'll probably send them after me, too!"

"You seem to have been wise in running for cover," Gar told him.

Ralke frowned. "Where did a mere steward find money enough to hire a whole company?"

"Yes," Gar said. "That is an interesting question, isn't it?"

He reported the information to Magda at the end of his watch, and she received it with indifference. "If they're here for one of you, why not have them here for both?" But she was holding Dirk's hand, and the glow in her face might have had more to do with her indifference to threat than logic did. For Dirk's part, he could scarcely take his eyes off her, and Gar felt a stab of envy. "Where's Cort?"

"Haven't seen him much," Dirk answered. "Kind of strange, isn't it?"

"Absolutely," Gar told him, poker faced.

Dirk managed to tear his eyes away from Magda. "Any ideas on how to save us all yet?"

"Aside from the obvious," Gar said, pointing upward, "not much. A merchant just arrived tells me that *two* mercenary companies are marching toward us, as well as a boss with all his bullies."

Magda finally looked up, dismayed. "Those are great odds indeed!"

"Can't you bring any other kind of force against them?" Dirk demanded.

Magda turned to frown at him. "How could he?"

Gar sighed. "We've met a duke on our travels. He's going to dream about a wizard tonight."

"How will that help us?" Magda asked, then frowned. "There are no dukes in this land, only bosses." Again, the implications hit her, and she stared, then exclaimed, "And how would you know what he'll dream?"

* * *

The duke did dream. He usually slept without disturbance, but this night, he dreamed of a void, and a white spot appeared within it, a spot that grew and swelled, until he could see it was a face, a human face, with long, long white hair and a longer white beard that swirled about it. Closer it came and closer, until it stared him eye to eye and intoned, "Avaunt! Avoid the dark giant!"

"What giant?" the duke demanded in his dream. "Do you mean that loutish outlander who overtopped even the Fair Folk? If I never see him again, it will be too soon!"

"You lie," the wizard intoned. "You plan to track him as the quarry of the Wild Hunt at Midsummer! But that will be too late, for the armies gather to besiege Quilichen and seize the outlander! They will put him to the torture, they will tear his knowledge from him!"

"Then we must capture him at once, and not wait upon them!" the duke declared in his dream.

"Harm him not!" the face commanded, its voice echoing all about the duke.

The duke quailed within, but hid it well—after all, he knew the trick of the reverberating voice, had used it often enough himself. "I might have let him be, but not after you have come cawing to disturb my slumber. Who are you, anyway?"

But the face was receding, shrinking, too fast to catch even if the duke had had hands in his dream. The mystic voice echoed again, "Harm him not!"

"I shall harm him so that he wishes he'd never been born!" the duke roared. "Tell me your name!"

But the hair and beard swirled up to hide the face, and the wizard shrank to a dot, a point, and disappeared, leaving behind it one last echo: *Harm him not!*

The duke awoke, trembling, but covering his fear with rage. "Not harm him? I shall harm him most shrewdly, once I catch him—if for no other reason than to make him tell me how he has put this dream into my mind!"

* * *

The people of the farms and villages streamed into Quilichen, driving their cattle with them and carting their household goods and food stocks. There was amazingly little confusion.

Dirk stared down from the castle wall at the farmers driving their cattle into hastily built pens in the park at the town's center. "And I thought you folk had just had the good sense to leave a large common for recreation!"

"We could not have justified so much space only for pleasure," Magda said with a smile, holding onto his arm.

"But they're all going right to the pens, then directly to a section of campground, without even asking!"

"They have done this before, haven't they?" Gar asked. "And frequently, too, to judge by the smoothness of it all."

Magda nodded. "At least once every three years, and sometimes more often than that."

Dirk shuddered.

By the end of the second day, the farmers were all inside, setting up housekeeping at their campsites as though they had lived there for years, and the town was rancid with the smell of livestock. The next morning, the besiegers began to appear. By the afternoon of the fourth day, they had surrounded the city in five separate camps, with space for a sixth.

"Three bosses?" Gar asked, looking out at the banners.

Magda nodded. "I see the insignia of the Boss of Loutre; him alone I did not expect. But the other two are my neighbors, the Boss of Knockenburg and the Boss of Scurrilein. I knew they would come to pick the carcass—and be sure none others took the land."

"Which means that if they defeat you, they'll fall to fighting over the spoils," Gar said grimly.

"Even so," Magda said. "It will be shrewd fighting indeed, for each has hired a mercenary company to protect his interests." She pointed. "Behold the banners of the Hawk and the Bear!" Her fingers dug into Dirk's arm. He winced and patted her hand.

"The Hawks were hired by the steward of the Boss of Loutre, and I've no doubt that boss is here on my account," Gar said darkly, "though I would love to know how his steward persuaded him to march against you."

That was code for Gar to be able to tell the results of his mind-spying publicly, and Dirk knew the response. "Make a guess."

"I would conjecture that he has told the boss that I cheated him, and that rather badly," Gar said, "perhaps even that I'm trying to persuade Quilichen to attack, and giving Lady Magda details of Loutre's defenses."

"Sounds probable," Dirk allowed, then stiffened, staring out over the fields. "Who's that coming?"

Drumbeats came faintly as a host of men came marching down the road toward the gap in the enemy lines.

"The missing ally," Gar said.

All four strained to make out the symbol on the company's banner that streamed over the heads of the marching men. Closer they came, closer and closer . . .

"The Blue Company!" Cort cried. "My own men to me!" He turned to Magda with a face twisted by anguish. "My lady, I can't fight against my own company!"

"That you cannot," she agreed, troubled.

"Would they march on Quilichen if they knew one of their officers had been given sanctuary here?" Gar asked.

Cort stared at him, hope rising, then turned to gaze out at the approaching troops. "Most likely not! But how shall I tell Captain Devers?"

"Call for a parley," Dirk suggested, "and let Cort carry the flag of truce."

So Cort rode out with a white flag and an honor guard of a dozen archers, their bows ostentatiously slung across their backs. They rode around the castle to the eastern quadrant where the Blue Company stood. Devers took one look at the blue livery under the pale banner and came riding.

"How did you come here, lieutenant?" he demanded.

Cort gave him the condensed version, and Devers's face swelled darker and darker as he heard how two strangers had fought beside his men, enlisted in the Blue Company, and been chased for days by the Hawks, then taken shelter in Quilichen.

"Sergeant Otto told me some of this when he met me on the road," he told Cort, "but I hadn't known you had taken sanctuary in Quilichen again. There can be no question of our fighting against your hosts. Come back to our camp now."

"By your leave, captain," Cort said, bracing himself, "I'm honorbound to help defend the city that has saved me."

"Of course you are, and so am I! The company shall march to resign the contract with the Boss of Knockenburg, and pay back the moneys he has advanced us—but bid your folk be ready to open their gates, for we may have to fight our way to you, and be in need of shelter quickly!"

"Captain, I thank you with all my heart," Cort said fervently.

Devers shrugged impatiently. "The soldier is loyal to the company, and the company is loyal to the soldier. No mercenary band can hold together otherwise. Go ask your hosts for hospitality for more guests."

No one tried to stop the Blue Company from entering the city, though—the sight of all those men marching in perfect formation to confront the Boss of Knockenburg seemed to give them second thoughts. They were almost to the city wall before the boss gave the order to charge. Devers relied on Magda and ordered his men to run, telling only the archers at the rear to fight. Two flights of arrows gave the Boss's army second thoughts; they veered aside as the gates opened and the Blue Company went pelting in.

The Hawk Company, though, was more alert than the boss; when the gate opened, the brown-coated soldiers charged with a roar. Improbable though it seemed, one flying squad made it to the gate before it closed. They shot the porters, then hauled the great doors open. The rest of the company came thundering up, but a flight of arrows from the wall slowed them, while Gar and Cort came bellowing out with a score of Blue soldiers behind them, to knock the Hawks away from the gates. Arrows from the wall pierced the men. They fell howling, and the gates closed again, leaving the Hawk cavalry no choice but to swerve aside, cursing. Arrows stitched a dead-line across the roadway, and the infantry fell back, seeing no purpose in risking their lives to reach closed, guarded doors.

Cort brought his captain up to the wall to meet Magda. Devers bowed over her hand. "My lady! My deepest thanks for having sheltered my men!"

"It was our privilege, captain," she said. "May *we* hire the Blue Company now?"

"You may not, lady! We are already in your debt, and will pay it with blood and steel instead of gold!"

"You are too generous." Magda had to blink a few times before she could go on. "How did you come here?"

"We were hired by Knockenburg," Devers told her. "The boss told me that the Boss of Loutre had allied with him and persuaded both himself and Scurrilein to bring down Quilichen, because he felt that all merchants, and therefore all free towns, were growing too strong, and would eventually corrupt all the bosstowns with their notions of freedom and prosperity for all."

Magda stared. "Wherever would the Boss of Loutre have garnered such an idea?"

"From his steward," Gar said grimly. "Torgi wouldn't care what arguments he used, so long as he maneuvered his boss into marching. He's seen that the Hawk Company alone can't kill me, especially not while I have your protection, my lady, so he has stirred up a war to destroy Quilichen, all to make sure I won't tell his boss what he's been doing." He turned to Magda, bowing. "My lady, once again I offer . . ."

"No!" she snapped. "When we say we have given you shelter,

we stand by our word! So, captain, the bosses have decided to attack the free towns and conquer them before we grow any stronger, and they mean to begin with Quilichen. Is there no thought that they will abandon this madness even if Quilichen falls, or do they truly mean to destroy all?"

"I fear they will finish what they've begun," Devers said heavily. "No matter where the idea came from or why, once it's born and about, it won't die, but will grow."

"So all the free towns will be destroyed, just for one steward's vendetta," Dirk said bitterly.

"Can this steward Torgi really have stirred up a campaign against all the free towns just to rid himself of the evidence against him?" Cort asked in disbelief.

"He certainly can," Gar said grimly.

Magda asked Devers, "How much chance have we of holding against them?"

"Two Free Companies, with the weight of three bosses' forces behind them?" Devers looked out over the field, his face grim. "Your walls are stout, my lady, and your archers skilled and brave. With my men beside them, we have a chance—but I cannot say how strong that chance may be."

"Will nothing turn them aside?"

"We can always parley," Gar said.

Devers shook his head. "It will do no good."

"Perhaps not," Gar said, "but it will do no harm, either—and it will, at least, postpone their first attack."

So the trumpets sounded, the gates opened, and Gar rode out under a white flag—with Cort and Dirk beside him to make sure he didn't try to give himself up. But they were scarcely clear of the gates when a trumpet blew, men roared, and the Boss of Knockenburg charged them with all his men, while the Hawk Company came riding from the left, along the wall, and the Bear Company came riding from the right. They had chosen their moment well—the porters had to keep the gates open until their men were back inside. The archers laid a row of arrows in front of the boss's men, and they shied, enough so their brutes had to roar and rant to make them start again. That bought enough time for the parley party to turn back—but the cavalry companies were another matter. The archers shot down at them, but they were so close to the wall that the arrows couldn't reach them. Archers fired their next volley straight down through the slots in the battlements that were usually reserved for boiling oil, but they weren't big enough for good aim, and only a few soldiers fell from their horses. The others thundered closer, nearly to the gate . . .

A hundred trumpets blasted, and lances of light stabbed the foremost riders on each side of the gate. They fell, and their horses reared and turned as thunder cracked all about them, deafening in its intensity. The light-lances stabbed again, scoring the walls, and all the riders pulled up, crying out in fear. Then a huge voice bellowed over the whole plain, "Now I say *hold*!"

All the fighting men froze, looking about them, then up to the hilltop where the Fair Folk stood, tall and severe, cloaks whipping in the wind, cowls deep to shield them from the sun, huge dark blisters where their eyes should be, making them seem half-human and half-insect. Only Dirk and Gar recognized those blisters as sun goggles.

There were a hundred of them at least.

"We hold all the heights!" the duke's voice thundered. "Look about you! If any disobeys the Fair Folk, he shall die on a lance of lightning!"

To emphasize the point, a lance from the east hissed through the pole holding the Boss of Loutre's standard. It fell, and the assembled soldiers raised a torrent of talk. Some turned to run, but laser-bolts burned the grass at the back of their armies, and they froze in fear. Finally they looked around, and saw more Fair Folk darkening the summits of the hills to every side.

"Where did he get them all?" Dirk wondered, amazed.

"I suspect he called in allies from other hills," Gar told him, "and half of them are wearing skirts, if that makes any difference."

"When they're holding laser rifles? It sure does make a difference, to these medieval militarists!"

"You talk as though you know the Fair Folk," Magda quavered.

Dirk turned to her, suddenly intent, taking her hands. "We spent a night in their hill, my lady, hiding from the Hawks. They would have kept us there, but we escaped. I suspect they don't feel kindly toward us because of that."

Fear was still there, but anger rose in Magda behind it. She trembled and her voice shook, but there was iron resolution in it. "They shall not have you!"

"Not while you're here to come to," Dirk whispered.

"Room for the Duke of the Hollow Hill!" another voice blasted, and the duke and an entourage of twenty rifle-bearers strode down the hillside. An avenue opened for them like magic, steadily expanding as they strolled along it, rifles at the ready. All eyes were on them, everyone silent in superstitious fear as the Fair Folk exerted what they regarded as their inborn right to rule.

Squarely between armies and wall, the duke stopped and glared up at Gar, where he stood near Magda, somehow conveying the impression of looking down his nose. "This tall Milesian and his friends have angered the Fair Folk! We have come forth by daylight to hale them home! Give them up to us, and no harm shall befall you!"

Magda stood forth, trembling, but her voice was iron-hard as she called down, "Never! They are our guests, and we shall never give them up! It is our honor!"

"And it is the honor of the Fair Folk to have them!" the duke bellowed. "Let fire fall upon this city!"

On the hillside opposite the gate, Fair Folk stepped aside, revealing a squat cylinder as wide as a human arm was long.

"They brought a beam projector!" Dirk hissed.

Lightning spat and exploded against the gates of the city. They flew apart, bits of wood raining down everywhere. The gateway to the city stood, open and empty.

The assembled armies strained forward with a roar.

The ball of lightning exploded before them, blasting a crater in the ground. With a moan of superstitious dread, the soldiers pulled back.

"Give them up to us," the duke commanded, "or every building in your town shall suffer that fate!"

Dirk exploded louder than the cannon. "Get back into your Hollow Hills!" he bellowed, stepping forward on the ramparts. "Who do you think you are, coming out here and threatening good people whose only fault is sheltering fugitives? Who gave you the right? Do you think your ancestors would be proud of you? With every word you say, you bring down their wrath upon you!"

"Be still!" the duke roared, his voice thunder that echoed off the hillsides. "You are a troll of a Milesian, and unworthy to so much as look upon the Fair Folk!"

Magda tugged at Dirk's hand, trying to pull him back to safety, but he bellowed on. "And you are unworthy of your lineage! Your ancestors were men and women of peace! They came here so that all people could be equal to one another, none oppressing the other! If they look down upon you now, they're turning their faces away in shame!"

"Slay me this Milesian!" the duke demanded, and rifles from every hillside centered on Dirk.

Before they could fire, though, he bellowed in full rage. "Oh, yes, slay me on lightning! Shoot me down from a mile's distance! Bravely done, very bravely indeed! You don't even have the courage to come against a Milesian face-to-face!"

The whole valley was silent, frozen, aghast. Then the duke's voice answered, softly, but amplified so that everyone could hear: "Is that a challenge, small man?"

"Dirk, no!" Magda gasped.

"It's the only way," Dirk muttered to her. Then to the duke, "A challenge, yes, and if I win, you and all your people shall go away, and drive these bosses and their cattle before you!"

"Done!" the duke said, and the gloating was plain in his voice for all to hear. "Come down, little fellow, and you shall be privileged to die upon a sword of the Fair Folk!"

Dirk stepped down, and Magda clung to him, weeping openly. "My darling, no! To have found you, only to lose you!"

"All I care is that you come unscathed through this mess I've brought down on you," Dirk said, then as an afterthought, "and all the people you care for, too."

Magda straightened, imperious and commanding. "I am the castellan of Quilichen, and while you are here, you are under my authority! I command you not to go!" She turned on Gar. "You! Go in his place!"

"Gladly, for it is I who have brought these Fair Folk upon you," Gar said, frowning, "and all the bosses and their mercenaries besides. Let me fight him, Dirk." The look he gave his friend said plainly, *For no lover shall miss me if I die.*

"I can't send another man to fight my battles," Dirk told Magda gravely.

"Then let him fight his own! I am mistress here, and you must obey me!"

"So you think I can't defend myself from this lanky lout?" Dirk demanded. "But the giant can?"

"It's not that at all," Magda snapped. "It's simply that I don't mind losing *him*!"

Dirk took her hand, staring into her eyes. "Does that mean that you don't want to lose me?"

"Haven't I only now said it?" Magda demanded fiercely, then wilted. "Yes! It does mean that I do not want to lose you! I have lost one love—I do not wish to lose another! O my darling, if you die in this duel, you shall break my heart again!"

Dirk gazed into her eyes, face totally serious, then very deliberately gathered her into his arms and kissed her.

Everyone on the battlements was quiet, watching. Gar glowered down, his face stone.

Dirk ended the kiss and stepped away, still holding his gaze on hers, still holding her hands. "I have to fight him now, for I've given him a challenge, and if I don't meet it, he'll take it out on you and your people."

"Is that all?" Magda cried.

"No," Dirk said evenly. "The real reason is because if I don't, I'll never be able to look in a mirror again, much less look at you without shame." He released her hands and turned to the stairway—and to Gar, who stood at their head. "Out of my way, old friend. It's time to earn my life."

Gar glowered down at him a moment longer, then bowed his head and stepped aside. The ranks of soldiers parted for Dirk, many removing their hats in respect as he passed. Out the main gates he went, striding to meet the duke.

"He must not die!" Magda stepped close to Gar.

He reached out to put an arm around her shoulders. "He won't, my lady. That much I can promise you."

19

Dirk bowed to the Fair Man, who stood easily a foot and a half taller than he. The duke grinned down at the smaller man. "Do you truly believe you can best a duke of the Fair Folk?"

"You don't seem all that fair at the moment," Dirk retorted. "Where I come from, I'm not exactly what people call a true believer—but I do think I can fence you to a standstill, yes."

"Then be on your guard!" the duke cried, and drew his sword.

But Dirk's blade was shorter, and cleared the scabbard first. He only held it on guard, but everyone could see his sword leveled as the duke's came up, and knew he could have lunged and brought first blood. The duke reddened and tapped Dirk's blade to open the duel, then instantly circled and thrust.

Dirk parried and counterthrust without riposting. He aimed for the duke's shoulder, but the tall man was quick enough to pull back so that Dirk only grazed his knuckles. Still, a line of blood showed on the duke's hand, and the crowd burst into furious comment, amazed that a mortal should draw first blood after all.

The duke sprang back, eyes narrowing, sword and dagger up to guard, lips pressed against the pain in his left hand. Then his rapier began to whirl in a mad figure eight, and he sprang in.

Dirk gave way, and gave and gave, parrying madly as the duke's blade sprang out of its whirl to slash at him, then sprang back into its spin. Again and again he struck, slamming through Dirk's defense to score the shorter man on cheek, hip, ear—none more than a scratch, but enough to leave his opponent bleeding. Once Dirk didn't leap back quite far enough, and the duke's point ripped his doublet. Redness welled through the cut, and Magda screamed, but Dirk fought madly on, crying, "Only a scratch, Lord Duke! Can't your long arms strike farther than that?"

The duke reddened and threw himself into a lunge. Dirk hopped nimbly to the left, pressed the duke's sword down with his own, and stabbed his dagger into the duke's shoulder. The duke cried out and went pale with the pain, nearly dropping his blade, and Dirk leaped back, sword and dagger up to guard, then quickly leaping in with a double thrust.

But the duke sprang back and managed to hold his sword securely enough to parry Dirk's dagger while he caught the rapier on his own poniard. Dirk leaped back good and far, and the duke took advantage of the pause to switch blades, his dagger now in the weakened right hand, his rapier in the left. Then he came after Dirk, blood in his eye, sword whirling just as deftly in the left hand as it had in the right, and the crowd murmured in awe; true switch-swordsmen were very rare.

Dirk gave ground, wary of the ambidexter, unused to the sword coming at him from his right. He parried it well enough, though, and caught the duke's dagger-stabs on his own shorter blade. The duke was clumsy enough to give him several openings, but Dirk couldn't take advantage of them, because the sword was on the wrong side. Seeing his discomfiture, the duke grinned and thrust straight for his belly. Dirk leaped aside, but the left-handed blade sagged and sliced across his thigh. Dirk's leg folded.

The duke cried out with triumph and leaped in, blade darting downward. But Dirk parried with his own sword, forcing himself to his feet—and the duke pivoted in, dagger plunging straight toward Dirk's eye.

Swordsman the duke may have been, but not a black belt. Dirk ducked under the dagger and thrust his own upward. He was inside the duke's guard, and his blade jabbed deep into the duke's triceps. His Grace howled with anger and pain, leaping away, and his dagger dropped from nerveless fingers.

The crowd roared.

Dirk followed up the advantage, limping after the duke, but the taller man held him off left-handed, rapier weaving an incredible pattern as it beat off first sword, then dagger, then sword again. Apparently thwarted, Dirk gave ground again, but the duke followed him closely, thrust—and Dirk's blade spun in a tight circle, then away, and the duke's sword went spinning through the air.

Then Dirk ducked and swung back in, once more inside the duke's guard, sword edge swinging up to press against the duke's throat, dagger poised before his eyes. The duke froze.

Dirk waited while the crowd went wild.

The duke's glare was pure venom, but finally he moved stiff lips enough to say, "I yield me."

Dirk leaped back, lowering his blades. The duke's dagger arm twitched with the urge to run him through, but honor won out; he reversed his weapon, and held it out hilt first to Dirk.

Dirk took it and bowed. Then his right leg crumpled under him again. The duke tensed, ready to spring, but he had yielded already. Besides, Dirk held both daggers and his own sword, still up to guard, his glare still alert. Muscle by muscle, the duke relaxed.

Cort stepped forward, offering his arm, and Dirk took it, pulling himself up, as Gar stepped between the two combatants. He bowed and asked, "My lord duke, is honor satisfied?"

"It is," the duke said, though each word cost him dear.

The Fair Folk erupted into shocked and furious denunciations. The duke held up a hand to stop them. "It was fairly fought, and fairly won!"

Dirk stopped and turned back. "Thank you, Your Grace, but I had an advantage—I was shorter."

In spite of himself, a thin smile tugged at the corners of the duke's mouth. The Fair Folk fell silent, staring in amazement.

"You were a worthy opponent," the duke replied, calling out so that everyone could hear him. "Never have I seen a Milesian who fights like one of the Fair Folk."

Dirk only bowed in mute acknowledgement of the compliment—and nearly fell. Cort hauled up on the shoulder and snapped, "Inside the gates and lying down! Now!"

"Go, worthy adversary," the duke said, managing to regain both his poise and his air of authority.

Dirk bowed again, but not so deeply, then turned to limp with Cort toward the gate. A dozen men of the Blue Company came running out to meet him, scooping him up, hoisting him to their shoulders, and carrying him through the gateway in triumph—where they instantly lowered him, and Magda ran to him with a cry of anguish, then tore his hose off, crying, "Hot water! Soap! Bandages!"

"Brandy," Dirk croaked. Magda glared at him, and he explained, "For the wound. You're the only intoxication I need."

She melted, her eyes misted over, and she caught him up in her arms for a kiss that lasted until the bandages came.

On the battlefield, Gar said, "A word in private, if I may, lord duke?"

"Only if you can explain how a Milesian bested a duke of the Fair Folk," the duke snapped.

Gar smiled and stepped close, speaking softly. "Easily done, Your Grace. To you and your people, fighting is only a game, a matter of skill in competition, but these whom you call Milesians are bred to war; to them, it's a way of life."

The duke's face darkened with anger, and he started to speak.

"More politely put," Gar said quickly, "the Fair Folk have only trained themselves for individual combat of a sporting kind, but the Milesians are trained to fight as armies, and to them, it's anything but a sport. They will do whatever they must, in order to win."

The duke knit his brows in thought.

"Can you imagine," Gar asked, "what a troop of professional mercenaries could do against a troop of Fair Folk, if superstitious fear didn't stop them? And I assure you, they would lose their awe of your lasers very quickly."

The duke stared, horrified at the image Gar's words conjured up. Shaken, he protested, "Enemies could never break into the Hollow Hills!"

"True," Gar agreed, "but the Fair Folk would thereby be imprisoned in their domes, never to ride in procession again, nor to visit one another's hills. Moreover, if the Milesians lay siege to you, and you dare open your portal for any reason whatsoever, they'll find a way to jam it before you can close it."

"We shall burn them by the hundred with our lasers!"

"And a thousand more will come streaming in, when your power supplies are spent. They have what you have not, lord duke: numbers."

The duke stared off into space, his attention on the inner picture, shaken to his core. Then he frowned, turning to Gar again. "You do not tell me this out of concern for my welfare. Why do you strive so to convince me? What do you want me to do?"

"The only thing you can, to assure the safety of your people," Gar said, "for your only true defense is to come out of your hills and go among the Milesians, taking your rightful places as wise people and councillors, teaching them the ways of peace—while your people can still intimidate them with the force of legend."

The duke glowered, but turned to look out over the field, then gave a reluctant nod. "You have chosen the right time and place to speak of this, for we have cowed these armies, and if ever this process of our leading is to begin, it must be now. I shall call a council of the dukes who have brought their people here. What measures do you suggest I take with these recalcitrant warriors for the moment?"

"To establish your authority," Gar said carefully, "I would insist they resolve this war without bloodshed."

The duke spat an oath and asked, "How shall they do that?"

"They have all come because the Boss of Loutre stirred them up," Gar explained, "but Loutre has come because his steward Torgi has persuaded him to do so. Torgi, though, spoke not out of concern for the bosses' welfare, but for his own selfish reasons: he wanted myself and a merchant named Ralke slain, because we know that he has been cheating his boss by mistranslating when he talks to the merchants, telling the boss the prices are higher than the merchants are really asking, and keeping the difference for himself."

"Treachery!" The duke's eyes glittered. "Yes, that they will understand, and will turn their anger away from this town and direct it toward the swindler! But what evidence shall we bring?"

"My own statement, and that of the merchant, who is sheltering here," Gar said. "There is also the testimony of a sergeant of the Boss of Loutre, who was the first to accept payment from Torgi to kill us, and the captain of the Hawk Company, whom Torgi hired to catch and slay us—and I'm sure the Boss of Loutre will want to know where his steward found money enough to hire a whole company."

The duke's thin smile widened. "What punishment shall I suggest?"

"They will want to hang him at the least," Gar said, "but may also want to draw and quarter him first. However, it would increase the prestige of the Fair Folk if you demanded the privilege of punishing him yourself, taking him back to your hill for a lifetime of servitude, never to be seen by mortal folk again."

"You hint at some other fate," the duke accused.

Gar nodded. "It occurs to me that you might place a sumptuous meal before him, watch till he falls asleep, and place him in one of your cryogenic chambers. Then, if the Milesian leaders grow too arrogant, you might find use for a mischief-maker who could ingratiate himself into court after court and foment dissension, setting the Milesians against one another, until only the Fair Folk could resolve their disputes and restore order again."

The duke glared at him. "Are you always so devious?"

"Only when I'm inspired, my lord."

"Then I trust you will find yourself inspired to leave our world quickly, as soon as you have seen that we have done as you suggest."

"I know you will do whatever is best for the Fair Folk," Gar returned. "If by some accident it is also best for the Milesians, I'm sure that's none of my concern."

"No, now that you're done with it. Very well, I shall talk to my fellow dukes. Do talk to the captains, and to the castellan of this town."

Gar took that as a dismissal. He bowed, then straightened and turned away.

"Oh, and Milesian!" the duke called.

Gar turned back, his expression all polite inquiry. "Yes, my lord?"

"How did you send that wizard into my dream?"

Gar fought to keep his smile from becoming too broad. "Only a favor between friends, my lord."

"You know this wizard, then?"

"As well as I know myself, my lord."

The captains and bosses came reluctantly to the council commanded by the Fair Folk, but under the muzzles of six beam projectors, they did come. The duke had commanded a dais be placed and a canopy raised above it, to shelter himself and his retinue, a dozen of the Fair Folk in their most lavish finery. Those whom the scowls of the tall men did not intimidate were charmed by the beauty and grace of the fairy women. The Milesian leaders came and sat in the semicircle of hourglass-shaped chairs, richly carved of glossy dark wood, facing the dais and the gilded chairs in which sat the Fair Folk. Magda sat with Dirk beside her, holding tightly to his hand and not caring who saw. On her other side sat Captain Devers, then the other captains, and beyond them, the bosses. Behind all of them stood their bodyguards, but none wore weapons, for the mighty beam projectors frowned on all of them.

The duke sat in front of all the other Fair Folk, glaring down sternly at the Milesians through his bulging dark goggles. "I shall tell you what you will do," he declared, bluntly and brutally.

Milesian faces darkened; captains and bosses shifted in their chairs, anger warring with superstitious fear—but none spoke.

"Good. You understand that you shall obey, if you wish to live, and your people with you." The duke left them no room for pride. "You will return to your strongholds and castles straightaway, with no attacking of one another on your journey—and be sure that Fair Folk eyes shall watch your every step! Once home, you will never war upon one another again without permission of the Fair Folk!"

Now, even among the watching officers and bouncers, faces darkened with anger, and several of the bosses and captains reached for their swords, on the verge of rebellion.

The duke touched his medallion, and his words broke over them like thunder. "Do not even think to disobey!"

They all jumped in their seats and gripped the arms of their chairs, eyes wide and backs chilling with terror.

The duke touched his medallion again, and his voice was normal once more. "Know that this whole war on Quilichen is misbegotten and misguided! You think you come to destroy a threat to your established order, but you have been deceived and cozened into fighting a baseborn knave's cause!"

The bosses stared, then turned to one another in furious question.

"We knew this from the beginning," the duke lied, "and laughed at your folly, at how easily you let a liar lead you by the noses! But when so many come against one on the word of a cutpurse, the Fair Folk are filled with such outrage that we can no longer be still, nor let you tear one another apart!" He gave them a thin and nasty smile. "After all, it amuses an idle hour. Know, then, that this whole campaign is due only to the selfish intriguing of the steward Torgi!"

The bosses and captains turned to one another with astounded questions. Behind the Boss of Loutre, Torgi looked wildly from one side to another, but grim-faced bouncers stepped up on his left and on his right, and he could only stand trembling.

"He has cheated the Boss of Loutre by misinterpreting merchants' prices, then keeping the difference between what they charged, and what his boss paid!" the duke snapped. "He has practiced this deception for years, but two weeks ago, he tried it once too often! The merchant Ralke came before him with a guard who knew both the language of the merchant and of the boss!"

He had to wait for more furious babble to quiet, watching the Boss of Loutre turn to demand the truth from Torgi, and to see the steward shake his head in a panic of denial.

"Be sure that he did!" the duke thundered.

The crowd fell quiet, whirling to face him, and he spoke normally again. "The guard, Gar Pike, now a sergeant of the Blue Company, will bear witness to this, as will the merchant! Worse, though—to hide this evidence of his crime, the steward hired his own boss's brute to take a squadron of boots to kill the merchant and the guard! They failed, so Steward Torgi hired the

Hawk Company to slay Gar Pike and Merchant Ralke! When they failed, and the merchant and his guard took shelter in Quilichen, Torgi twisted a cable of lies to bring both his boss, and Quilichen's neighboring bosses, to besiege the city with the aid of the mercenaries they hired! That is the tale of how you have come here today, and why even the Fair Folk, in our amused dispassion, could not stand by and watch the comedy of your mutual annihilation!"

The crowd burst into a torrent of talk, and the bosses turned to unleash their rage and humiliation on the hapless steward. Torgi fell to his knees, hands upraised in pleading.

The duke sat back and waited.

Finally, the crowd quieted, and the Boss of Loutre rose. "Lord duke, we must insist that this miscreant be brought forth to trial and your charges proved, for we find it difficult to believe that any steward could be guilty of such perfidy!"

"And because they need to save their faces," Dirk muttered to Magda.

She nodded, not looking at him, but murmuring back, "They'll raise this siege and go to their homes, but they must prove that they had reason not to fight the Fair Folk."

"He is the Boss of Loutre's man," the duke told them. "Therefore, it is fitting that Loutre preside over his trial."

He gestured to Cort, who stepped forward with two Quilichen archers. They lifted the boss's chair and set it before the duke, facing the other bosses and captains, but on the ground below the dais. The Boss of Loutre stared for a moment, then stepped up, swelling with the self-importance of being designated by a duke of the Fair Folk. His fellow bosses bristled with envy, but had to sit and watch.

The duke watched, too, but somehow his whole posture told all the watchers that he was there to make sure Loutre did it right.

The boss sat, lifting his head high with all the dignity he could muster. "Bring forth the accused!"

His bruisers hustled Torgi out in front of his boss, and threw him down kneeling before Loutre.

"You are accused of treachery and theft from your own boss," Loutre intoned, then lifted his gaze. "What evidence is there against this man?"

Gar stepped forward. "I am the guard who caught him out in his mistranslation."

"Yes, I recognize you," Loutre said slowly. His jaw squared with determination not to be intimidated by Gar's sheer size. "Tell us what happened as you saw it!"

Gar told, carefully naming all the other witnesses in his testimony. There followed a small parade, with Ralke, then the brute, then the captain of the Hawk Company stepping up to tell their tales. When they were done, the boss turned to Torgi, face swollen with rage. "What have you to say for yourself?"

Torgi had a great deal to say, a chain of rationalizations and excuses that might have deceived his boss at any other time, but now only sufficed to make him even angrier. "Enough!" he finally exploded, and a bruiser stopped Torgi's babble with a backhanded slap. Loutre lifted his gaze to his fellow bosses and the mercenary captains. "You have heard the witnesses, and his defense. What is your verdict?"

"Guilty!" they all cried, then elaborated: Torgi was guilty of treachery and incitement to war, and should be hanged, drawn, and quartered. Loutre smiled vindictively and opened his mouth to pronounce the sentence.

But the duke of the Fair Folk stepped in again. "The verdict is sound and the sentence just, but I find this rogue so nefarious that I claim him as my own."

Furious babble erupted again, and Loutre whirled about to protest, but the duke only raised a hand, as though in promise. This time, he let the clamor run its course. One by one, the watchers noticed the locked stares of boss and duke, and quieted.

When all was silent, the duke assured them, "We shall see

that this perfidious steward receives just punishment for his crimes, as only the Fair Folk can mete it out."

Everyone in the crowd, even the bosses and captains, remembered gruesome tales from their childhoods, shuddered, and subsided, convinced that Torgi would fare far worse with the Fair Folk than with any punishment the Milesians could devise.

"Take him away," the duke commanded, and two men of the Fair Folk stepped down to haul Torgi off, as though they'd been expecting to. The crowd relaxed, falling into a buzz of talk. The duke sat back, letting it run for a while, then suddenly, thundered, "Be still!"

The people fell silent, all eyes upon him.

"I do not wish do be troubled so again," the duke snapped, voice still amplified. "It is high time you Milesians put your own house in order!"

A buzz of trepidation went through the crowd.

"Apparently you do not know how to manage your own affairs," the duke went on, "so we shall have to teach you! To that end, all you seven leaders, and all other bosses, captains, and squires within a hundred miles of my Hollow Hill, shall assemble in the plain about that hill to meet with me on the forty-fifth day after Midsummer! There we shall discuss issues of concern, and shall hear and decide disputes between you, captains, squires, and bosses alike!"

A roar of incredulous talk went up from the crowd. The leaders remained silent, though, glowering up at the duke, but not daring to defy him. Magda alone fairly beamed.

"Be not affronted," the whip-crack voice commanded. "All other dukes of the Fair Folk will expect gatherings of the same sort within their own districts. Emissaries of the Fair Folk shall go among the bosses and captains and squires throughout the land, summoning all to assembly, and woe betide the boss who refuses, for lightning shall break and crush his walls, and his enemies shall swarm into his town to loot as they will, at the command of the Fair Folk." Then, before the talk could start again, "Go now! Strike your camps and march out of this valley, and do not even dream of disobeying me, for Fair Folk shall watch your every step, and lightning will strike the man who dares to rebel against my words! Go home to your towns, and let each boss send forth messengers to other bosses and squires, spreading word throughout the land that the Folk of the Hollow Hills will no longer tolerate war!"

He turned and strode away. His retinue followed him, hauling the hapless steward with them, and the crowd stood, riveted in silence, as the Fair Folk marched back up to the duke's pavilion on the hillside. He went through the door—and a storm of talk burst forth in the valley.

Cort helped Dirk to rise, and supplied an arm for him to lean on, asking, "Why a month and a half after Midsummer?"

Magda explained, still beaming. "It will give him time to make sure report of this day is sent to all other Hollow Hills."

"Midsummer is one of their festivals, when they travel to one another's hills," Gar explained. "It's the perfect opportunity for each hill to send troupes of messengers to other hills. Word will spread through them all quickly enough, and they can capture Milesians and send them home with their summonses to the bosses and captains and squires."

"What sort of issues shall they discuss?" Magda asked, frowning.

"They're all so cussedly independent that I don't think there'll be any shortage of quarrels," Gar answered, "but I've put a bee in Master Ralke's bonnet. He's going back to Loutre, to point out to the boss how much money all the bosses will have saved by not fighting, and how much more they could make if all the men left alive spent their time farming and making trade goods, instead of taking up valuable farmland for mass graves. He's going to tell the boss about the profits that can come from protecting merchants and increasing their trade, but taxing them only a little—especially if each boss is a silent partner with each merchant."

Cort stared, amazed, then slowly smiled, and Magda turned very thoughtful. "If each boss has an interest in his merchants' profits, he will have an excellent reason for maintaining peace."

"Merchants do much better with stability," Gar agreed.

"And with money from a boss, or even a squire, to invest in goods to trade, he could reap golden profits indeed! I think I shall have to see to greater support of my own merchants."

"See how good ideas catch on?" Gar asked Cort. To Magda, he said, "When the assembly of rulers meets, perhaps you can talk them into guaranteeing safe passage for merchants—if those merchants pay a hefty tariff, a tax for bringing goods into or through a domain. That way, each boss's merchants will receive safe-conducts from all the other bosses—and will pay the same tariff."

"Why should they bother?" Magda asked, frowning. "Surely the tariff you pay will cancel out the tariff you collect!"

"Perhaps, my lady, but the taxes your own merchants generate can be very impressive—especially since the money they will bring in will come from your neighbors. Besides, you'll benefit from their goods."

"I have benefited well enough already." Magda caught Dirk's good arm, smiling into his eyes. Dirk returned the smile, his face softening amazingly.

Cort watched them with envy, then turned to Gar with sudden hope. "Do you suppose the Fair Folk will stay in this valley a while?"

"They have to make sure none of the bosses tries to come back," Gar mused. "Yes, I'm sure she'll stay—or rather, *they* will, at least for this one night."

Cort turned to bow to Magda. "By your leave, my lady, may I be excused?"

"I don't think she heard you," Gar said with a smile. "Yes, by all means, go."

20

That evening, Magda's people celebrated wildly inside their town. She herself held aloof from the drinking and dancing, though, and assigned half her army to stay sober, some to patrol the walls, some to rebuild the gates. Magda walked the battlements to make it clear she was asking no more of them than she was willing to do herself—and if Dirk limped beside her, why, surely that only set all the better an example for her soldiers.

Outside the walls, Cort walked with Desirée between the castle and the encampment of the Fair Folk, their pavilions lighting the night like glowing jewels, the sounds of their merrymaking faint but entrancing.

"What a foolish custom!" Desirée exclaimed. "Must man and woman stay together even if they tire of one another?"

Cort looked up at her sharply. "Will you tire of me so soon, then?"

Her face softened, and she reached out to caress his cheek. "Not soon, my darling, and perhaps not at all—but my people say that life is long, and love is short."

"*My* people dream of love that lasts until death parts the two," Cort countered, "and perhaps after—but maybe that's because once man and woman really fall in love, they expect to have children."

"Ah! Well, if *everyone* were to have children, that might be different," Desirée allowed.

"You don't wish to, then?" Cort braced himself for a life without offspring.

"Oh, in silly, childish dreams," Desirée confided. "I have always yearned to have a child, perhaps two, one of each kind . . ."

"Kind?" Cort frowned.

"One boy and one girl. But the grown folk assured me that it was only a childish fantasy, and I would outgrow it."

Cort felt a flood of relief, and a huge stock of tenderness washed in its wake. He stopped and held her hands, looking into her eyes. "You might not have to outgrow it."

"Oh, but I would," Desirée said, "for our hill, and every other, has a computer—think of it as a guardian spirit—that advises us. It speaks to us from a console—a little table with buttons—and among the many things it tells us is how many people can live in the hill without hunger or thirst. Simply put, no one can have a baby unless someone else dies, and surely it is terribly selfish to have more than one, when so many want them!"

"I could bring in extra food and water," Cort offered.

Desirée tilted her head, smiling merrily. "The duke might countenance that. He seems seized with a sudden desire to open the hill to contact with you Milesians—thank our lucky stars!"

"Thank them indeed," Cort breathed, unable to believe how her touch still seemed to make him burn with desire.

"But other women tell me that the little creatures can be quite demanding," Desirée told him, "indeed, that they can wear a woman out so that she even loses interest in lovemaking! Many who want babies sorely and have them, love them for a few months, then wish just as sorely that they had never seen them!"

Cort stared in horror. "Surely not! Children are the second greatest blessing known to Man!"

"What is the first?" Desirée asked, then saw the answering look in his eyes and blushed. "Well, if Man thinks children are so great a blessing, he can help to rear them, and not only in playing with them, but in walking the floor with them and arguing with other parents whose children they anger, and feeding them when all they can do with food is make messes, and . . ." She paused for breath, then summarized, ". . . and all of that!"

"Man can," Cort said thoughtfully. "Man will, if we're lucky enough to have them."

"I'm sure the duke would also say that you must rear them in such a fashion that after they were grown, they would go outside the dome to make their ways in the world, so that they did not burden the resources of the hill—and it is you who would have to do that, for I know nothing of the outside world!"

"Yes, that part would fall to me," Cort agreed.

Desirée frowned. "You are a most strange man, to agree so readily."

"If I didn't agree readily, you should be suspicious if I agreed at all," Cort countered, "for how much is agreement about children worth, if you have to argue a person into it? If they do anything, they must do it wholeheartedly, not grudgingly."

"I can see some truth in that," Desirée said slowly.

"The world is changing, my love," Cort said softly. "It will be a better world, but in many ways, it will be a world we don't know. We will have to change with it, you and I."

"Some things are hard to change," Desirée countered. "Remember that among my people, coupling rarely lasts longer than a few months, though a bonding of three or four years is not unheard of. In rare, very rare, cases, two Fair Folk bond for life—but because of this, we have none of your quaint wedding ceremonies, though parties celebrating the beginning of a pairing are common."

"Can we plan such a party, then?" Cort asked her.

Desirée gazed at him for a moment, then gave him a sultry

smile and said, "A week ago, I taught you how to make love to a fairy. How well do you remember it?"

Cort gave her a sizzling smile of his own and answered, "Try me."

"I will," she said, "and if you prove to have learned your lessons well enough, you may ask me again."

Three hours later, he did. She gasped, "Yes!"

Atop the castle wall, strolling slowly between sentries, Dirk and Magda looked down on the jewel camp of the Fair Folk and talked.

"When you rode away with your soldiers," Magda told him, "I felt you had deserted me, that I would never see you again."

"You don't know how badly I wanted to stay!"

"I think I might." Magda smiled into his eyes. "At least, I hope that I do."

Dirk smiled slowly, caressing her hand. "It wasn't just duty that took me away. I knew that I was a liability to you—that if I stayed, I'd bring the wrath of the Hawk Company upon you. And I was right, though I didn't know the real reasons."

"That duty is satisfied now," she reminded him, "and the danger past."

"Yes," Dirk agreed. "You shouldn't be in danger from me any more."

"I hope that I am," she murmured.

Dirk smiled slowly. "If I endanger your heart, the more lucky I—but I have to tell you the other reason that I rode away: that I knew I had no chance to court you."

"Why ever should you think that?" she breathed, leaning closer to him.

Dirk didn't bother answering—he kissed her instead.

When they parted and he caught his breath, he explained, "I knew that I couldn't possibly be worthy of you."

Magda nodded, with a self-satisfied smile. "Yes," she said. "I think that is an excellent way for you to feel. But do not let it grow too strong, sir." And she kissed him again. Somewhere in the midst of it, as his breathing grew heavier, he began to believe that he might have a chance of courting her, after all.

When they parted, Magda said, "Worthy or not, you should have at least a bit of audacity."

"So much audacity as to ask for your hand in marriage?" Dirk asked.

Magda tilted her head to the side, considering the question. Then she nodded. "Yes. Perhaps even so much audacity as that."

Slowly, Dirk knelt, still holding her hands. He hid the wince at the pain of his wound and asked, "Most beautiful Magda, I'm only a poor wanderer, but I'm a genuine knight, and I'll work as hard at staying as I have at wandering. Will you marry me?"

"Yes," she breathed, then helped him stand again so that he could wrap her in his arms for a very long kiss indeed.

Within the Fair Folk encampment, there was some revelry, but it was far more subdued, as though they weren't sure they had won a victory. Gar had no difficulty hearing the duke's words as they sat in satin camp chairs under a silken canopy at the door of the duke's pavilion, with old wine between them on an intricately carved table of dark wood made three hundred years before.

The duke looked up sharply at Gar's last statement. "Surely you do not believe that the Milesians could ever match our weapons!"

"Not easily or quickly," Gar agreed. "You and your beam projectors will be a deterrent for a while, able to keep the peace, perhaps long enough for the bosses to begin to like the taste of the prosperity they gain when they don't have to spend three-quarters of their income on their armies. But there will be some fighting, my lord. Many of the bosses will take your interference in their affairs as a challenge, and will start attacking you. If even one of the Fair Folk is killed in battle, they'll realize that you are as human as they."

"So! I had wondered why you felt we must abolish war for them!" the duke said. "I know why I wish it—since we have once come forth in force to judge between armies, they will expect us to do so again. It could become quite tedious, hearing every grievance of neighbor against neighbor, and knowing always that the truth of it is simply that one boss wanted another's land and people. Far easier to bring forth our beam cannon and blast them all to atoms if they dare to fight one another again!"

"That will do for a while," Gar agreed. "Do it too often, though, and they will learn that your only strength is your 'magical' weaponry. Then the bosses will start trying to develop their own."

"They cannot!" the duke spat. "They lack the knowledge, they lack even the tools to make the tools!"

"Oh, it might take a hundred years or more," Gar agreed, "but the knowledge that it could be done would be an amazingly sharp spur, and they'd develop defenses as impregnable as your domes first, then go on to making their own laser weapons. Some of them might even have the old science books squirreled away."

The duke's eyes flashed, and he hissed, "I wish I had never listened to your poisoned advice!"

"But you did," Gar countered, "and it's too late for you to retreat into your Hills now."

The duke replied with a spate of curses that Gar either had to admire, or savagely return. Under the circumstances, he chose admiration, and listened to the steady stream of invective, marveling at the duke's originality and gift for metaphor. When His Grace ran down, Gar said mildly, "I can see that you must be a student of literature, my lord, for it has given you great skill in your use of language. Still, I think you have very little to regret, or to fear. Look at those two couples out there, strolling arm in arm in the moonlight." He nodded toward the young folk in question.

The duke turned and looked, seeing Cort and Desirée in earnest conversation that ended in a very long kiss, while not too far away, a tall man of the Fair Folk walked with a woman from Quilichen. "She is not so young as all that," the duke said sourly.

"Nor is your man," Gar returned. "Of course, this woman is still single, despite her maturity, because she is too tall to attract a husband, despite her beauty—and your warrior is single because Fair Folk seldom wed. Nonetheless, both are taking pleasure in one another's company."

"What of it?" the duke snapped. "The Fair Folk have always taken pleasure of the Milesians when it suited them—most particularly of the Milesian women!"

"Then the Fair Folk have always been open to the Milesians in one way at least," Gar said, "and are the Fair Men completely indifferent to the children they sire outside the Hill?"

"Of course not! If the child is fair enough, mother and babe are brought within the Hill until the child is grown. Then the woman is sent on her way with a gift of gold."

Gar felt sorry indeed for the Milesian women thus transformed into glorified wet nurses and nannies for their own babies, and probably scorned by their Fair Folk lovers after the first year or so, then cast off without a thought. "What if the baby isn't so beautiful as to be brought into the Hill?"

"Then the father gives the woman a gift of gold, and now and again goes by night to be sure his child is well treated. Usually, with Fair Folk gold in her pocket, the woman has no difficulty in attracting suitors."

Again, Gar felt a pang for the women who had probably fallen in love with the tall and charismatic men, only to be virtually deserted even before their babies were born, then condemned to marry men who didn't love them, but wanted their dowries. "Either way, my lord, and even more in the second, the Fair Folk have concerned themselves with the fates of Milesians for many generations." Again, he nodded at the tall townswoman. "Can you be sure she is *not* of the Fair Folk?"

"That one? We know she is," the duke said. "She is the granddaughter of a Fair Man who is now dead—Geiroln, his name was."

"Then you even keep track of their genealogy," Gar said, "yet you tell me you're indifferent to the fates of the Milesians."

The duke flushed. "It is one thing to stay aware of the life-progress of individuals, and quite another to take a hand in their governance."

"There's really no other way to be sure of their well-being," Gar said quietly, "and with the Fair Folk openly abroad in the land, I think you'll find that such bondings occur far more frequently. The Fair Folk can increase as much as they wish now—they no longer need to limit their reproduction according to the capacities of their Hollow Hills."

"Yes," the duke said bitterly, "and we will dilute our blood in doing so! You have condemned me to having ugly descendants!"

"Those mortals don't look particularly ugly," Gar observed.

The duke looked again and nodded, frowning. "Perhaps . . . after all, Fair Folk would be attracted to only the best and most beautiful of Milesians . . ."

"And will find themselves far more concerned with the fates of their offspring," Gar concluded. "In fact, some Fair Folk might even wish to stay with their Milesian mates for life."

"Unnatural!" the duke scoffed.

"Only to Fair Folk," Gar said, unperturbed. "But with so many of your people outside the Hollow Hills, you will have to take a hand in governing the Milesians simply to protect your own—and to make sure no soldier kills a Fair Man."

"I knew you should have frozen the instant I saw you!"

"So did some of your women," Gar returned. "But you will have to involve yourselves with the Milesians most carefully, for the bosses will band together against you, and will form their own council to coordinate them in their opposition. If you lead all the free towns in leaguing together, you can outnumber them and outweigh them."

"But would we be the ones to lead such a league?" the duke asked, frowning. "Or would the Milesian towns lead us, and eventually enslave us?"

Gar shrugged. "The Fair Folk already have a Council of Councils, my lord, though you don't call it that, and though it never meets face-to-face, and all together. It deliberates by duke talking to duke at the solstice festivals, then discussing the results of those conferences with other dukes at the equinox festivals."

"Quite true," the duke said, frowning. "How did you know that about us?"

"I listened carefully to what you told me." Most carefully; Gar had listened to the duke's thoughts as well as his words. "That's an excellent way for your Council of Councils to meet, for if all the dukes were to assemble, it would be a great temptation for a Milesian boss to seek to assassinate them all."

The duke turned very thoughtful.

"Still, you do have your Council of Councils, your way of coordinating all the Hills—and the free towns do not. You'll be leading them in that, as in all else; they'll revere you as their teachers and benefactors. With that kind of initial advantage, there's no reason why you shouldn't remain the leaders."

"We shall, be sure of that!" the duke said, his eyes burning. "But take my curse with you when you go, Gar Pike, for you have tricked us into accepting responsibility at last!"

They all rose late the next day and met later for breakfast. One glance, and Gar knew what was to come, for Dirk looked inspired and determined, while Cort was dreamy-eyed, not quite touching the ground when he walked.

"She said yes, then," Gar inferred as Cort sat down with a steaming cup.

"She did!" Cort virtually glowed.

"I congratulate you," Gar said. "When will you wed?"

"We won't, alas." Cort seemed to come down a little closer to earth. "But when her Fair Folk return to their Hill, I'll go with them. I don't mean to surrender my commission, of course, nor does Desirée want me to—she will take what time she can with me, between battles."

Gar suspected what plans Desirée had for Cort's absences, and suspected further that the young woman would be sadly disappointed, for there wouldn't be anywhere nearly as many battles for the Blue Company as there had been. Nonetheless, the Company would become a political force, and Cort would no doubt be gone from the Hollow Hill often enough, and long enough, to prevent her frustration from mounting. "So Desirée isn't quite ready to break the Fair Folk custom against weddings."

"Alas not," Cort agreed, "and I'll have to work most strenuously to keep her!"

Gar made a mental note to give him a copy of the *Kama Sutra* before he left. "I understand that there have been one or two cases where Fair Folk bonding has lasted lifelong."

Cort nodded. "I have hopes of making it so with Desirée, of being so excellent a mate that she will want it thus."

Gar hated to prick Cort's bubble, but he felt the question had to be asked. "What if she doesn't?"

"If she doesn't," Cort said sighing, "I'll abide by her wish, and go."

"What if there are children?" Dirk was suddenly very intense about it.

"If we *are* so blessed, I suspect none shall wish to keep me from taking the children to rear outside the Hill."

Gar had a notion Desirée wouldn't object either, so long as she was able to visit the children whenever she wished. "Then for a while at least, you'll be the Milesians' man on the inside," he said, carefully changing topics.

"Man on the inside?" Cort frowned. "Of what?"

"Of the councils of the Fair Folk. If you're very discreet and very tactful, you'll probably find the duke willing to listen to your information about how bosses and captains think and act. Play that card carefully, and you'll work your way into being his advisor."

"Why would I wish that?" Cort asked, frowning.

"Because it's the best way to insure Desirée's safety, and that of any children you may have." Gar waited until he saw the idea register and take root, then launched into a major conference on ways and means of advising and influencing the duke in coping with the mercenaries and bosses. He also hinted that if Cort could become indispensable to the Fair Folk, Desirée might want to keep him around longer. When he was done, and Cort wandered off with his head spinning, Dirk said to Gar, "You don't mind playing dirty, do you?"

"Not as long as I'm telling the truth," Gar replied, "and his chances of a lasting bonding *are* much better if he gains status among the Fair Folk."

"You have a very cynical view of feminine nature, Gar."

"Really? I thought it was merely realistic." Gar hurried on before Dirk could take offense. "Actually, though, I only thought I had a cynical view of *all* human nature."

"There is that," Dirk admitted.

"And my great disappointment is that I'm so often proved right," Gar sighed.

"Of course," Dirk said, "you're really hoping that Cort will become one of the forces for keeping the peace and developing a sort of confederation-style government, aren't you? And you don't care what emotional blackmail you apply to get him to do it."

"Someone has to. But you must admit that I didn't tell him any lies."

"No, but you sure told him every reason for him to work his way up the political ladder."

"I did not," Gar stated. "I didn't play on his desire for personal power at all."

"Only because he doesn't have one," Dirk retorted, "or at least not much. That's why you had to try to kindle one."

"I only kindled a desire for public service," Gar said, with the stiffness that bespoke suppressed laughter. "What about you, my old friend? Are you going to stay and become a politician too?"

21

What more natural place for a scheming fighter to go into government?" Dirk retorted. "You might consider settling down here, too."

"No, I don't have your reason." Gar sighed, "and I'm afraid it's the only one strong enough to make me want to stay on one single planet. Have you asked her to marry you?"

"Yes." Dirk grinned.

So did Gar. "I see she said yes. Aren't you worried about not having children?"

"Not really." Dirk shrugged. "We both know she didn't have a decent chance to get pregnant in that first marriage. But if she doesn't, well . . . children would be nice, but real, lasting love is more important."

"Yes, because if you have children and don't have love, the poor things grow up as blighted as plants in the dark," Gar agreed. "You understand, of course, that marrying the local squire's sister doesn't automatically make you his heir, or give you any significant portion of her power."

"Oh, I do understand that," Dirk said, "but I'm not sure she does."

"She will, believe me."

"Never doubted you," Dirk said, "unless you were talking about your own unworthiness. But I am braced for giving her all the support I can in her political struggles."

"You can't possibly do that without becoming involved in those struggles yourself."

"Of course not." Dirk grinned. "I have learned something in our wandering and revolution-mongering, after all."

"Then you've realized that Quilichen will become the leader of all the free villages of this district."

"After what's happened here? Of course." Dirk smiled. "But let's not forget that none of it would have happened if Magda hadn't been so merciful as well as being so excellent a leader."

"Yes. That's the main reason." Gar nodded. "She's a very intelligent woman, and it won't take her very long at all to realize that the only way the free towns will stand together is if she manipulates them into it. That kind of intriguing can have only one of two ends."

"Assassination," Dirk said grimly, "and you can damn well bet that isn't going to happen. Oh, they'll try, all right, but they won't succeed."

"I suggest you do all you can to strengthen ties with the Fair Folk to help ensure that," Gar said. "And the other end?"

"She becomes leader of the free-town party."

Gar nodded. "That *will* happen."

"Which means that, like it or not, I now have a vested interest in developing enough of a government to give this land a fair chance of peace," Dirk said, with a sardonic smile.

"Oh, come now," Gar protested. "That was your aim all along. Magda only gave you a personal reason for it."

"It was your aim, too," Dirk accused.

Gar raised a hand. "Guilty."

"Well, everybody who's been making a living from war won't like it," Dirk grumbled, "which means that for the first generation or so, we're going to be supporting one hell of a police force."

"And *that* means the taxes will still be heavy," Gar agreed, "but at least the peasants won't see their crops destroyed by armies chasing across their fields every other year."

"And in ten years or so, we ought to be able to get that massive police force out to protect the villagers against banditry and rape," Dirk agreed, "if for no other reason than to give them something to do."

Gar smiled, eyes glowing, pleased. "You have the nucleus of a government now, with the Hollow Hills leading the free towns in developing a parliament. If you take care to include the bosses on the pretext of resolving disputes with the free towns, you'll have an opposition party, but not an enemy, and the majority of the people will always vote with you."

"Yes, if we make the signing of a Declaration of Rights the price of membership in that parliament, and insist on free and mandatory elementary schooling for everyone." Dirk smiled. "You've taught me well, Gar. If you educate the people and guarantee their rights, some form of democracy will follow sooner or later."

"Yes, unfortunately," Gar said with a sardonic smile. "I do wish I could have developed more variety."

"Variety? The people we've helped have developed forms of democracy no one else ever heard of! Oh, I think you're doing just fine for variety."

"Yes, but only in democracies. I can't help thinking some people are better off with monarchies or dictatorships."

"Only when they haven't learned enough to be able to rule themselves." Dirk reached up and clapped his friend on the shoulder. "Trust me, old son. You're giving them what they want, what people will always want—the only possible compromise between anarchy and tyranny."

"I suppose that's true," Gar sighed, "and I suppose I can always console myself with the thought that they always get what they deserve."

"I'm not sure about that," Dirk said darkly, "or that even if it was, we should let them have it."

"Who are we to say otherwise?" Gar demanded.

"People who want to be free," Dirk answered. "People who want our rights guaranteed."

Gar couldn't get used to a wedding without a church, but since the planet didn't really have religion, they had to manage with the castle itself. As many of the townsfolk and yeomen as could, crowded in to watch their castellan marry. Music came from every side, musicians throughout the crowd playing the same tune on fiddles, bagpipes, hautboys, gambas, all manner of instruments. It set Gar's teeth on edge, but the locals seemed to enjoy it.

From the shelter of the barracks, Dirk said, "I'm not too sure about this."

"You will be in half an hour." Gar flicked an imaginary speck of lint off Dirk's doublet and adjusted his cloak for maximum effect. "I have it on good authority that grooms always get cold feet."

"I'm sure being married will be great. It's just the wedding I can't stand!"

"All of Quilichen must see that their castellan is well and truly married," Gar told him severely. "You've faced battles—you can face a bride, a sage, and a crowd! Come on, let's go."

Trumpets burst forth in fanfare as the two men stepped out of the barracks—almost enough to make Dirk go right back in. But the honor guard of archers closed about him, and there wasn't much he could do except march in their midst to the sage who stood in the center of the courtyard, his humble peasant tunic and leggins made festive for the occasion by the chains of flowers the village maidens had festooned all over him.

The honor guard halted near the sage, and Gar nudged Dirk's elbow to make him go on three paces more, to stand before the old man.

"Thank Heaven I've got you with me," Dirk muttered to Gar.

"We've been companions in danger for eight years now," Gar reminded him.

Then the trumpets blared again, and all the instruments burst forth in a tune that Dirk was amazed to realize was the age-old wedding march from Earth! He turned to the castle portal—and his jaw dropped as he saw the most beautiful sight he had ever seen.

Magda was resplendent in golden embroidery and lace, her veil thrown back so that he could see her face, more lovely than it had ever been. Three children carried her train of cloth-of-gold, and two more sprinkled flower petals in her path.

She came up to Dirk and flashed him a smile that told him her full intent. He couldn't smile back—he was too thoroughly paralyzed. Together they turned to face the sage . . .

And Dirk was jolted back to reality. The sage, severe at first, asked them each a set of searing questions about living together and making their lives one, but still respecting each other's identities. It would have thrown them both for a loop, if he hadn't challenged them with worse when they'd come to him to ask to be married. Then the sage told them both, loudly and clearly enough for the crowd to hear, that they must never make the mistake of thinking that they could become one person, for they were really two independent people, and must always respect that independence in one another—but that they could form a solid relationship in which each would help fulfill the other's needs, and receive as well as give.

It was intended as a reminder to the crowd that marriage wasn't for everybody, and Dirk took it in good part. Then, and only then, did the sage turn to the couple and ask Magda, "Do you take this man for your husband?" And in spite of everything she had just heard, Magda said "Yes!" loudly and clearly, then turned to Dirk, her gaze challenging, but also burning with ardor. Dirk stared back, more lost than ever in those beautiful, deep eyes . . .

"He asked you if you take Magda as your wife," Gar muttered.

"Oh, you bet I do," Dirk said, softly but with great intensity. Then Gar's elbow jolted into his ribs, and he came out of his trance long enough to call out, "Yes!"

"Then I pronounce you husband and wife!" the sage declared. He said something after that, too, but Dirk couldn't hear what it was, because the people were cheering too loudly.

The celebrating went on all afternoon, with Magda and Dirk growing quite weary from going to as many people as they could, yeomen and merchants and craftsmen and mothers and maidens and bachelors and . . . well, virtually everybody, accepting their good wishes and thanking them. Finally, as the sun was setting, they managed to sneak out the main gate with Gar, leaving the sage to keep an eye on things for an hour. They stepped into the town's single coach to ride out to the top of the ridge overlooking the town. There they stepped down, and Gar told the coachman, "Drive the horses down into the fields, and come back in fifteen minutes."

The coachman nodded and slapped the reins; the horses trotted off down the road.

Dirk looked around. "This should be high enough."

"And dark enough," Gar agreed. He touched his medallion and said, "Let it come down, Herkimer." Then he looked out over the lights of Quilichen, the castle on the hilltop in its center almost garish with the lamps of the celebration. Even at this distance, they could hear the music and the noise of revelry, though it was faint.

"You have a lovely town," Gar told Magda. "You have made it into something of which you may be proud."

"I am," Magda said, and reached out to take his hand. "Are you sure you won't stay in it with us?"

"I thank you," Gar said gravely, "but I have work to do in this life before I may settle down, and it's not done."

"It has to end sometime and somewhere," Dirk said. "Why not here?"

"Because I haven't found what you two have," Gar said, struggling for composure. Magda saw, and let out a little cry, reaching up toward his face, but hesitating.

"Are you sure you're going to be okay?" Dirk asked.

Gar managed a sardonic smile. "I traveled alone before I met you, Dulaine. Don't worry about me—just do the best you can to take care of each other, and of your world."

The couple exchanged a glance that lingered, then smiled and turned back to Gar, holding hands. "I hope you will find what we have found," Magda said.

"A woman with the key to a golden box," Dirk seconded.

Gar looked up in surprise, almost alarm, then frowned. "That's right, I did tell you about that dream once, didn't I? Well, don't worry about me. I'll be fine. After all, I have Herkimer for company."

"Who is this Herkimer?" Magda asked, frowning.

"That." Gar pointed upward.

Dirk had told her about it, warned her about the impact, but still Magda cried out and clung tight to him as she saw the huge golden disk falling out of the sky.

It landed on the hilltop, and the ramp slid down. "Ready to board, Magnus," said the resonant voice within.

"Good-bye." Gar clasped Magda's hand, then leaned down to kiss her cheek. "Best man's privilege," he explained, then turned to clasp Dirk's hand and arm with both of his own. "Good-bye, my old companion. Fare you well."

"Oh, fare you well!" Magda cried, tears in her eyes, and Dirk blinked once or twice himself as he said, "Fare you well, old son. Stop by to visit some day."

"I will," Gar promised, then grinned. "Probably with pursuit hot behind me."

"I shall have the porters ready to open the gate, and the archers ready to fire," Magda promised.

"I thank you," Gar said softly. He pressed a quick kiss on the back of her hand, clapped Dirk on the shoulder, and turned to mount the ramp, alone.

He came into the control room, sat in his acceleration couch, and fastened his shock webbing across his body, not speaking. The computer read his presence in the acceleration couch and rose. Gar felt the weight press down on him as the ship hit escape velocity. Then it eased off, and Herkimer's voice said, "We are in orbit, Magnus. You may move about."

Gar unfastened his webbing and stood up, feeling the persona of Gar fall from him like a travel-worn cloak, becoming only Magnus again. Slowly, he moved to the shower cubicle, undressed, stepped under the ultrasonic beam, waited as dust drifted from him, then hit the spray and let himself linger under the warm water for a good half hour.

Finally, cleaned, dried, and wrapped in the sybaritic luxury of a soft white robe, he stepped out, dialed a drink from the dispenser, and sat down in the acceleration couch again, to sip and contemplate the image of Durvie on the viewscreens. Herkimer, correlating his needs from his unusual silence and Dirk's absence, kept soft music and the sounds of distant chatter going on, careful not to let the ship seem too empty. Finally he asked, "Where shall we wander, Magnus?"

"Oh, choose a planet at random," Magnus said carelessly. "Just take the next one down that index of human misery Dirk worked up."

"As you wish, Magnus." The computer was quiet for a few minutes, then said, "Course plotted. Leaving orbit."

There was no change in weight, no sensation of movement at all, but Durvie began to shrink in the viewscreen, very slowly at first, then faster and faster.

Gar watched the planet recede and whispered softly, "You lucky knave, Dirk. You lucky, lucky prince!"